W9-BUU-044

THE
SILENCE
OF
SIX

Copyright © 2014 Adaptive Studios Inc.

Visit us on the web at www.adaptivestudios.com

Library of Congress Cataloging-in-Publication Data

Myers, E.C.

The Silence of Six / by E.C. Myers

ISBN 978-0-9960666-2-4 (hardcover)
eISBN 978-1-6346186-6-3 (eBook)

[1. Conspiracy—Fiction. 2. Technology—Fiction. 3. Friendship—Fiction. 4. Suicide—Fiction. 5. Internet Privacy—Fiction. 6. Computer Hackers—Fiction. 7. Government Control—Fiction.]

THE SILENCE OF SIX

E.C. MYERS

ADAPTIVE BOOKS

An Imprint of Adaptive Studios
Culver City, CA

@adaptivebooks

For the everyday heroes who stand for truth and justice and strive to make the world a better place for strangers like me.

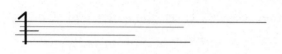

MAX STEIN BOUNCED ON THE BALLS OF HIS FEET. The line was moving way...too...slowly. He should have been at afternoon soccer practice or running around the track, not zombie-shambling down this hallway to the school auditorium. But since hosting a presidential debate was such an honor for Granville High, attendance was mandatory.

"Man, this blows," Isaac Ramirez said in front of Max.

Max scratched his right wrist where the sleeve of his wool blazer kept itching. He was always uncomfortable in a jacket and tie; he felt less like himself. His black Chucks were a small act of rebellion against tonight's draconian dress code.

"'Don't you think it's exciting to see our political system at work firsthand? We're participating in history.'" Max quoted his girlfriend Courtney. "And so on and so forth." He followed

Isaac as they shifted another foot toward their destination.

"You don't want to be here any more than I do," Isaac said.

"Guilty. Just don't tell Cort."

The Commission on Presidential Debates had decided to bring one of the events to a high school because internet regulations and education were both major topics in this year's election. Courtney Garcia's essay about her digital detox efforts and her recent suspension for criticizing the school's "no use" policy for mobile devices had won the national competition for Granville.

It was ironic that, as a result, students were being encouraged to use their cell phones in school tonight to post live on Panjea, the debate's biggest sponsor.

Two men in black suits flanked the doors to the auditorium, hands clasped in front of them. The small stars pinned to their lapels and the coiled earpieces winding behind their left ears marked them as United States Secret Service.

"Hey! It's the S.S.," Isaac said. One of them flicked his eyes at Isaac then continued gazing straight ahead.

"I'm sure they love it when people call them that," Max said.

A female agent was running a wand over students before allowing them into the auditorium, which seemed excessive since there were already metal detectors at each of the building's entrances. When his turn came up, Max palmed his cell phone in his right hand, his keys in his left, and spread his arms.

He wondered what the life of a Secret Service agent was like. Max was athletic. He had a knack for assessing situations quickly (at least on the soccer field), and he had a freakishly good memory, which his best friend Evan Baxter called his superpower. On the other hand, he had problems with authority, and he wouldn't want the government looking into his past too closely. He had just been a kid having what he'd considered harmless fun, but he knew they would love to make an example out of him now.

The agent waved Max through. He passed between the silent sentries guarding the doors and joined Isaac inside.

"Wow," Max said.

The debate's public relations team had transformed the auditorium in only a week. The shabby old curtains along the walls and on the stage had been replaced with red velvet drapery. A large projector screen now stretched across the stage, with two walnut-grain podiums situated on either side of it. There were enough cameras, floodlights, cables, and speakers to make it resemble a movie set.

Mr. Kelley ushered Max and Isaac into a row. "File in. All the way to the end."

"Axe! Ram! Down here!" Walt Smith called them down to the third row, where he was holding two seats. Max tensed up as the Secret Service agents stationed around the auditorium focused in on Walt and murmured into their earpieces.

Mr. Kelley sighed and let them join their teammate. "Just get settled quickly, will you? And no more shouting, huh?"

They made their way down to the front. Max grabbed the seat on the aisle; he hated being boxed in.

Isaac gave Walt a fist bump. "Good looking out."

"This is great, Walt. Thanks," Max said.

They were close enough to the front to see everything, even the laptop screens on the moderator's table below the stage—all except for Courtney's. The privacy filter he'd bought her for their one-month anniversary blacked out the screen at this angle.

Max texted her. Look behind you.

Courtney picked up her phone from the table, read the message, and then turned around. She smiled and waved when she spotted him.

Isaac whistled. "That outfit really shows off her rack."

"Come on." Max forced a cheerful tone to hide how pissed off he was. But he had to admit: Courtney *was* stunning in a gray striped pantsuit. Her honey-brown hair was twisted into a business-like bun that made her look older.

"I still can't believe you scored Full Cort," Isaac said.

"Don't call her that," Max snapped.

Guys had started chanting "Full Cort!" at basketball games whenever Courtney appeared, because of the way she filled her cheerleading uniform.

"You used to call her that too," Isaac said quietly.

"Yeah, but—" *I was just trying to fit in*, Max wanted to say. He'd just been pretending to be one of the guys, because that's what you did to be popular. Just as Courtney had pretended the nickname didn't bother her.

Eventually she quit the squad and joined the school newspaper, where she quickly developed a reputation as a tough reporter. After a brutal interview with a teacher about the Common Core, a reader commented that she had given the interviewee "the *Full Cort Press*," and the less offensive meaning soon stuck. Courtney had even taken the name for her personal blog.

Max's cell phone vibrated with a text from Courtney: I'm so nervous!

Max typed back. You'll be great!

I've got butterflies in my stomach. Or maybe one giant butterfly.

If it escapes your chest Aliens-style, you'll steal the show, Max wrote.

Courtney laughed then covered her mouth. Ew, she wrote.

I thought you'd be in the gym, he typed. The gym had been designated the "Spin Room", as it was the only space large enough to accommodate all the reporters covering the debate. Max didn't see the point, considering the internet would decide the winner almost instantaneously.

I couldn't turn down the best seat in the house. I'm going to liveblog the whole night and record video for my blog post, Courtney typed.

Good luck! he wrote. He added: BTW, you look amazing. ;)

We're about to start!!! See you after? <3

Max started to put his phone away when it buzzed again.

It wasn't from Courtney this time. The text message was

encrypted, which meant it could only be from Evan.

Max scanned the crowded auditorium. He didn't see Evan's trademark red hoodie anywhere. A dress code wouldn't have prevented him from wearing it; he would happily play the autism card if someone raised a fuss.

Max swiped his finger from right to left across the phone's screen and a password field popped up—Evan's handiwork. Concerned about telecom companies storing the communications of their customers, he had created an app called Lemon-Juice for secure SMS texting. If Evan had sold the app, he'd be raking in money, but instead he had offered it for free as open-source software.

Max shielded his phone and tapped in his encryption key, then pressed his palm against the screen for three seconds.

The text message faded in.

hey, bud stop i need your help with this stop i know you'll figure out what to do with it stop good luck stop

Hairs rose on the back of Max's neck.

The ominous message was followed by a string of jumbled letters, numbers, and symbols.

"Hey. Have you guys seen Evan?" Max asked.

"Who?" Isaac asked.

"Does that dork even still go here?" Walt asked. "I thought he had Asperger's or something."

"He can still attend school. He's just in different classes this year," Max said.

The diagnosis had changed more than Evan's class schedule,

though. The meds that helped control his anxiety and paranoia also made him slower and more withdrawn.

Maybe he had decided to stay home to watch the debate on his computer, while doing ten other things simultaneously. But Max now realized he hadn't seen Evan around much at all lately. Which didn't necessarily mean he hadn't been coming to school—Max could have missed him because he hadn't been looking for him until now. Max had barely spoken to Evan since school started, but in the old days, whenever they weren't hanging out in real life, they were communicating with each other online.

Max typed back: What? Where are you???

The lights over the audience dimmed as the stage lit up. The entrances and exits around the auditorium were closed, each guarded by Secret Service agents.

Max checked the time on his phone. 4:59. Still no response from Evan.

A woman dressed all in black beside one of the cameras raised a hand. She spoke into a headset.

"We are live in ten, nine, eight, seven, six. . ." She finished the countdown silently on her fingers: five, four, three, two, one.

The red light above the cameras blinked on and a sign mounted above the stage displayed "On the Air."

A graphic of the billowing "Presidential Debate" banner and the CNN and Panjea logos blossomed on the giant video screen. It was then replaced by a shot of the dark school auditorium, students' faces lit eerily by the glow of their phones and tablets.

"Good evening from Granville High School in Granville, California. I'm Bennett Avery of the *CNN Newsroom*." Over the speakers, Avery's rumbling baritone sounded like the voice of God, if God had a southern twang. The screen transitioned to a shot of the desk, making him look fifteen feet tall. "I welcome you to our second presidential debate between the Republican nominee, Senator Clancy Tooms, Jr. of Utah, and the Democratic nominee, Governor Angela S. Lovett of Tennessee. Panjea is the sponsor of this event."

Avery quickly explained the debate format. The candidates would be fielding questions from pre-screened web videos submitted through Panjea. They would have two minutes to respond to questions, then have the opportunity to address each other and answer follow-up questions from the moderator.

"The audience in this auditorium has promised to remain silent throughout the evening. No applause, no cheering, no ringing cell phones. The one exception is right now: Please join me in welcoming Senator Tooms and Governor Lovett."

Avery rose and began clapping as Senator Tooms entered from stage left and Governor Lovett from stage right. Max joined in the applause and stood with his classmates. He was finally feeling some of the excitement that he'd been resisting until now. Max had never been this close to a celebrity before, and one of the people only one hundred feet away from him was going to become the next President of the United States.

Tooms and Lovett met in the center of the stage and shook hands as camera bulbs flashed around them. They paused and spoke briefly to each other while more photos were taken. The microphone didn't catch what they said, but they were acting more like old friends than opponents.

Tooms was about Max's height, six feet tall, and built like a football player, with close-cropped, silver hair. The fifty-one-year-old Senator was a striking contrast to Lovett's slim, five-foot-one-inch figure and auburn hair in a trendy style. Courtney was Lovett's biggest fan, but she often complained about the Governor's outfits getting more attention in the news than her views on the issues.

Sure enough, the Panjea commentary scrolling on the bottom of the screen with the hashtag #webdeb was now almost entirely focused on her "smoky blue" business suit, her makeup, her new haircut, and her "chic" glasses.

Despite Max's lack of enthusiasm for the debate itself, the issues under discussion tonight mattered to him. Everyone who cared about net neutrality knew that Senator Tooms, the GOP nominee, was all for limiting the government's role in regulating the internet. Although he supported the "defensive" use of computer viruses and malware to spy on other countries, he was strongly opposed to monitoring American citizens.

Even though Lovett had once headed the government's top spy agency, she had pledged to end surveillance of the American public. However, she also supported *more* government regulation of the internet. She claimed that it would help protect everyone's privacy because it would be easier to identify security flaws in software and share them with businesses and users before they could be exploited.

The candidates separated. Lovett paused on the way to her side of the stage to take a picture of the audience with her phone. She typed on it as she walked, and by the time she reached her podium, a note was scrolling across the screen.

AngelaLovett: Hello, Granville HS! :) #webdeb

Max checked Lovett's feed on his phone. The image she had just taken already had over three thousand Amps—and as more users shared it, it was getting even more Amplified. Front and center in the photo, Courtney grinned ear to ear.

Lovett was making great use of Panjea to connect with voters and raise campaign funds. She had more than thirty million Peers on her Panjea profile, where she ran weekly chats and shared video messages. Most of that online success was attributed to her senior strategist and media advisor, Kevin Sharpe.

Avery briefly introduced Courtney and the assembled students immediately broke the debate's rule about staying quiet. But how could they not cheer for their own classmate? As the official representative for Granville High, she would ask the last question of the night. Max knew that she was planning to ask how Panjea could be considered an impartial supporter of the debates when its CEO, Vic Ignacio, was Lovett's biggest donor.

The lights brightened and the camera panned across the audience, beaming their images out into the world. Max smiled and tried to look thoughtful and engaged.

"Candidates, are you ready?" Avery asked.

Tooms flashed a thumbs-up and Lovett nodded.

Avery consulted his laptop screen. "Our first question comes from Kennedy Richards of Bangor, Maine."

A pixelated video speckled with a lot of low-light noise showed a teenage girl in a white tank top, her black hair in a braid draped in front of her right shoulder. A silver stud in her right nostril glinted in the white glow from her computer screen. Kennedy's name and location were listed in the graphic under her image.

"Hot," Isaac breathed. "I'd like to *Bang-or.*"

Max forced a short laugh.

Kennedy's voice boomed from the speakers. "I would like to know, if you're voted into office, how are you going to address climate change?"

"First response to you, Senator Tooms. You have two minutes," Avery said.

"I'm glad we're starting off with an easy topic," Tooms said.

The audience laughed.

Tooms looked straight into the camera. "First of all, I'd like to thank Principal Zimmerman and the faculty, staff, and students of Granville High School for inviting us and hosting this event. You all know education is an important part of my campaign, and it bothers me as much as I'm sure it bothers you that you had to give up a day of classes to prepare for our visit."

More laughter and some clapping.

"But I hope we'll all learn from each other tonight." Tooms smiled. "Thank you for the question, Kennedy."

Then he launched into a carefully phrased, party-approved response that cleverly avoided acknowledging that climate change was an actual threat.

Lovett was up. "I had the opportunity to tour Granville this afternoon, and it's a lovely city. In many ways it reminds me of where I grew up, in the small town of Alexandria, Tennessee. It feels like home here. . . the kind of American town we used to see on television when I was growing up.

"I know Granville is also one of the oldest cities in California, dating back to 1850—at least according to Wikipedia." Laughter rippled through the audience.

Lovett told them Granville was a vibrant part of the nation's history, and it would be a shame if it weren't part of its future because of rising sea levels.

"Climate change is real, it's happening now, and it affects all of us," she said.

And so it went. Questions about foreign policy, internet regulation, nuclear power, national debt. Several questions touched on education and student loans. And sprinkled among these heavy topics were "fun" questions, such as: Did the candidates prefer cats or dogs? Lovett said she'd always wanted a potbellied pig.

The ninety minutes flew by. In no time, Avery said, "Our

last video question comes from Samir Gupta in Bakersfield, California."

Pixels danced in the video box onscreen.

"I'm sorry. We're having some technical—" Avery had one finger pressed to the earpiece in his left ear. Then the distorted pattern of blocks resolved into a face. "Oh, here we are."

But the face wasn't human: It was a sinister mask.

A bright light gave its bone-white surface a ghostly glow and plunged the background into shadows. It had a grotesque expression, with demonic eyes, a furrowed brow, and a horrible grimace.

Kids around Max gasped and murmured. Several students said the words that were also running through Max's head: *Dramatis Personai.* The mask was reminiscent of the ones worn by members of the well-known hacker group when they addressed the public.

Avery turned to the technicians working in the wings. "That's the wrong video," he hissed off-mike.

"Hello?" the figure said. The voice was as unsettling as the mask, digitally altered to be flat and low-pitched.

The figure turned to the right and stared into the darkness for a moment. It wore a red-hooded sweatshirt, the hood drawn over the head.

Max's heart beat faster and his palms prickled with anxiety.

The figure turned back to face the camera and took a deep breath. "My name is STOP."

What? No.

STOP was Evan's online handle.

STOP leaned closer to the camera and Max instinctively leaned closer too, trying to get a better look at him. There were twin glints behind the large, dark eyeholes of the mask, like light reflecting off lenses. Evan was practically blind without glasses.

It couldn't be.

"What's going on?" Avery asked in an exasperated voice.

"Do you really want to know?" STOP asked.

Evan, what are you doing?

"He answered me! Is this video *live*?" Avery looked at the screen with his hand cupped over his mike. "What do you mean, you don't know where it's coming from?"

"Just listen," STOP said. Even through the audio filter, there was no mistaking the urgency and desperation in his voice. "Please listen."

Three loud tones punctuated the audio. Max and his classmates flinched.

"I have a question." STOP took a deep breath and looked straight into the camera. Max shivered. From where he was sitting, it was as if STOP was looking straight at him.

"What is the silence of six, and what are you going to do about it?" STOP pushed his hood back. Evan's usually wispy brown hair was greasy and dull, matted against his head.

He reached off screen with his right hand and used his left to slowly lift his mask enough to reveal his nose and mouth.

He had a few days' growth of stubble and his pale skin glistened with sweat.

Max gripped the armrests of his seat. *What the hell was he doing?*

In his own undisguised voice, Evan mumbled. "I'm sorry, I'm sorry, I'm sorry. . . ."

Light from the desk lamp flashed against something dark. It took Max a moment longer to figure out what Evan was holding in his right hand. It didn't register immediately because it didn't belong there. It didn't belong in Evan's mouth.

Shit, that's a gun, Max thought.

The sharp pop of a gunshot tore through the quiet. The video jumped as Evan's body jerked and fell backward into the shadows with a sickening, wet thud. Blood speckled the camera lens and the light turned red.

The audience gasped then fell quiet.

2

MAX STARED AT THE BLANK WHITE SCREEN. HE wanted to scream, but he could barely breathe. That couldn't have happened. That couldn't have been real.

Evan.

The auditorium was bright and the stage was empty but for a fallen bottle of water spreading a dark, wet stain on the crimson carpet. Like blood.

He had a vague recollection of the Secret Service agents whisking Tooms and Lovett into the wings. Courtney was standing in front of the stage, clutching her closed MacBook, while Bennett Avery talked to someone over his headset.

Some students hovered near the closed doors, which were still guarded by Secret Service agents. Most had stayed in their seats, typing on their phones, huddled with their arms around themselves. Kids talked loudly and over each other.

"Oh my God. . . ."

"Can you believe that?"

"What did he say? The 'silence of six'?"

"Creepy."

"Obviously delusional."

"WTF."

"I'm gonna need therapy."

"This still isn't loading. How's yours?"

"Who was that loser?"

He was one of us! Max wanted to shout. *He wasn't just some stranger. His name was Evan Baxter. He was only seventeen years old. He walked the halls of Granville High with us. Not that any of you ever gave him the time of day.*

Of course, Max hadn't done much better lately.

Max closed his eyes, wishing he could shut out the sounds too. He saw blood and brains explode from the back of Evan's skull in slow motion, like some over-the-top horror flick.

Max heaved. He tasted the chalky protein shake he'd guzzled following his afternoon run.

"Max? You don't look so good," Isaac said.

He swallowed and opened his eyes. He took deep breaths.

"We just watched someone die," Max said.

Could people be so used to violence and gore that it didn't affect them anymore? God, kids were actually taking *selfies* now.

"I can't believe he did that on national television," Isaac said.

Max squeezed his hands into fists. "That didn't happen," he said.

Evan would never kill himself. Where would he even have gotten a gun?

He remembered: Mr. Baxter hid a gun under a loose floorboard in the master bedroom closet. Evan had discovered it years ago while looking for Christmas presents. He and Max took turns holding it and pretending to be CIA agents tracking down terrorists. Dumb, but Evan had at least made sure the gun wasn't loaded and that there were no bullets in the chamber.

So Evan wasn't stupid enough to kill himself.

"It wasn't real," Max said. "Videos can be faked."

Evan was good at that sort of thing, special effects. If it could be done with a computer, Evan could pull it off.

"It looked real," Isaac said.

"It happens," Walt said. "Things get bad, people can't deal anymore. It's a shame."

Max pressed his lips together. They didn't know it was Evan. They didn't know how impossible all this was. Evan was often depressed, but his hacking activities and friendship with Max kept him in check.

Only Max didn't know how bad it might have gotten, or how his medication might have affected him, because they hadn't talked in a while. The Evan that Max knew wouldn't have done this, but maybe he hadn't been the same Evan.

Max pulled his phone out of his pocket. He turned it on

and swiftly tapped in his twenty-digit PIN to unlock it. That last text message from Evan had to mean something. It had to tell him why.

"Don't bother. No signal. Must be overloaded or something," Walt said.

Max checked his signal strength and saw the phone was in roaming mode and had zero bars. He had no internet access either. "What the hell?" he said.

"My Panjea note still hasn't gone through," Isaac said. He showed his phone screen to Max. The progress circle in the center of the Panjea app kept spinning around and around.

"Everyone's having the same trouble?" Max asked.

"Seems like."

"Hmm." Max noticed that the doors around the auditorium were still closed and guarded, which didn't make any sense. The gun hadn't been in the school, and they didn't even know that the masked caller was a Granville student. So why were they acting like there was some immediate threat?

"What?" Isaac asked.

Max lowered his voice. "If I didn't know better, I'd say someone's using a frequency jammer to block our phone signals."

"Like, terrorists?" Panic crept into Isaac's voice.

"I don't think so," Max said. "Frequency jammers are illegal, but the government sometimes uses them during protests and in prisons, that kind of thing."

Max switched on the wireless radio on his phone. The student Wi-Fi network had been disabled, but the faculty network was active. The agents might need that one to keep their computers online. Or maybe they just neglected to turn it off.

"Why would they jam us?" Isaac asked.

"That's the question. Maybe something's going on out there they don't want us to know about. Or they don't want anyone out there to know what's happening here." Max nodded at their teachers, who kept trying to make calls.

"Come on, man," Isaac said. "This is getting freaky."

Having something to do, a problem to solve, would help Max deal with what he'd just seen. It was either this or shut down.

Max connected his phone to "Granville_FAC." The administration thought it was secure enough, but he and Evan had figured the password out on their first day of school. The router's default factory settings had never been changed: username "admin," password "00000." Brilliant.

He was online. He opened his browser to CNN and read the headline: "Breaking News: Presidential Debate Hacked," with a still of Evan in his mask. Max skimmed through the transcript below the news video:

"Moments ago, tonight's presidential debate at Granville High School in Granville, California was interrupted by a pirate video transmission from a hacker who identified himself only as 'Stop'. . ."

"You're online?" Isaac leaned over Max's shoulder.

"Shh." Max lowered his phone and looked around. No one was paying attention to them so far.

Max opened the Panjea app on his phone. People were going wild on social media with speculations on what was happening inside the school and what Evan's video had meant. The #webdeb hashtag had been joined by #Granville, #WhatIsTheSilenceOfSix, #STOP, and #coverup. The messages scrolled up like movie credits, almost too fast to read.

"No one's talking about the suicide," Max said. "You'd think they'd be all over that."

"Can I borrow that?" Walt asked. "My family's gotta be worried."

Max shook his head. "I only have an internet connection. My phone signal is still blocked."

Max could call out over the internet using his VoIP account, but Walt would draw attention if he were the only person talking on a cell phone.

Max looked around again and froze when he noticed someone watching him from the stage's left wing: a man in a gray turtleneck, black jeans, and white tennis shoes. Kevin Sharpe.

His grizzled face had recently graced the covers of *TIME* and *Wired*, where they referred to him as "the Architect" who masterminded Lovett's entire online campaign. Of course he was here tonight, but why hadn't he left with her? And why was he interested in Max?

Max casually slipped his phone into his pocket. Sharpe tapped on his tablet and disappeared into the shadows backstage.

"Now what?" Isaac said.

A stern-faced Asian man with thinning gray hair and a paunch walked on stage.

"I'm Agent Richard Kwon, with the FBI." A badge dangled from a chain around his neck.

"What's happening? Why can't we leave?" That was Jenny McIntyre from Max's social studies class. "Why don't our phones work?"

Agent Kwon held up a hand. "We have just experienced a serious security breach. We are locking down all network traffic while we attempt to trace the transmission. We greatly appreciate your patience and understanding as we deal with this. We are going to send you home shortly." He nodded and the doors at the back of the room opened. "However, as this is an ongoing federal investigation, you are prohibited from discussing this on social media of any kind. Anyone who posts about what happened here tonight will be prosecuted for obstructing justice."

Students began muttering.

"Thank you for your cooperation. We'll begin dismissing you from the back forward," Kwon said.

The students in the last row lined up in front of the doors and were escorted out of the auditorium.

Soon Max heard raised voices in the hallway outside, but he couldn't tell what they were arguing about. Finally it was Max's turn to line up, and as his row approached the hallway, they learned what the hold-up was.

"They're taking people's cell phones," Isaac whispered.

Max squeezed the phone in his pocket. He was suddenly acutely aware that he had received a text message from the very hacker who had interrupted the debate moments before killing himself. Even encrypted, the message would invite uncomfortable questions. It was only a matter of time before they connected STOP to Evan and back to Max.

Kwon had just said that anyone interfering with the investigation would be punished. Could Max be charged with withholding information if he didn't come forward with what he knew? He was probably the only person who could tell them who STOP was. Maybe that made it his responsibility to help, and sharing what he knew with Kwon could help Max understand why his friend had done this.

Damn it, Evan, Max thought. *Why did you send me that? What did you send?*

In retrospect, the message—the first communication between them in months—should have told Max that something was wrong. Maybe Evan had been reaching out for help, and Max had shrugged it off. If he had called his friend back, perhaps he could have stopped him from killing himself.

"They aren't getting my phone without a warrant," Walt said. He set his jaw and went through the doors ahead of them.

Shit. Just the fact that Max had encryption software was going to raise red flags. They would probably be able to crack the algorithm eventually.

An agent beckoned Isaac out of the auditorium. Max was next.

He pulled his phone out. Too late to remove the SIM card.

He didn't even have time to wipe its contents. If only he'd deleted Evan's message as soon as he memorized it, but he'd been waiting for some kind of explanation from his friend. As the agent nodded to Max, he did the only thing he could.

He thumbed the power switch and turned off his phone. When they turned it on, it would require his twenty-digit password to unlock it. There were ways around phone security, but it would delay their access to its contents. Max was embarrassed that he hadn't gotten around to installing kill switch software to wipe the phone remotely. He had been more focused on winning soccer games than having his phone seized by government agents.

The agent led Max to a security station where they had a plastic bin filled with student cell phones in zipped baggies labeled with their names and school ID numbers.

"We need your cell phone," she said.

"What for?" Max asked.

"We're reviewing all the pictures and videos taken during the debate for our investigation."

Max remembered what Walt had said and wondered if it had worked for him. "Don't you need a warrant?"

"You signed a waiver when you consented to be in the audience," the agent said.

He should have read that form more closely—not that the school had given students a choice in attending.

Max forced himself to keep an even tone. "I didn't record anything. I didn't even update Panjea. Will I get my phone back? Will my data be secure?" He almost couldn't keep a straight face while asking that of a government employee.

"You'll have it back as soon as we're done with it. Everything will still be there," she said.

"As long as it doesn't have anything to do with that weird video, right?" Max asked.

She looked surprised. *That was interesting.*

"I know it's an inconvenience, but this is a matter of national security."

She held a plastic baggie open for Max's phone.

"National security? Because of that depressed, crazy conspiracy nut?" Max felt a twinge of guilt. "What's to investigate?"

"Do you have something to hide?" she asked.

"No, and you know that's beside the point," Max said.

I should just tell them, Max thought. They were going to find out he was lying anyway. He just didn't know how he could best help Evan, if he wasn't already beyond help.

"We can always hold *you* and go through the phone's contents together after everyone else has been dismissed in five, six hours. Maybe longer," she said.

Evan had sent him that text for a reason. Max would never have the chance to figure it out if he told them everything now. He should try to find out more on his own first. When he knew what he was dealing with, he could still come forward if he had to. Say he was afraid, or shocked, or something. That much was true.

The agent made eye contact with someone behind Max. He

didn't turn around.

He didn't need the phone. Handing it over would be a sign of cooperation.

He offered it to her. She held out the baggie again. If she wouldn't touch it, they were probably interested in lifting fingerprints, too. In Isaac's words, this was getting freaky.

Max dropped his phone into the baggie.

"Thank you." She smoothly sealed the bag and uncapped a blue Sharpie. "Student ID number?"

"Two-four-six-oh-one," Max lied.

She raised an eyebrow, but then she scribbled the number on the bag and placed it in the box.

"Have a good night." Her tone suggested he should consider himself lucky. "Go straight home. Don't loiter on school grounds."

Isaac and Walt were loitering on school grounds, waiting for Max at the end of the hall. Another Secret Service agent stationed there was giving them the stink eye.

Isaac raised his hand for a high-five. Max slapped it unenthusiastically.

"Isaac folded right away," Walt said. "More like a lamb than a ram. That agent practically laughed at me when I mentioned a warrant."

"Makes you wonder, don't it?" Isaac said.

"What?" Max asked.

"If that guy in the video was legit. Would they go to this much trouble over nothing?" Isaac asked.

Max bit his tongue. In some ways, it bothered him that no one else knew it had been Evan. His own classmates, people who had been going to school with him since middle school, didn't know him well enough to recognize his unfiltered voice at the end of the video.

They hurried toward the exit to the parking lot. There was a guard posted at every junction in the hallway, keeping a close eye on them.

When they got outside, Max gulped in the night air, cooler than it should be for October. He shivered, which had nothing to do with the cold.

Knots of tension loosened in his neck and shoulders, until he remembered his best friend was dead.

If he could figure out Evan's last message, maybe he would know why. He just had to do it before he ended up in government custody.

MAX DIDN'T HEAR THE INSISTENT KNOCK ON THE
passenger side window of his car at first. He instinctively
closed the screen of the laptop balanced on the steering wheel
as he turned his head to see Courtney glaring at him through
the glass. He unlocked the door and she climbed in, slamming
the door.

"They took my computer!" she said.

Max curled his fingers protectively around his laptop.
"Why?"

She was shaking so much it took her three tries to fasten
her seat belt.

"I mentioned that I'd filmed the debate," she said.

Max's pulse quickened. "Including STOP's message?"

"Yeah. I know. It was a rookie mistake. I thought I was

being helpful." She seemed to shrink into her black wool coat.

"The Feds would have taken it anyway."

"The way Bennett Avery looked at me. Like I was an idiot. God! I *was* an idiot." She pulled her hair out of her bun and ran both her hands through her hair in frustration. "He said they cut off the broadcast before the end of STOP's video. I might have had the only copy."

So that's why no one was discussing the suicide online, Max thought.

"Can we get out of here?" Courtney asked.

Max slid his laptop onto the center divider and started the engine.

"Where to?" Max asked.

"Home." Her expression softened. "My home. I'm sorry. I'm not in the mood to celebrate after all."

"Nothing to celebrate tonight," he said.

Max drove east towards Courtney's house on the other side of town, near Harbor Park. Not too far from Evan's.

"Did you get all of that guy's video?" Max asked.

"Yeah."

"Did you make a backup?"

"I tried to put it on the cloud, but the Wi-Fi went wonky in there."

"Is 'wonky' a technical term?"

"It's as technical as I get. That's why I keep you around."

Max's eyes burned and the orange streetlights smeared across his vision. He slowed the car and blinked rapidly until he could see again.

"You okay?" Courtney asked.

"The. . ." He cleared his throat. "That 'wonkiness' only started after the debate ended. The Feds disabled the wireless network and jammed our phones."

Courtney drew in a sharp breath. "That's so illegal. Why would they go that far?"

"They don't want this getting out. Only the people in that auditorium know that STOP killed himself," Max said.

"I wish I hadn't seen it." Her voice caught. "That was awful."

"Are you thinking what I'm thinking?" Max asked.

"If the government doesn't want his video getting out, maybe it's important that it does," Courtney said.

Evan had to have had a good reason to kill himself, especially so publicly. Max needed to find out why.

He noticed Sunset Lane was the next street up. He made the sudden decision to turn onto it.

Courtney grabbed the dashboard. "Whoa. You were supposed to go straight there."

"Sorry, my mind wandered and I went on autopilot. Evan lives on this street." He squeezed the steering wheel.

"I didn't see him at the debate." Courtney turned and gave Max a searching look. "Max, is there something you want to tell me?"

The end of the street was flashing with red and blue lights.

"Uh-oh," Max said.

He pulled up behind a police car near the corner of Hillcrest

Avenue. He turned off the engine and studied the white two-level house. All the lights inside were on. His eyes went to the window in the attic bedroom. Silhouettes moved back and forth on the drawn shade.

"That's Evan's house," Courtney said.

Max nodded.

"Max, tell me what's going on."

Mrs. Baxter was standing on the sidewalk in front of the yard, with Mr. Baxter's arm around her. They looked back at their house. Evan, of course, was not with them.

Is this where it had happened?

As torn up as Max was by Evan's death, he knew it would destroy his parents. Had they been home when he did it? They had probably been watching the debate downstairs, not realizing that their son was the masked hacker, broadcasting two floors above them. He wondered if Evan had left a note, something more direct than what he said in the cryptic video message.

Max opened his car door.

"Where are you going?" she asked.

"To find out what's going on," he said.

"Max, think about this. Are you sure you want to get involved?" Courtney asked sharply.

Cold air seeped inside the car. Max unbuckled his seat belt. "He's my best friend."

Max closed the door softly behind him and walked briskly up the sidewalk. In addition to the police car on the street, there was another in the driveway. Its headlights were turned all the way up, casting bright spotlights on the front of the house. He didn't see an ambulance or a coroner's van.

Could they have already removed the body?

"Max?" Allie Baxter wiped her eyes and managed a shaky smile. She was a computer graphics teacher at ITT Tech, and one of the sweetest people Max knew. She'd been like a mother to Max.

Tony Baxter nodded in greeting. Max didn't know the man very well. He did something with stocks, and he was away from home a lot of the time. When he was around he kept to himself.

"Hey, Mrs. B. Is everything all right?" Max asked.

"Oh, sweetie. We're all right. But the house. . . ." She looked at their home. "We were robbed."

"Oh," Max said.

They didn't know.

He put his hands in his pockets. "I can't believe that. Did they get anything?" he asked.

"We haven't had a chance to look around yet," Mr. Baxter said. "We called the police as soon as we saw the broken door."

"Of course." Max licked his lips.

He couldn't tell them about Evan, and not just because he didn't want to tip off the Feds. Max didn't want to be the one to tell them their only son was gone.

"Are you looking for Evan?" Mrs. Baxter said.

"No, I was just . . . I was just driving Courtney home from

the debate and I saw the commotion. I was worried."

Mrs. Baxter smiled. "Thank you. I'm glad Evan wasn't home. When he's on his computer, he doesn't pay attention to anything else. As long as we're all okay, none of this matters."

Oh, God.

"It's just stuff," Mr. Baxter said gruffly, as if he were trying to convince himself. The Baxters had *nice* stuff, and a lot of it.

"Where is Evan?" Max asked. It was unusual for Evan *not* to be home on his computer. In fact, a robbery in this part of town on the night that Evan killed himself had to be more than a coincidence.

"He had to work tonight. He's been spending all of his free time at the office."

"Work," Max said. He nodded, pretending he knew what she was talking about. It was perfectly natural that Evan would be working, except that as far as Max knew, Evan didn't have a job.

"At first I was happy he was getting out of the house, but he's really just spending more time behind another computer, isn't he? I wish he was more like you, Max," Mrs. Baxter said. "But don't tell him I said so."

Max's mouth went dry. "I won't," he rasped.

"They're ready for us," Mr. Baxter said. A cop came down the walkway toward them.

Mrs. Baxter pressed closer to her husband. "I can't bear going in there right now. I want to go stay in a hotel tonight."

Mr. Baxter sighed.

Max took a couple of steps backward. "Sorry again. I've got to get going." He didn't want the cop to see him and possibly remember him later.

"I'll tell Evan you came by," Mrs. Baxter said.

"Oh, sure," Max said.

"You should visit more often, Max. I feel like we haven't seen you in a while."

"Will do." Max turned away as the cop looked at him, and walked back to his car.

Max slid into the driver's seat and closed the door. He crossed his arms on the steering wheel and rested his head for a moment.

"What happened? Max?" Courtney asked.

"The Baxters were robbed," Max said.

"Max, did Evan have something to do with that video?"

Max looked up. He waited until the cop and the Baxters had returned to the house before starting the car. He drove past slowly and turned the corner in the other direction.

"Headlights," she said.

"I know."

He waited until he was half a block away before he switched the low beams on.

Courtney was typing on his laptop with what he called her "thinky look"—the distant expression that told him she was far away from him, lost in the words flowing from her fingers.

"What the hell, Courtney?" he said.

"Relax. I'm using the guest profile, okay?"

"Still, you have to ask first," Max said. "What are you working on?"

"My blog post about the debate."

"The one the Feds told you not to write about for a few days?"

"They said not to say anything on *social media*. Besides, I'm a reporter; I have a responsibility to the truth. They won't be able to keep this out of the news for long anyway." She looked at him. "Your computer connected automatically to the Baxters' Wi-Fi. I just checked Panjea, and there's nothing about what happened. It's weird that it isn't all over Panjea by now, right?"

"Maybe the Feds are forcing Panjea to censor posts." Max laughed.

"Don't joke. If they can do that, we're all screwed," Courtney said. "That's what oppressive governments do."

"Considering what happened tonight, I'm ready to believe anything." Max glanced in the rearview mirror. Was that car following them? No, it was pulling into a driveway. Wow, he had really spooked himself.

"This is a big deal. If I break the story, the rest of the media will get it from Full Cort Press. I bet we could even get Fawkes Rising to blog about it," Courtney said.

"I guess some poor guy killing himself live makes a great story." Max pulled off his tie and tossed it into the back seat. He loosened his collar.

"It would be even better if we knew the identity of STOP," Courtney said.

Max hunched over the steering wheel.

"Max?" Courtney asked.

"What?"

"It was Evan, wasn't it?"

The car veered to the right. Max yanked it back onto the road.

"I thought that was his voice at the end," she went on. "It makes sense. He's a computer genius. He has the video equipment and experience. He obviously knows everything about how to get into the school's systems. You said you used to be a hacker, and I assume he still is. . . was."

"You're a great reporter, Cort," Max said.

"Thanks." At least she didn't sound happy about it.

"But you're not a great friend."

"Max!"

Max pulled the car onto the shoulder of the road and switched on the emergency blinkers. He stared straight ahead at the dark road for a moment before turning to her.

"What do you expect?" Max asked.

"Talk to me." She closed the screen and folded her hands over it in her lap.

"Yes, it was Evan. Do you know what that means?" he asked.

"He's dead."

"Cort, my friend died tonight."

"Evan made a choice. And so did you."

"What do you mean by that?"

"You have to tell them who he was," she said.

"You volunteered information and you lost your laptop."

"This is different."

"They'll figure it out soon enough," he said.

"All the more reason not to keep it to yourself. How is it going to look when they find out you were friends?"

He didn't say anything.

"Not good," she said. "Really not good."

"It looks pretty bad from here already," he said. "Did you say anything to them about Evan?"

"I didn't know before. Do you know what he was talking about?"

"I have no idea. I haven't talked to him in a while. You're the reporter. What do you think?"

"I think you knew him better than anyone," Courtney said.

"Until he pulled the trigger, I never thought he was capable of something like that. What's going to happen when they do identify him?" Max asked.

"They'll interview kids at school, anyone who knew him. Our classmates will say he was a quiet boy, that they don't know why he did this. They'll dredge up some meaningless interaction they had with him once that makes them feel better about the way they treated him or that gives them some insight into his character. Some kids will say they always thought there was something 'off' about him and that they aren't surprised. He was obviously very troubled, and they wish he'd only talked to someone, or gotten the help he needed." Courtney tapped her fingernails against the lid of his laptop. "They'll learn you were his only friend. What will you say about him?"

"Nothing. Evan's a private person, and so am I."

"You're the only person who can speak for him. Set the record straight, so people know he didn't do this because he was bullied or depressed."

"I can't even do that much. I don't know why he did it. If I had been a good friend, I would have seen this coming."

"Oh, Max." She placed a hand on his knee.

"I could have stopped him."

"You don't know that. Evan planned everything, right? He didn't do things spontaneously. He must have worked on this plan for a long time, and if he didn't reach out to you, of all people, I don't think anyone could have changed his mind."

Evan *had* reached out to him though. He'd sent a few chat messages to Max earlier in the week, at odd hours in the middle of the night. But Max had been offline, and he hadn't had a chance to get back to him. He hadn't bothered to. Evan had even resorted to leaving a voicemail, but all he'd said was "Call me."

That should have told Max something was up. Evan only used his phone as a phone when he really needed to talk or didn't want to put anything in writing over e-mail. But he was also paranoid about leaving voice records that could be used to identify him. Max had been too busy with school and family and soccer practice and. . . Courtney.

He and Evan had been inseparable once, but he hadn't even had time to return a phone call. Max had figured he'd see him tonight at the debate, where he could find out what he wanted in person.

"Max?" Courtney said.

"Huh?" She had just asked him a question but he hadn't heard it.

"I said, what was the last contact you had with Evan?"

"A text," he said automatically, then realized he'd said too much.

"What did it say?" she asked.

"Just some nonsense," he said.

Max started the car. They were only a couple of blocks away from Courtney's house. He looked over his left shoulder and pulled back onto the road.

"You're hiding something," she said.

"I'm upset that my best friend is gone."

"Is that all it is? How many times have you even seen Evan since we got together? I spend all my free time with you, so when do you talk to him? And if he is such a good friend, why wouldn't you want to help the Feds figure out what he was trying to tell us? This was more than just a suicide."

"I don't want to end up in one of your goddamn articles!"

The silence between them stretched on for a long time.

"Can't you turn the reporter off for a minute?" Max asked.

"No, I can't. That's the definition of a reporter," Courtney said.

"Then I have nothing else to say."

He pulled into Courtney's driveway, behind her mom's Prius. He left the car running.

They sat there and looked at each other with uncertainty. This was more awkward than when they'd said good night after their first date—then they had both known what they wanted, and that they were going to get it. The future was far less certain here.

"Thanks for the ride," Courtney said.

"Thanks for the interview," Max said.

He regretted it as soon as he said it, but the damage was already done, and Courtney didn't need a reporter's instincts to know the truth when she heard it.

She blinked rapidly and turned away. She drew in a shaky breath.

"Good night, Max." She opened the passenger door. "Be careful."

"Hold on," he said.

She turned around. "Yes?"

"My computer," he said.

She put his laptop down on the empty passenger seat. She opened it and pulled a USB drive from her purse. "Can I at least grab what I wrote?"

Max snatched his computer back before she could plug it

in. "I don't know where that's been. I'll send your post to you."

She straightened, slammed the door, then stalked up the walkway to her house.

Max waited until she made it safely inside before he drove away.

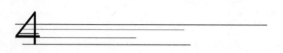

4

MAX OPENED THE FRONT DOOR AND FOUND HIS dad waiting for him in the foyer, balancing his open ThinkPad on one arm.

"Thank God," Bradley Stein said. "Are you okay?"

After one look at Max's face, Bradley put down his computer and pulled him into a hug.

His dad's hugs were legendary. They had miraculously taken away the pain of scrapes and bumps and life's assorted disappointments since Max was little. Being home, warm and surrounded by the comforting smell of musty old books and Chinese takeout, made Max feel like everything was going to be all right.

For a few seconds, Max forgot that things were seriously screwed up and that his world would never be the same again.

But only for a few seconds.

"Tell me what happened." Bradley picked up his laptop and led Max into the living room. The TV was tuned to CNN, still covering the aftermath of Evan's video, but what Courtney said was true—the news still had no mention of the video's gruesome ending.

Bradley pushed aside some stacks of paper on the coffee table to make room for his computer. Most of the time, this was his office. He was a web developer for WriteOn!, a nonprofit organization that provided a range of services for human rights initiatives. Max's dad worked from home all day, right there on the couch, and often late into the night.

Max sat on the sagging end of the couch and sank deep into the cushions. Bradley picked up the TV remote.

"No, leave it," Max said. "I want to hear what's happening."

A CNN reporter was saying, "*Both Senator Tooms and Governor Lovett have issued official statements regarding the question posed to them tonight by the hacker identified only as STOP. They both claim to know nothing about the so-called 'silence of six' and dismissed the message as a stunt to disrupt. . .*"

Bradley muted the television.

"What did you see in there?" Bradley prompted.

"Did that hacker in the mask seem familiar?" Max asked.

"Should he have?"

Max put his hands on his knees and squeezed until his knuckles were white. "That was Evan."

"Holy shit," Bradley said. He dropped the remote on the

coffee table with a hollow thud. "Holy shit. Are you sure?"

"Evan goes by the handle STOP. He dropped the voice filter near the end when he lifted his mask. It was definitely him."

Revealing his real voice could have been a calculated move. Or maybe he was just too distraught, or had stopped caring, because he was about to shoot himself.

"I didn't see that part. Where is he now?" Bradley asked.

Max leaned forward. He felt like he was going to throw up. He squeezed his eyes shut, but that didn't prevent hot tears from leaking through. His body shook as he sobbed.

He felt his dad's hand on his back.

Max heaved a ragged breath. He swiped the back of his arm over his eyes and nodded.

"Evan's dead," Max whispered hoarsely.

His dad stiffened beside him. "How?"

"He shot himself. Courtney said they cut the live feed before everyone watching saw it."

Bradley held Max tight. Max turned and pressed his face against his father's polo shirt.

"Max. . ." His dad's voice broke up. "I'm so, so sorry."

Just as Allie Baxter had been like a mother to Max, Bradley Stein had treated Evan like a second son. He'd been a big part of why Evan and Max had gotten so interested in computers in the first place.

Max described what had happened.

"So Evan's parents have no idea?" Bradley asked. He handed Max a bottle of water.

Max drained it and rolled the empty bottle between his hands. The thin plastic crinkled as it went back and forth.

"I couldn't tell them," Max said. "I can't even be sure he's really dead."

"That would be some hoax. Why would he pretend to kill himself?"

"Why would he do any of it?" Max asked.

"He sure got people's attention."

"The government can't keep this quiet. Especially if Courtney publishes her blog post," Max said.

"The smart thing to do is stay out of it, as much as we can. Courtney's right: As soon as they establish a link to you, they'll come knocking. Especially if they learn he sent you something just before he died. I assume you memorized his text. Have you tried to figure it out?"

"I haven't been able to think straight. I need to write it down, work with it a bit to see if it's a code or a passphrase...."

"Maybe I can help." Bradley handed Max a yellow legal pad and a pen.

Max wrote out Evan's message and the string of forty-two characters, counting spaces:

a9 %_!;e3 Z_j*g29@X; aso] dr23\\8i #qWd|0?

He handed it to his dad.

Bradley studied the message. "Evan asks you for help, but he's awfully vague."

"That video was vague too."

"Is there any chance those agents will find this on either of your phones?"

"Evan would have zero filled his phone's memory." Writing over his phone's contents with junk data should make the data irrecoverable. "That's what I should have done, but I didn't know it was important until it was too late. If they break the encryption on my phone, they'll see it. They'll know who it's from, but that's all. Hell, maybe they'll have better luck figuring it out."

Max's dad scribbled on the edges of the page, his eyebrows furrowed in concentration.

"Evan obviously didn't want them to have this," Bradley said. "It has to be something that either means something to you, or will mean something later."

He tore the first few pages off the pad and crumpled them up. He stuffed the ball of paper into a coffee mug.

"Max, are you still hacking?" Bradley asked. "It's okay if you are. But we need to know what we're in for here."

"No!" Max said. "Not since I started playing soccer last year."

Bradley nodded.

"I think Evan might have gotten deeper into it. Like, maybe he was mixed up with Dramatis Personai."

"The hacktivist group? Because of his mask?"

"That, and they've been targeting this election a lot."

Some people claimed Dramatis Personai was a spinoff of

the larger hacker group, Anonymous. It wasn't trying to make a name for itself, and it didn't follow a clear moral code. No one ever knew why it attacked a certain company or individual, leading many to assume it was just a bunch of troublemakers.

Anonymous operated as a collective, with an ominous, drone-like mentality: "We are Anonymous. We are legion. We do not forgive. We do not forget. Expect us." But Dramatis Personai acted as though it actually *was* a single entity, posting notes on Panjea like:

Hello, I'm Dramatis Personai. Life is theater. Watch. Laugh. Weep. The curtain is rising.

I decided it was finally time to teach the cable news networks a lesson in objectivity. They're too weak to break free from their corporate puppet masters—so what happens? They force-feed us with their one-sided agendas until our craniums are fat with propaganda.

I strongly object to their existence, so for ten minutes this morning, they didn't exist. Fox, MSNBC, CNN, and all the other acronyms were off the air.

If they insult our intelligence one more time, I'll do it again.

You're welcome.

No one was safe from their wrath or whimsy, not even Panjea.

It was only a matter of time before a social media giant like Panjea would take over. Information that we create, our data, is now theirs to sell to—guess who?—the corporate world. We do the heavy lifting, Panjea sits back and collects the cash.

Sure, we don't have to go on the site in the first place, but don't lie to us and say you offer your service for free. All of us are paying with a new currency: our privacy. We pay a price for living. And soon, we're all gonna go broke.

The social media companies know way too much about us; we can't escape them. So for the last two hours, I turned every post on Panjea into useless strings of the pig snout emoji. Google, you're next.

You're welcome.

Dramatis Personai passed itself off as a machine mind, an artificial intelligence with a snarky teenage personality, but it was definitely a group of talented geeks. Geeks just like Evan.

"The government's been making examples of the high profile hackers they catch more than they ever have before." Bradley said. "If Evan was involved, they'll investigate him in the hopes it will lead to his co-conspirators. It's possible this will all lead back to your old alter ego. I think I'd better phone my lawyer in the morning."

"Okay," Max said. "But I didn't do anything wrong, Dad."

"Even so, that doesn't mean you can't be charged with anything. Believe me, I know."

The reason Bradley had a lawyer was because he'd been a political activist—until Max's mom, Lianna, had abandoned them and left him solely responsible for Max. He still did web work pro bono for human rights organizations and had expressed his approval of how hacktivism groups kept the government in check.

"Why don't you get some rest? It's been a rough day. In the morning things will look different and we'll figure out what to do next," Bradley said.

"Aside from lawyering up?" Max asked.

"Evan was counting on you. At the very least, his parents deserve to know what their son gave up his life for."

"I thought you said the smart thing was to leave it alone."

Bradley smiled. "Your mother used to say I was far too clever to be smart. She also said you take after me."

"Like that's a bad thing," Max said.

"We'll see. Whatever you decide to do about all this, I'll support it."

"Thanks, Dad." He grabbed the edge of the couch and pulled himself to his feet. "Good night."

Max didn't sleep. He couldn't have if he'd tried.

He huddled in front of his desktop computer in the dark. He hadn't done this kind of thing in a while, but he still had all the tools he needed.

He used Tor, a web browser which masked his computer's location, but unfortunately was the equivalent of waving a big red flag and shouting, "Hey, I'm doing something interesting over here!"

In this case, Max wanted to search for information about STOP and Evan, to know what the FBI would be able to discover once they had a name. He also looked for information on 503-ERROR, his old hacker handle.

He didn't come up with anything. They'd thoroughly covered their tracks over the years, thanks to Evan's skills and caution. The only connection between Evan and Max existed in real life.

An hour after Max heard his dad finally go to bed at two a.m. he slipped out to the garage and wheeled his bike to the street. The squeaking rear tire made him grit his teeth. He didn't want to risk waking his dad by starting the car, and it would only take thirty minutes to bike to the Baxters' house. There was no traffic at this time of night.

He hid his bike behind some shrubs and walked the last block, in case the house was already being watched. The cop cars were gone, the driveway was empty, and the windows were dark. They must have gone to a hotel after all, which made this easier.

If the house was under surveillance, it was well hidden. Hopefully he wouldn't be mistaken for another burglar; he just wanted to take a quick look around Evan's room, and it wasn't breaking and entering if he had a key.

He went around the back and unlocked the kitchen door. Somehow it always smelled delicious in there. Max's stomach gurgled loudly. He pressed his hand to his belly. He hadn't eaten anything since lunch.

He helped himself to a cookie from the jar on the counter. He cupped a hand under it as he bit in and walked into the living room.

He was worried about dropping crumbs, but the room was already a mess: chairs knocked over, table upended, the couch cushions were in a pile on the floor and ripped open. He stood and stared at the carnage. It didn't look like a burglary at all— it looked more like someone had been looking for something in particular.

The expensive things in the room were untouched: the television and entertainment center, the paintings and knick-knacks on the mantle, even Mr. Baxter's Rolex, which he always forgot in a bowl by the front door. So if those things were still there, what had been taken?

The rest of the first floor had been similarly tossed, but he didn't see anything specifically missing. Finally, he crept slowly up the stairs. The master bedroom was open and empty. He went past it and took the narrow, winding staircase into Evan's attic.

It was in chaos. Books had been pulled from shelves. His desk drawers had been dumped.

And his computers were gone.

Evan had several laptops and a few desktops, all of them in active use for various tasks such as file sharing and gaming. He had probably needed his workhorse laptop to stream the video, but he wouldn't have taken all of them. Even his stacks of external hard drives and bins of memory cards were missing.

Max sat in Evan's desk chair. He swiveled slowly, taking in the whole room. He suspected the rest of the house had been ransacked to disguise the real target.

There was another possibility: Maybe Evan had seen all this before his parents did. It had spooked him, sent him on the run. And ultimately, it had convinced him that the only way out was to kill himself.

"Jesus," Max said.

He poked around the mess of books and loose cables scattered around the carpet.

He didn't know what he was looking for. A suicide note? A pay stub from Evan's supposed job would be nice, if that hadn't been a cover story to get him out of the house without arousing suspicion. Wherever it was, he must have stayed out late often, or else his parents would have been alarmed when he didn't come home. Maybe they were already wondering where he was.

Max looked at the posters on Evan's wall. Above his bed, close to the ceiling, was a long strip of paper: a reproduction of the first long-distance telegram, transmitted by Samuel F.B. Morse in 1844. It was a series of Morse code notations with the translated letters written below: WHAT HATH GOD WROUGHT?

Evan said that the telegraph, one of the many obsolete technologies that he was infatuated with, was the first internet. His online handle had been inspired by the telegram's use of "STOP" to indicate a period at the end of a sentence.

Max climbed onto the bed and reached his hand up. He swept it along the printout, feeling for anything behind it.

There was a slight, rectangular bump in the middle. He peeled the paper from the wall and turned it over.

A white plastic card was taped to the back. Next to it, Evan had neatly handwritten the lines "HTTP Error 503 Service Unavailable" and "A patient waiter is no loser."

Error 503 was the inspiration for Max's online handle. His specialty had been implementing Distributed Denial of Service attacks to take down websites. He'd had a fleet of botnets, computers infected with malware so that with a click of his mouse he could use the network to cripple a site with requests in a matter of minutes. It had seemed like fun at the time, but Max wasn't proud of it now. He'd given Evan access to the botnets when he got out of hacking, but as far as he knew, he'd never used them.

Max examined the quarter-inch thick plastic card. It was about the size of his palm, and from the embossed "HID" in one corner, he knew it was made by one of the world's top manufacturers of security systems.

A keycard? For what?

He added it to his pocket with the folded printout then took one last look around before heading home.

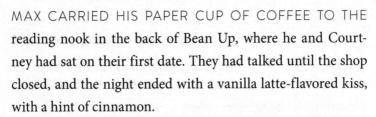

5

MAX CARRIED HIS PAPER CUP OF COFFEE TO THE reading nook in the back of Bean Up, where he and Courtney had sat on their first date. They had talked until the shop closed, and the night ended with a vanilla latte-flavored kiss, with a hint of cinnamon.

The empty chair across the small round table seemed accusatory. Courtney must still be angry with him; she had sent an e-mail early that morning saying she would drive herself to school. She'd likely stayed up all night writing her article. It wasn't online yet, and he wondered if she really would post it.

Max yawned. He drank half his coffee, letting the hot liquid do the work of waking him up until the caffeine kicked in. The scalding black brew tasted like punishment.

He stifled another yawn and opened his laptop.

After getting home from Evan's the night before, he'd curled up in bed with his computer and ran every decryption program he had against the text Evan had sent him. Considering what Evan had done a short while after sending it, Max believed the message was important, and that he was meant to decipher it.

A coffee grinder droned behind the counter. The gay barista who always gave Max free refills smiled when Max looked over.

In junior high, Max and Evan used to trade notes encrypted with the simplest of substitution codes, the kind where *A* equals *one*, *B* equals *two*, and so on. They soon moved from that basic cipher to devising their own, more complicated ones, and their interests gradually shifted to computer hacking and decrypting databases of passwords to get access to people's e-mails, social media accounts, and private systems.

Most computer systems stored passwords as encrypted hashCodes. It took a long time to crack them by brute force with software, but dictionaries of words and their corresponding hashCodes—called rainbow tables—made it much easier.

If someone used a common word like "password"—which plenty of people actually did—it would take under a second to crack the hashCode by checking it against these tables. And once you had one password for a site or system, you often had access to that person's other accounts. Lots of people sacrificed security for convenience by using the same password everywhere.

Max was starting from scratch, though, with no hint at a possible cipher key that could help him translate Evan's text. He didn't even know where to begin.

He stared at the forty-two characters on his screen, which he had meticulously retyped. There were few repetitions and he could see no discernible pattern. He checked them over carefully once more. If he misremembered even a single character, the code would be much harder to crack—if not rendered entirely useless. But his memory hadn't failed him yet. He routinely recalled passwords as complicated as this one.

Max lifted his heavy head and rubbed his eyes. They stung from fatigue, and his neck ached from craning it forward. When he picked up his cup, he was surprised it was empty. He checked the time in the corner of his screen: seven-thirty. He should have left two minutes ago to get to school on time.

He didn't move. The only reason to go to school was to act normal, and he didn't think he could go through the day pretending that he wasn't mourning his best friend. He might be able to reclaim his cell phone, but he'd already written it off; if the FBI had checked it, they would want him to answer some difficult questions.

In fact, once they cracked his phone or otherwise discovered STOP was Evan, they would be looking for Max. No reason to make it easy on them by being exactly where they would expect him to be.

He wasn't ready to face Courtney yet either.

Max fired off a short e-mail to his dad inquiring about the

lawyer. It might be a good idea to have that phone number with him if things went south today.

He loaded Full Cort Press. Courtney's most recent blog post was from yesterday where she said she was excited about the debate. He cleared the cache and refreshed the page to make sure she hadn't published her exposé yet. If she blew Evan's cover, Max would have even less time before the Feds became interested in him. He couldn't even be sure that she wouldn't mention Max in the story, after the way they'd left things last night. She'd made it pretty clear that getting the scoop was more important than anything, including him.

Max looked around the coffee shop at the other early risers. A guy in a red and gold Los Medanos College hoodie sat at the table next to him, typing on his MacBook with just his index fingers, as if he were playing "Chopsticks" on a piano. A copy of *Cat's Cradle* by Kurt Vonnegut and a messy stack of index cards rested beside him.

Max leaned over. "Excuse me?"

The student glanced at Max and plucked one white earbud from his ear.

"Could I borrow a pen?" Max asked.

The guy rummaged in the messenger bag on the chair beside him and pulled out a red ballpoint pen without a cap.

"I think this writes." He handed it to Max.

"Thanks." Max scribbled on a gray napkin made of 100 percent recycled paper. The ink was sticky and the pen tip almost tore the thin paper, but it worked.

Some things were better done on paper than on a computer. He scribbled Evan's code across the top of the napkin. It stood to reason that it wasn't as easy as a substitution of one for one, with all those random numbers and punctuation marks and other characters.

"Do you want something better to write on?" the LMC student asked.

Max smiled. "That would be great," he said.

"I don't need these anymore." He passed Max a short stack of index cards with almost illegible notes on the front of each. "The backs are clean."

"Thanks," Max said.

Max messed around with the text message for about an hour while his second cup of coffee went cold. He tried dividing it into words based on where the spaces were and applied every cipher he remembered, backwards and forwards. He tried merging some of his and Evan's favorite ciphers. He pulled out all the numbers then put them back again. He arranged the sequence in different patterns, sorted them by length, built intricate matrices until it resembled a cracked-out game of Scrabble.

Max shredded the last index card. He hadn't done cryptanalysis in a long time. Either this was the toughest code Evan had ever devised, or it wasn't a code at all and he was just wasting time.

If it was a passphrase, it was way too long to be useful to most people, even for Evan and his astonishing mnemonics. But it was possible that he had created a one-off passphrase, knowing that only Max's memory could retain one this complicated.

So if it was a passphrase, the trick was figuring out what it was for—just as he had to do with the keycard he was carrying, which unlocked a door somewhere in the world. Until he found out where they fit, he would have to keep them safe from whoever had ransacked the Baxters' house.

"Hey, can you watch my stuff for a minute?" the college student asked.

Max nodded absentmindedly, gazing out the wide front windows.

After a minute of staring at the street in front of the shop where he'd parked his dad's Impala, he registered a black sedan that was now parked in the spot behind his. The side windows were tinted, but Max could see the occupants through the clear windshield. The driver wore dark sunglasses and a green polo shirt under a gray windbreaker. His passenger had on a black T-shirt and a blue and white varsity jacket, and was typing on a bulky black laptop balanced on the dashboard.

Max was getting an ugly vibe from these guys. They looked too old to be college students and more like actors hired to play teenagers on television. He glanced at the LMC student's table suspiciously. Was he with them?

Max's laptop screen had gone dark to conserve power, so he tapped a key to wake it up. He refreshed Courtney's blog, but the browser was suddenly sluggish. He was still connected to the shop's Wi-Fi network and the signal looked strong, but the page wasn't loading. Something else was slowing it down.

Something like a man-in-the-middle attack, which two men logged in to the same network could execute from a car parked outside the coffee shop. Max had been careless to connect to a public router without masking his IP address.

"Shit." Max's heart was pounding and the palms of his hands tingled.

This had to be connected to Evan. But were these guys federal agents, or with someone else?

Not knowing their identities made Max even more nervous. It didn't matter who they were—they either wanted the message he had, or they wanted to prevent him from sharing it. Max couldn't wait around to find out.

He scanned the coffee shop, mapping an escape route in his mind. He visualized his path through the tables, chairs, and scattered early-morning patrons the way he kept in mind the positions of his teammates, their opponents, and the soccer ball on the field. Only right now, he couldn't see the ball or his way to the goal.

His attention returned to the car in time to see the driver remove a hand from inside his windbreaker.

Shit. Shit. Shit.

Max's time was up.

Whoever these guys were, even if they couldn't circumvent half a dozen of his security precautions and compromise his computer, he had to assume they now knew a few things: One, he was trying to crack Evan's code. Two, he had just e-mailed his dad about a lawyer. They probably had access to his unencrypted e-mails, which included that last one from Courtney—so if she hadn't published her post yet, they could be reading it from her hard drive right now.

The upside was that monitoring his computer wasn't the same as monitoring *him*. They couldn't tell that he was on to them or see him quietly freaking out because his webcam was covered with black tape, a low-tech precaution.

The front doors of the sedan opened and the guys stepped out. Sunglasses walked to the sidewalk and kept an eye on the entrance to Bean Up while Varsity strolled over to Max's car holding a small black box. He held it close to the lock on the passenger side—then opened the door.

What the hell?!

Max patted his pocket. His key fob was still there, so they must have had some way of bypassing the electronic lock. Max knew how to do this too, but it was scary to see it in action, against him. Varsity rummaged through the glove compartment and came up with Max's backup laptop. *Great.* Thankfully, that one was configured to delete all his activity and files whenever he logged out.

As much as Max wanted to, he didn't dare send his dad a second e-mail right now to tell him what was going on. They might be recording his every keystroke, but it wouldn't matter after this. He started the process of deleting and zero filling the drive. It felt like putting down a beloved pet.

Max reverently closed the laptop lid while the self-destruct sequence ran and stood up. Now they could have it, for all the good it would do them.

He slid the pen into his left front pocket with the uncapped end sticking out. It made for a sad weapon, despite the old adage. Of course, even a sword wasn't much use against fire-arms, but if they got rough with him, he would get rough right back.

Max spotted the torn index cards and napkin with Evan's code written on it. He couldn't just leave them there or throw them away; you could find all sorts of useful things about peo-ple by going through their trash.

He popped the lid off his full cup of coffee and quickly sub-merged the thin strips. He covered the cup again and swirled the coffee around.

Now Sunglasses was walking toward the entrance. Max had to get out of here.

He remembered the emergency exit past the bathrooms, which led to the narrow loading area between this building and Bow Wow!, the dog boutique next door. This was defi-nitely an emergency.

Hands trembling and slick with sweat, he walked by the college kid's table. He closed the lid of the kid's silver MacBook and smoothly tucked it under his arm. No one even looked up from their laptops or paid him any attention. He walked at a leisurely pace toward the restrooms, resisting the urge to bolt.

It was a dick move, stealing from someone who had been kind to him, especially when he was working on a paper for school, but Max needed it more than he did. And if he had the chance—if he stayed free and alive—he would try to return it later.

Max paused at the back door with his free hand on the crossbar. What if they had backup waiting for him right outside?

A toilet flushed in the bathroom by the emergency exit. He clutched the stolen laptop under his arm tightly. Water ran in the sink.

Max pushed the door open and slipped through. As it swung shut behind him, he heard a bell jingle back in the cafe. They were inside.

Max tossed his coffee cup into a small dumpster then dragged the rusty metal bin over to block the exit. It scraped against the concrete with a horrible, prolonged shriek.

The college kid was going to raise a fuss over his missing computer, and then Max's followers would know he had it. But they wouldn't be able to catch him. Not on foot, in his hometown.

Max ran.

He cut over to One Tree Way and ran along it, passing the parking lot. When he turned onto Deer Valley Road at full speed he actually laughed from the joy of wind against his face and pavement under his soles. He was running, and he was fast, even if he didn't know where he was going yet.

The only things Max had ever stolen before were records from clueless companies' servers, passwords, some e-mails. But digital files couldn't be missed, since he had only copied them, and no one had ever suffered anything worse than embarrassment, because he hadn't ever done anything with what he took. In fact, he and Evan had always alerted the companies to their security holes, without even bothering to claim credit or the financial rewards some of them offered.

Whatever those guys wanted him for, he was now definitely a criminal. He'd just taken some innocent guy's laptop.

And his pen.

MAX PUSHED THROUGH THE REVOLVING DOORS into the Gateway Suites.

He stood just inside for a couple of minutes, pretending to check the time on his new burner phone, until he was certain that the gentleman behind the concierge desk had seen him waiting. He pretended to dial a number then held the phone to his ear. Max paced slowly back and forth in front of the doors.

"Hey. Yeah, I'm here," he said into the phone. His voice carried well in the marble-floored lobby. "Just a few minutes. I'm downstairs. . . . Really? Okay. Sure. I can come back if—No. No, that's fine. Yeah, I'll wait."

Max made eye contact with the concierge and mouthed the word *sorry*. The man looked at him sympathetically.

"Sure, I'll stay right here," Max said. He shrugged and

pointed over to the lounge area and raised his eyebrows. The concierge nodded.

"Take your time. I'll sit tight," Max said as he made a bee-line for the seat in the farthest corner, near a mahogany baby grand piano. He sat in one of the lush armchairs facing the desk, where he could see the concierge and everyone who walked in, but where visitors would not be able to spot him immediately because of a marble pillar in the center of the room. He noted the emergency exits to his left, as well as the open space leading to them.

He'd nearly been cornered back in the coffee shop. He had narrowly escaped, but he wanted to have plenty of notice before he was caught off guard again.

Max settled back in the wide chair and put his new back-pack on his lap. After successfully evading capture at Bean Up, he'd made a quick stop at Staples at the Granville Square Shopping Center for some vital supplies. He needed a bag because he would have been more conspicuous walking around with a naked MacBook. Along with the prepaid, disposable smart-phone that offered him anonymity, he had also picked up a universal AC adapter for the stolen computer, a pack of two 32GB USB sticks, a microSD card and adapter, a bottle of Goo Gone, a roll of black electrical tape, and earbuds with a built-in microphone.

He couldn't keep using his bank cards, so he'd risked a one-time withdrawal at an ATM near the Amtrak station, tak-ing out the daily maximum of eight hundred dollars—most of his savings from caddying at the Old Mill Golf Club over the summer. After this morning's shopping trip, he was down to $637.66 in cash—all the money he would have until this blew over.

Max pulled out the MacBook and got to work. He applied Goo Gone to the "Los Medanos Mustangs" and "Small World Amusement Park" stickers on the cover. After a couple of minutes, the liquid had loosened the glue enough for the stickers to slide right off. He rubbed it dry with the sleeve of his jacket.

Next he peeled off a strip of electrical tape and stuck it over the web camera lens inside the MacBook's lid, then powered on the computer.

It didn't even require a login password when it woke from sleep mode. This guy had just been asking for it.

Max rebooted the machine, thinking through what he had to do next. His skills might be a little rusty, but hacking had been his life once; it had been second nature to look for flaws everywhere, from systems to people to places.

He and Evan had talked about how they would go on the run if they were caught for their cybercrimes, but they'd just been fooling around. Now that he was suddenly an actual fugitive, Max had instinctively begun following their imagined escape plan, and improvising with tactics he'd seen in thrillers over the years.

When he heard the computer's startup chime, Max quickly held down the Command and S keys. He glanced up and caught an annoyed look from the concierge. He initiated the commands to delete the computer's setup file and rebooted it.

Max plugged his earbuds into the headphone jack and stuck one in his left ear. If he'd done this correctly, he had just tricked the computer into thinking it was brand new.

He logged in to the hotel's guest Wi-Fi network—he'd chosen Gateway Suites specifically because they advertised complimentary wireless internet in the lobby.

It worked. He created a new administrator account with the username "Maskelyne" and a ten-character passphrase, using his usual system to scramble the phrase "this machine was stolen" with numbers and other punctuation marks. Then he enabled firmware password protection to prevent anyone else from doing what he had just done, and deleted the computer's tracking software so it couldn't be used to find him.

He scouted the lobby. Not much traffic on a Thursday afternoon. He picked up his burner phone and tested one of the ringtones. He faked answering it and carried on another one-sided conversation for the benefit of the concierge: Yes, he'd be happy to keep waiting, he had a lot of work to catch up on anyway, and the concierge was nice enough to let him hang out in the lobby.

Then he went fishing through the true owner's files.

Hi, Jeremy Schaal. Thanks for loaning me your laptop, Max thought.

He looked up information on Jeremy on both his computer and the internet. He was a second-year English major at LMC.

E-mails from his advisor (his browser was set to remember his passwords, another no-no) indicated Jeremy was not a particularly good student, and e-mails from three women he was dating at the same time suggested why. One of the women was a teaching assistant for one of his classes, so at least Jeremy was doing something to try to improve his grades.

Max zipped up all of the academic documents and sent them to Jeremy from his own e-mail address. In the e-mail, Max promised to ship the computer back or send money to replace it when he could, because of course he knew Jeremy's home address now too. He signed his message "Anonymous." He smiled, thinking that Jeremy would assume he'd been hacked by someone from the infamous group.

That was fun. He'd missed doing stuff like this.

Now to get down to his real business.

First, he launched a secure web browser and ran a search for the latest information on the debate. It looked like Courtney was still sitting on her blog post, but media was now buzzing about the suicide. Max knew it was inevitable the story would come out eventually—how long could they keep an auditorium full of teenagers from sharing information online? Yet there was still no public video footage of those final seconds of Evan's video.

Agent Kwon was quoted as saying, "We're following up on some promising leads. Right now, we're focused on finding out who STOP was."

But since Max was clearly one of their promising

leads—perhaps their only one—they had to know that Evan was STOP. Had they found his body yet?

Kwon hadn't said anything about investigating the meaning behind STOP's message, which left it to Max.

He launched a new tab and opened Panjea, while running more searches in other tabs for "silence of six," "Clancy Tooms," and "Angela Lovett." He switched between them all, soaking in whatever information he could.

The only hits on "silence of six" were articles about the debate, which all showed the same short clip of Evan's question, "What is the silence of six, and what are you going to do about it?"

Commenters on the blogs were wondering if the phrase literally referred to six people who had been silenced, whatever that meant, or if there was someone or something named "Six," or some organization with a similar-sounding acronym that was "silent," as in secret. Someone pointed out that STOP was a hacker, and "SICS" was internet slang for "Sitting in Chair Snickering"—suggesting he had posted the video "4 the lulz."

If they had seen the video's dark and graphic finale, no one would think it was a joke.

The debate had ended prematurely, but it had been nearly over anyway; most pundits declared it a win for Lovett, mirroring overwhelming online sentiment in her favor. Senator Tooms's team tried to spin STOP's interruption as another attack against Tooms by Dramatis Personai.

Governor Lovett had opted to issue a simple, personal

apology for the debate being disrupted. She invited anyone with questions or concerns to participate in her Ask Me
Anything beginning at five o'clock Pacific time in the Panjea
forum, promising that she would answer as much as she could
in an hour.

Max collapsed the other tabs and returned to Panjea. To
find out what "the silence of six" was, he had to get into Evan's
head—which was all stored online. His friend was brilliant
when it came to computers, and he referred to off-line storage
and the cloud to host his brain. His hard drives and online
backups were now all that was left of Evan.

And those were just as inaccessible as he was. Of course
his accounts were too secure for Max to guess the passphrases,
and he struck out with the characters from Evan's text message
as well.

He browsed Evan's public Panjea pages, but Evan hadn't
made any notes since May, or he had purged them. There could
be a clue buried deep in his pages of notes, but Max didn't have
the time to go chasing ghosts right now.

Ghosts.

There was one last place Max could check online to see if
anyone knew anything about Evan's plan—if he could find his
way back there. As far as most people knew, it didn't exist.

Max typed in an IP address he hadn't visited in over a year.
For a while, this site had been his whole world, but now it just
seemed like a tiny part of it.

He was in. The address for the hidden hacker chat group

was still alive in the so-called "Deep Web," the intricate network of unpublished IP addresses on the internet. No search engine crawled through the Deep Web indexing webpages. Like the most exclusive clubs, you had to know it existed before you could go there, and you had to have an invitation. The question was, had his invitation expired after a year away?

Max clicked his cursor into the first of two unmarked text fields on the screen and typed "503-ERROR". The box disappeared and he entered his passphrase. That box disappeared too, leaving a blank white screen.

After ten seconds, he thought the slow Wi-Fi was to blame. After thirty, he wondered if the page had timed out, or if the chat rooms were no longer active. After fifty seconds, he started to get worried.

Loud high heels clacked on the marble floor and echoed throughout the lobby. Max watched a woman in a short red mini dress cross the lobby from the elevator bank and push through the revolving door. Outside, she opened the back door of a waiting taxi.

His computer screen faded to black. He started to panic, but a flashing green user prompt appeared in the top left corner, mimicking an old style computer terminal. Green type scrolled in a retro font: Welcome back, 503-ERROR. Long time no see.

A shiver ran down his spine.

The cursor flashed. Anyone who just stumbled across this

and somehow gained access would probably start typing commands, but those in the know understood that there was one more passphrase needed to get past this screen. Max typed: You are standing in an open field west of a white house, with a boarded front door.

The old lines from *Zork*, the first text adventure game, came back to him easily. He'd never even played the original game, but he appreciated the analogy: Every target was a puzzle to be solved, a place to be explored. And it took the right strings of characters to get you deeper. Every hack was a text adventure.

The screen displayed the next line from the game: There is a small mailbox here.

Open mailbox, Max typed.

A familiar robotic sound bite played "You've got mail." Max had never used America Online, but the early days of computing had been immortalized in pop culture.

The screen stuttered and suddenly Max was looking at a list of comment threads. The most recent thread, created just seconds before, was titled "back from the dead." It was about 503-ERROR's return after his long absence and whether they should give him access to the room or not.

Max wiped his sweaty palms on his jeans then flexed his fingers. The thread directly below the one about him, with thousands of page views and a few hundred comments, was labeled "Who was STOP?"

A new thread appeared: "503-ERROR." He debated

ignoring it, but he was in a tenuous position. He hadn't logged in for a long time, had disappeared without warning, and there were bound to be questions. If he didn't respond, or didn't give the right answers, he could be booted at any time and locked out.

Max clicked on the "503-ERROR" thread to expand it. There was only one post, which said: come inside.

He opened a chat window, clicked Join, and typed 503-ERROR. He was logged in to a private chat room that already had nine users signed in. He recognized only a couple of the names from his old days hanging out here with Evan: 0MN1, Edifice, and Kill_Screen. The rest were strangers, or might have been people he'd dealt with before under different handles: ZeroKal, print*is*dead, GroundSloth, Plan(et)9, DoubleThink, PHYREWALL.

Hackers changed their identities all the time, or maintained multiple identities: Anonymity was one of the last freedoms available on the internet, though even that was harder to come by now, unless you were on the Deep Web. And when you decided to give it up, as Max had, you could just disappear, without anyone ever knowing who you really were or what had happened to you.

A message from 0MN1 flashed on the screen: Who are u?

I'm 503-ERROR, Max typed.

Kill_Screen: the real deal???

503-ERROR: Of course I would say I was, even if I wasn't.

0MN1: Where have you been?

503-ERROR: I needed to take a break for a while.

He didn't mention that he'd never intended to come back.

Kill_Screen: why are you back now?

503-ERROR: I'm trying to figure out what STOP was up to.

0MN1: I thought u 2 used to be buddies?

503-ERROR: We were. But we haven't been in contact for a while.

print*is*dead: That could have been anyone behind the mask.

Kill_Screen: Shut it.

0MN1: When wass the last time u talkd, 503?

Crap. Max could lie now, but if he decided to trust them he wouldn't be able to ask for their help deciphering the text message later. They would refuse, and they might lock him out. Or worse, they could turn against him and make him another one of their targets.

If Evan had trusted them, maybe Max could too. And if they weren't trustworthy, there wasn't much they could do without Max's cooperation.

But something made him hold back from telling them everything just yet.

503-ERROR: Few months ago.

Had it really been that long? He'd been so busy with soccer practice over the summer. Then school had started, and they'd been in separate classes. And Max had started dating Courtney.

Max waited for a response. The others were probably

discussing all this in another private chat room and posting the news for others.

0MN1: Suspishius that your hear, now, after all this time. If u want us to believe, tell us something about STOP. Something real!

Max was asking a lot by coming here. If he wanted their help, he had to give them a reason to trust him, and show that he trusted them. He didn't want to tip his hand about seeing Evan's suicide just yet, though, because that would give them too much information about his own identity.

What if he told them something that they didn't know the Feds already knew? It was just a matter of time before the FBI had to share more information about the case, including STOP's identity. If it came from Max first, it might buy him some credibility.

503-ERROR: STOP and I sometimes talked IRL. His name was Evan Baxter.

It couldn't hurt Evan anymore to admit their connection in real life, but it still felt like a betrayal.

Another long pause—so long that Max had to check to make sure he was still connected to the internet and the program hadn't frozen.

Finally, nine chat responses appeared on-screen simultaneously in one block of text, as if sent by one user—which shouldn't even be possible.

0MN1: Hi, I'm Dramatis Personai

Kill_Screen: Hi, I'm Dramatis Personai

Edifice: Hi, I'm Dramatis Personai
print*is*dead: Hi, I'm Dramatis Personai
DoubleThink: Hi, I'm Dramatis Personai
GroundSloth: Hi, I'm Dramatis Personai
Plan(et)9: Hi, I'm Dramatis Personai
PHYREWALL: Hi, I'm Dramatis Personai
ZeroKal: Hi, I'm Dramatis Personai
No way.

MAX STARED AT THE GREEN TEXT THAT FILLED HIS black screen:

> Hi, I'm Dramatis Personai
>
> **503-ERROR:** Oh shit.
>
> **Evan really had been in Dramatis Personai.**
>
> **print*is*dead:** LOL
>
> **503-ERROR:** I can't believe I'm talking to Dramatis Personai. You guys are legendary!
>
> **Edifice:** Now that you know our handles, we'll have to kill you.
>
> **DoubleThink:** Seriously, this is a mistake. We shouldn't trust him. Why would he give up STOP's name like that?
>
> **PHYREWALL:** Assuming it's legit.
>
> **Kill_Screen:** Why should we trust *you*, DT?
>
> **DoubleThink:** I was here before you, KS.

print*is*dead: I remember 503 / He's a good guy

503-ERROR: Thanks, print*is*dead.

Max's surroundings dropped away as his focus narrowed to the rhythm of fingers on keys and the glowing fifteen-inch window into a digital world that often felt more immediate than his "real" life.

In high school, everything you said and did had consequences, and everyone had their own expectations and agendas. He spent most of his time there worrying about what others thought of him. People were sometimes turned off by interactions with strangers or shocked at how blatantly people acted in chat rooms, but their conversations were just unfiltered. Despite their layers of anonymity, hackers were refreshingly transparent. Usually, at least.

DoubleThink: Where's 503-ERROR been all this time? Like 0MN1 said: Why come back now, when the Feds are looking for info on STOP?

Edifice: He may not even be 503 anymore.

That comment struck a little close to home. Max hadn't thought of himself as 503-ERROR in a long time, but it was coming back to him, with startling ease.

Kill_Screen: Where you been, dawg?

503-ERROR: I had to lay low for a while. Had things to sort out. You know.

0MN1: Chill, guys. He knew STOP irl.

Max had interacted with a few members of this group before, so they knew how far back he and Evan went. He wondered if they secretly had been in Dramatis Personai even then, or if they'd also been recruited with Evan in the last year.

To think: If Max had stayed in this world a little longer, they might have invited him into the group too. Could he have passed up that opportunity? Joining Dramatis Personai meant you had leveled up as a hacker. You could have a bigger influence on the world and do something that mattered. But being part of it also came with greater personal risk, as Evan had probably learned.

503-ERROR: We talked sometimes on the phone. Never met in person.

This was an old lie. He and Evan had always been careful to act like they only knew each other through faceless communications, and rarely revealed any truthful information about their lives. If someone pieced together enough small, seemingly harmless personal details about you, they could figure out who you were. It was doubly dangerous for Max and Evan to be friends, because identifying one of them would inevitably lead to the other.

That was what had happened with the FBI in less than twelve hours: from the time Evan entered their radar at the debate to the agents who tracked him down the next morning at Bean Up.

Kill_Screen: then we have one up on you. we all met STOP once IRL

They had met Evan?

503-ERROR: When was that?

0MN1: @ Hackers Gonna Hack – you shoulda been there!

Max and Evan had planned to go to the annual gathering of hackers, but the conference had been scheduled for the last week in August, when soccer season started, so Max had begged off. He had assumed Evan would skip it rather than go without him.

PHYREWALL: We knew STOP, but even we didn't know his name.

Kill_Screen: that doesn't prove they were friends or that we can trust 503. if anything, the opposite.

503-ERROR: I'm just trying to do the same thing you are— figure out what happened to STOP. Knowing his name helps, right?

0MN1: STOP's video was intense, huh?

503-ERROR: Definitely.

0MN1: Thanx for the tip. I'm doxxing Evan Baxter now. Can u give us more 2 go on?

0MN1's attempts to research Evan's identity wouldn't turn up anything that Max didn't already know. Evan had been obsessively cautious with his identity, up until the end. Giving up his secrecy in such a reckless, public way was almost as shocking as giving up his life. It could have been a sign of mental instability. That might be enough for the media to feel satisfied by his motives, but Max believed there was more to it.

503-ERROR: I wish I did. Had he been planning that for a while?

print*is*dead: STOP talked about this debate for weeks / he told everyone to watch and spread the word / he signed out a few minutes before he hacked the video feed / didn't know it was for the last time :(

Kill_Screen: the video's on youtube! most of it. someone commented that he shot himself. that part was cut out.

PHYREWALL: I saw that. It was posted by "AHS_Student." He said STOP used a gun.

503-ERROR: God.

Plan(et)9: The video and those comments were DELETED. But there are SCREENCAPS.

The chat program *dinged* as a link came through to Max's computer. It only identified the sender as "Dramatis Personai." Wasn't he already talking to them?

Max clicked on the link and returned to the chat while his browser loaded the page. Everything was a little slower through Tor.

Edifice: Coverup! It's surprising there aren't more posts from kids at the school. Like, how do you get teenagers to ~not~ post notes on Panjea when something happens?

Plan(et)9: I saw a picture with a FRAME that wasn't in the released vid. STOP's mask's half off.

Plan(et)9 posted a bitmap image of the projector screen on the stage at Granville High. The picture was blurry, showing Evan reaching off-screen for the gun. It gave Max a chill to see it again. It had to have come from one of the kids at his school, probably around the fifth or sixth row on the left side of the auditorium. Max saved the image to his desktop.

503-ERROR: What do you make of this "Silence of 6" thing? Any guesses what STOP meant by that?

print*is*dead: I bet it has to do with the others who went offline. . .

ZeroKal: muy suspicious

GroundSloth: This again? STFU. 3 missing + STOP isn't 6, idjit. And quit the Spanglish ZeroK. We get that you're Latino, or want us to think you are.

503-ERROR: Hold on, 3 people are missing? Recently?

print*is*dead: 3 of us

Max felt a rush. Three members of Dramatis Personai disappearing went beyond suspicious. This could be a clue to what Evan had been talking about.

GroundSloth: Unverified.

ZeroKal: Already been over that, *amigo*. Read the threads. It don't make no sense.

GroundSloth: People have just been leaving lately. It happens. Right, 503-ERROR?

0MN1: 503, did STOP send you anything before his broadcast?

Max froze. How could 0MN1 know about the text message?

If anyone could help Max crack Evan's code, it was these guys. But Max wasn't ready to share it with people he didn't trust, especially not when any one of them could be logging the chat or have someone looking over his shoulder.

Max turned around, suddenly nervous about being watched. Two elderly women were now sitting on the far end of the lobby holding paper cups of coffee from the complimentary station in the corner. They didn't look like secret agents spying on him, but one of them did give him the once-over as she took a sip from her cup.

Max's earbuds dinged again. A small window popped up on his screen. Max clicked on it and found himself in another private chat room named "doubleplusungood." DoubleThink was the only user inside. Curious, Max logged in.

DoubleThink >> 503-ERROR: Do *not* share what Evan sent you with DP. Especially not with 0MN1.

It took Max a moment to realize DoubleThink had said "Evan" instead of STOP. He leaned closer to the screen.

503-ERROR >> DoubleThink: He didn't send me anything.

DoubleThink >> 503-ERROR: ;) He didn't send me anything either. Better write back to 0MN1 before he thinks something's up.

503-ERROR >> DoubleThink: What's the deal with 0MN1? Can we trust him?

DoubleThink >> 503-ERROR: Evan didn't trust him, so I don't either. Not sure why.

Max switched back over to the group chat.

0MN1: Hello? You disappearring on us again, 503?

503-ERROR: Sorry, spotty signal here. I didn't get anything from STOP. Like I said, we hadn't been in contact much since I went dark.

0MN1: OK. Did *anyone* get anything, or did STOP say anything unusual?

Boy, this guy was pushy.

503-ERROR: What do you think he had, 0MN1?

0MN1: STOP said he was working on something BIG. . .

Something worth dying for?

0MN1: . . . He wanted my help. Said he was gonna send me some 'insurance' in case anything happened to him, but I was offline most of yesterday. I thought maybe he got it out to someone else he trusted.

503-ERROR: I don't know anything else. I didn't even know STOP was part of DP :-/

DoubleThink: You must not have been that close to him after all. This was his life. We're his family.

That stung, mostly because Max couldn't deny it. Evan wouldn't have kept this part of his life from Max if he had shown any interest. It was Evan's way to respect Max's decision to cut off ties with this world, and to keep Max out of it for his own protection. So if Evan had decided to drag him back into it after all, it must be serious.

DoubleThink's last message had been in the group chat instead of in their private room, so it had to be for the benefit of the others. To throw them off?

Kill_Screen: i bet STOP was flipped. He probably informed on the others to the FBI and the guilt got to him. And now '503-ERROR' is here to pick up where he left off. Are you a puppet, 503?

Ding.

DoubleThink >> 503-ERROR: We have to talk. Let's go to voice.

print*is*dead: or maybe the fbi killed him / we won't know

what happened until we see the whole vid

Another link appeared in the chat room, from an unidenti-fied source. Max clicked on it, thinking it was another picture from the video. It launched a new tab in his browser and a dia-log box appeared with a warning: This program is requesting control of webcam and speakers.

"Oh no, you don't," Max said. Someone was trying to click-jack his webcam.

Max had already taped over the webcam and changed his computer's security settings to notify him of attempts to control hardware, so this was no threat. But it told him that someone wanted to know what he looked like or get a glimpse of his location. The simple hack was way too ama-teur for anyone in Dramatis Personai, but who else would be interested in him? It was too soon for the government to have tracked him down. Or so he hoped.

Max left the dialog box open without clicking Cancel, so whoever it was wouldn't know he was wise to the attempt.

503-ERROR >> DoubleThink: Is this you trying to get access to my camera?

DoubleThink >> 503-ERROR: Pffpt! If I was, you wouldn't know it. But it isn't me. You took care of it?

503-ERROR >> DoubleThink: Yeah, I got it. I'm surprised/insulted they thought it would work.

DoubleThink >> 503-ERROR: Someone must know more than he's saying.

Max switched back to the group chat.

503-ERROR: So who were the others? What happened?

Going to voice with DoubleThink would at least cut down on the likelihood of Max typing in the wrong window. He initiated a voice chat.

0MN1: No 1 knows for sure. they just went away.

print*is*dead: they go by L0NELYB0Y, Infiltraitor, and @sskicker / if they were arrested, they didn't expose us at least.

Kill_Screen: which probably means they weren't arrested. . .

0MN1: Oh? Would you turn us in to save yourself?

Kill_Screen: in a heartbeat

print*is*dead: maybe they turned each other in / they disappeared one at a time / like a horror movie

GroundSloth: As far as we *know* they didn't turn us in. But we should move servers again in case we're already being monitored. Like I've been saying for *months*.

In his ear, Max heard a synthetic voice—actually, *two* voices, only slightly out of sync with each other, and eerily similar to Evan's filtered voice in his video.

"Hello, Five-oh-three," DoubleThink said.

Max picked up his cell phone and once again pretended to be carrying on a conversation with someone while speaking to DoubleThink through the microphone in the cord of his earbuds.

"Hi," Max said. "Why do you want to talk?"

The concierge shot him an annoyed look. Max might have been wearing out his welcome.

"To see if I can trust you."

"You can trust me. I was Evan's best friend. You're the one using a voice filter."

"I know Evan vouched for you, but I still don't know if I can trust you not to do something stupid."

Max's face burned. "I'm not a noob."

"Pause your ego, hotshot. I'm trying to help. You have to start being more careful. Don't reveal anything to the group. I think one of them is working with the enemy."

"Who's the enemy?"

"That's the other thing we need to figure out."

While he carried on the conversation with DoubleThink, Max kept an eye on the ongoing text chat.

Kill_Screen: More worrying that one or more of us is probably already working with the Feds. . .

0MN1: If a hacker was busted the news would be all over it. They love to brag.

Plan(et)9: YEAH! Maybe they got to L0NELY, Infiltraitor, and @sskicker!

Edifice: Unless they're dead. Then we'd never know unless we find out who they are IRL.

0MN1: Told you—I doxxed 'em. No sign of anything bad. They're fine. . .

Edifice: Then why won't you tell us who they are so we can stop worrying?

0MN1: For the same reason I won't say who *you* are, Ed.

DoubleThink: I bet they just got scared and went into hiding like 503-ERROR did.

0MN1: Exactly, DT.

"Hey! Why are you giving me such a hard time in the chat room? Are you on my side or not?" he asked.

"I'm on Evan's side," DoubleThink said.

DoubleThink: No offense, 503! Just making a point.

"Happy now?" DoubleThink asked.

"Thanks. How are you doing that? Saying one thing while typing another at the same time?"

"I'm not called DoubleThink for nothing."

"I only left because I thought if I kept hacking, I would get in too deep one day."

"You were scared."

"Okay, sure. So what? I was scared."

"Hey, you were right to be, as it turns out," DoubleThink said. "I'd get out too if I could. Do you think there's a chance that's what Evan's doing?"

"I wish he were, but I don't think the FBI would say he'd committed suicide for no reason." Max didn't want to share why he was so certain that Evan was dead—not yet.

"They could have captured him. Saying he's dead would let them get away with silencing him too, if that's what they're doing. Evan was working on something major."

"Do you think he was talking about those three hackers in his video?" Max asked.

"He was kind of obsessed with their disappearances. It's weird enough that it happened to three members of Dramatis Personai. Now four."

"I keep trying to understand why Evan would kill himself. He wouldn't do it if the others had been arrested or gone into hiding. But *murder*. . . . Could they have been killed?"

"That's a bit dramatic," DoubleThink said. "That's not how the Feds work. And why wouldn't Evan just say that instead of this 'silenced' business?"

"Because people would dismiss the idea immediately, like you are. He obviously wanted someone to investigate this, but he was speaking in code to be sure it was the right someone. We don't know who or what Evan was trying to expose, but it seems to have something to do with Senator Tooms or Governor Lovett, and whatever 'the silence of six' refers to."

"You can silence people without killing them. Quite effectively, in fact. It happens every day. All you have to do is make them afraid. Maybe that's what this is. Making examples of people like Sabu and Manning hasn't worked—it just gives hacktivists like us something to rally around. But you put someone in prison, and you keep it quiet from the media, and no one knows what happened. Anything we imagine is probably worse than the reality. And pretty soon the rest of the group stops taking risks, because the unknown is scarier than the truth."

All of that sounded reasonable, except Max had seen Evan die. He didn't know for sure that the other "offline" hackers were dead, or were connected to Evan's message at all, but it had to be more than a coincidence. The truth had to be pretty freaking awful if Evan would rather take his own life than suffer the same fate.

503-ERROR: If you know anything that can help us figure this out, 0MN1, you should share it.

0MN1: We might know more if we had the rest of that video.

"Seriously, drop this for now, okay? We don't know who's involved yet," DoubleThink said.

"How do I know you aren't working with the 'enemy'?" Max said. "Maybe that's why you're called DoubleThink."

"Good. You should question everything and everyone. Maybe I'm not wasting my time with you after all."

"Yeah? Well. . . your robot voice is creeping me out. And you haven't answered my question."

"We all have to trust someone," DoubleThink said.

"You just said the opposite a second ago," Max said.

"DoubleThink, remember?"

"Right. But believing two opposite things at once is also called 'insanity.' You saying you're the exception to the rule?"

"Questioning people's motives doesn't mean you can't trust them. You can always trust them to do what's best for themselves, and you can use that."

"And what do you want?" Max asked.

"I want to help Evan," DoubleThink said.

0MN1: Someone at that school must have recorded it on a phone.

PHYREWALL: Word is everyone's phones were confiscated and wiped. Tell me that isn't suspicious.

"Tell him you'll work on it. Then log out," DoubleThink said. "We have our own plans to make."

503-ERROR: Good idea. I'll try to dig something up. Gotta go for now.

print*is*dead: good to have you back / you should come to haxx0rade nxt wk /it's gonna be epic

Panjea had recently announced their first annual Haxx-0rade for the end of October, a combination hackathon and costume party. They were inviting hackers from all over the world to work in their San Francisco headquarters, developing their own apps for Panjea over a twenty-four-hour period.

503-ERROR: I'll see, but I doubt it. SF's a long way for me to travel.

0MN1: Hope you can make it. Keep us posted if you learn anything else.

ZeroKal: Hasta la vista

Max signed off.

"Well, that was fun," DoubleThink said. "We have to meet. In person."

"Whoa. I don't know who you are. What can you say in person that you can't say here?"

"Um, everything? I don't trust talking about this online any more than we have to. Evan sent me something that you need to see."

Evan had sent DoubleThink a message too?

Max felt a mix of relief and jealousy. It was good to know he wasn't alone in this, but he'd felt a twisted sort of pride that

Evan had chosen him. What if Max were just one of several people he'd reached out to?

Of course all that mattered was finding out what Evan had died for.

"What is it?" Max asked.

"You'll see it when I see you."

If DoubleThink wanted to trick Max into the open, this was the way to do it.

"That's a big risk."

"For both of us."

"Still. You have to give me more than that," Max said.

"If I wanted to turn you in to the Feds, they would already have you surrounded, Maxwell."

It took a moment for it to sink in that DoubleThink had used his real name—sort of. No one actually called him Maxwell.

It also came as a shock to hear his name after just half an hour online. Despite his long absence, being 503-ERROR seemed to come more naturally to him than being Max, the popular kid at Granville High. It took effort to be one of the guys on the soccer team and Courtney's boyfriend. He doubted she would ever understand this part of his life—which meant she'd never really understand him.

"How do you know my name?" Max asked.

"Evan. He wanted me to contact you if anything happened to him. I just hope I don't regret it."

Max took a deep breath. "Okay, let's meet. But in a public

place, and I'll come to you," Max said. "Where is that?"

A short pause. "Seattle."

"Oh." That was a long way from Granville, especially without a car.

"Why don't we meet halfway? There's a Denny's just off Interstate five in Roseburg, Oregon," DoubleThink said.

"You want to meet at a Denny's?" That was always Evan's favorite spot to work.

"You don't like Denny's?" DoubleThink asked.

"It's fine," Max said.

"They have good pancakes and they're open twenty-four hours."

"Sold."

Max googled it. The map showed the diner was almost exactly halfway between Granville and Seattle.

"Um. Evan told you where I am?" Max asked.

"No, you just did. I knew where Evan lived, and I guessed you might be close by." DoubleThink said.

Maybe it wasn't such a great idea to meet DoubleThink after all. He knew way more than he should about Max. But Max didn't have any better leads at the moment, and it would be good to get out of town for a little while.

"Okay, fine. When?" Max said.

"Dawn tomorrow."

"Are we going to duel? Why such a hurry?"

"Just having this makes me nervous. The sooner I pass it off to you, the better."

And the sooner Max could get to the bottom of this, and hopefully back to his life.

"The thing is, I had to abandon my car today when some shady guys came after me," Max said. "I'll have to take a bus or train, if they even go to Roseburg."

"There's a Greyhound station, but that will take you too long. Just get a new car."

"For six hundred dollars?"

"That shouldn't be any problem for you," DoubleThink said. "Wink, wink."

How much had Evan told this guy about their past hacks?

"I don't do that anymore," Max said.

Max heard a garbled digital sound that he eventually identified as DoubleThink snorting.

"I don't care how you do it, just get to that diner by seven thirty tomorrow morning," DoubleThink said.

"I hope you're for real."

"I don't go into meatspace for just anyone. The only hacker who knows what I look like in real life is Evan."

"Then I'm honored."

"You should be. But, like I said, I'm doing this for him. As for whether or not you can trust me. . ."

A link popped into Max's chat window.

"It's okay," DoubleThink said. "That link is totally safe."

"Uh huh. You just sent me a link to prove I could trust you, but I have to trust you in order to follow it."

"Just click it."

Max did. A video window opened. When the image cleared up, he saw black and white surveillance footage of a familiar hotel lobby. He looked around. It was definitely the lobby of the Gateway Suites. And when he spotted the figure sitting in the corner of the image on a computer, he knew he was viewing a live security feed of himself.

"No way," Max said. "How did you. . ."

"It doesn't take a genius to realize that you'd favor free public Wi-Fi networks to get online to avoid being located. Lots of supposedly private security cameras all over the world have been hacked. Breaking into new ones is a hobby of mine, but ironically, this one was powned by Evan first.

"I just scanned the ones in your area for anyone using Tor on the same network. And here we are. Or rather, there you are. Try to be more careful. At least avoid cameras, unless you enjoy being the star of your own reality show. You should also try to disguise yourself to prevent face recognition."

"Oh my God," Max said.

"So now you see the urgency," DoubleThink said. "The FBI could find you the same way, especially if they do have hackers working for them. And if you logged in to one of your personal accounts, even while running Tor, they could twig to your location a lot sooner."

"Oh," Max said. "That's stupid. Of course I'd never do that." Not again, anyway.

The phone at the concierge desk rang and he turned his head to hear a little better.

"Why yes, there is." From his peripheral vision, it seemed as if the concierge was looking straight at him. "I thought so. Yes, sir. Understood. I'll do my best."

"You look nervous," DoubleThink said.

"I think I'd better go."

"Yeah, I think so. See you soon, Five-Oh-Three." Double Think signed off.

Max shuddered as he looked at the security feed again, thinking about all the cameras in the mall that had been tracking his movements that morning. The grainy video reminded him of those found footage movies; typically, this was what you saw just before something horrible happened. A monster attack, a paranormal event. . . or maybe a raid from the Feds.

He certainly hoped that Evan's mysterious friend was trying to help. If DoubleThink or Dramatis Personai at large was playing him, Max's skills were no match for theirs. He could lose everything by going to this meeting; it could be the government luring him in and entrapping him. But he knew he had to go. He'd just have to take whatever precautions he could.

Max closed the laptop and slipped it into his bag, resisting the urge to glance over at the concierge, whom he suspected was now closely watching his every move. He stretched his neck and massaged his left shoulder; he certainly hadn't missed this part of his old life in front of a computer. Spending all his time in the virtual world had had very real consequences in the physical one.

He stood and headed for the exit. By now the Feds could be on their way here—or outside already. Another reason to get as far away as possible. Oregon was as good a place as any. But he needed a way to get there, and all things considered, public transportation was too risky right now. It was time to put his dormant hacking skills to a real test.

8

MAX EXITED INTO THE HOTEL'S PARKING LOT.

Perfect.

He put his head down, hands in his pockets, and walked slowly past a row of cars. He glanced sidelong inside each vehicle, looking for a blinking amber light on the dashboard. After walking past one row and halfway up another, he finally found a dusty, blue 2002 Hyundai Elantra with the security system he wanted.

Not the fanciest wheels, but that was an asset when you didn't want to attract attention. He slid his laptop from his bag and scanned the wireless networks in the area until he found one he could hack. *1 2 3 4*…nice password. Most people never changed the admin password that came as a factory setting on their routers.

Max created a new guest network called "Change Your Admin Password," connected, then logged in to the cloud storage he shared with Evan. He searched for their old files on "war texting," a way to hack some devices that connected to the internet just like cell phones, via GSM modules. So-called "smart appliances" used cellular networks to send updates or even be controlled remotely.

Only they weren't that smart after all, because once a particular device was identified on the network, unauthorized users could send text messages to control it.

Inspired by a video showing how hackers used such a flaw in an alarm system to unlock a car and start it, Evan had spent a month war texting vehicles in his neighborhood. He and Max had left McDonald's Happy Meal toys on dashboards all over the city. They never took the vehicles for joyrides or stole anything from them—they had just been doing it to see if they could.

That was about to change.

After Evan pointed out the exploit to car alarm companies, many of them had updated their firmware to patch it. But one budget manufacturer, Hedgehog, never responded to his e-mails.

Max ran the script Evan had developed and searched for GSM modules on the network in the range for Hedgehog's devices. In three minutes he had located and disabled the alarm—he hoped. The telltale amber light was still flashing on the dashboard. He typed the command to open the doors and waited anxiously to see if the hack still worked.

"Locked out?"

Max jumped at the voice. He had been so focused on his screen he hadn't noticed the man approaching on his left, jingling his car keys.

"Sorry if I surprised you," the man said.

"I was just thinking about something," Max said. His heart was racing. What if the car's owner had come outside while Max was breaking into it?

Max closed his laptop screen halfway. The man was in his forties with graying brown hair. He was wearing a puffy black coat over gray sweatpants and Timberland boots. He didn't look like an FBI agent, but without the dark suit and badge, they probably looked like normal people, even with potbellies like this guy's.

"Shouldn't you be in school?" The man pulled a cell phone out of a pocket. To call the cops or snap a photo of Max?

Shit. Max concentrated on staying calm.

"I have a free period," Max said.

The man glanced back at the hotel and his brow furrowed, probably trying to understand why a high school kid would be hanging out at a hotel in the middle of the afternoon and not liking the conclusions he was coming to.

At that moment, the car's interior lights blinked on and off and the door locks clicked open. Max hurriedly pulled his key ring from his pocket and pressed the unlock button on the fob for his dad's car. Max was relieved that the hack had worked. Now came the tricky part—and he hadn't anticipated an audience.

He opened the driver side door and slid behind the wheel. The seat was obviously adjusted for someone much shorter than Max. He closed and locked the door and hoped the man would leave him alone.

The man stepped closer and tapped on the window. Max couldn't lower the window until the engine was on. He typed the command to start the car then rested his laptop on the passenger seat.

"Hey, is this your car?" the man shouted.

"No. It's my teacher's."

The start-up command was taking too long to process. Max slowly adjusted the seat and mirrors then buckled in. He inserted his key in the ignition, pointedly ignoring the inquisitive man.

Max glanced over at the hotel. Through the sliding glass doors, he saw two men in suits talking to the concierge. They had to be FBI, and they were only a few hundred feet away from him. If they went out through the same door Max had, they would see him.

The man tapped on the glass again.

Jesus. Why was this guy in his business?

Max looked at him.

"Where is she? Your teacher?" the man asked.

Max jerked his head back toward the hotel. "*He's* inside."

"Is there something going on that you want to talk about, kid?"

Max shook his head. "I'm fine." The agents were exiting the hotel. They were going out the front doors. They would see Max if they turned and looked to their right.

Max was not fine.

The car wasn't starting. He unbuckled his seat belt then held a finger on the unlock button. If they noticed him, he would grab his laptop, push the door open, and run.

The man tapped on the glass again then jiggled the door handle.

The car roared to life. Max choked back a giddy laugh.

One of the agents turned and looked right at him.

Max pointed. "There he is! Tell him I'll see him at school." The man jumped back as Max pulled out of the spot. The only problem was: He would have to drive past the FBI agents in order to get to the highway.

The agents were standing by a black car like the one he'd seen earlier. They were not the same guys who had tracked him to Bean Up. If the search for him was widening, now was the perfect time to get out of Granville—if he could make it out of the parking lot first.

As the stolen car approached the black sedan, Max felt the urge to speed by before they identified him. Instead, he looked straight ahead and drove at what felt like a snail's pace, willing them to ignore him.

When he was only two car lengths away, Max casually leaned over as though he were reaching for something in the glove compartment and turned his head away from them. Not a safe driving practice, but safer perhaps than getting arrested. He popped back up as soon as he had cleared their car and glanced in his rearview mirror. They weren't paying any attention to him.

Max turned onto 18th Street and headed west, away from Lake Alhambra. He reached the highway and wiped the sweat from his forehead and the back of his neck. He lowered all the windows to let the cold air rush in. He whooped.

Once he was driving past the Los Medanos College campus, he relaxed his grip on the wheel. He'd gotten a rush both from the successful war texting and another close call. It felt wrong to be doing this without Evan; now he kind of wished they had taken a car for a spin after all, at least once.

As "gray hats," they had hacked only for the intellectual challenge and to point out security flaws, like the ones they found in those car alarm systems. Max liked improving overall security and raising awareness of weaknesses that could harm the public, but Evan had wanted to do more. Instead of helping companies get richer, he wanted to change the world—even if he had to do it by leaking sensitive information or bringing down systems to make a statement.

Max should have suspected long ago that Evan was in Dramatis Personai—his philosophy was a perfect fit for their specialized brand of controlled chaos. That was where Max had drawn the line, but now he was edging over it into Evan's world. Unlike Evan, Max was raised by a father who was a "hacktivist" before the term existed, so he knew what the risks were. And he also knew that the stakes had to be high for Evan to involve him. Evan's death meant Max couldn't wash his hands of this situation. As scared as he was of what had backed Evan into this corner, Max couldn't go on as if nothing had happened. He had to understand, and maybe even finish, whatever Evan had started.

Burner phone or no, Max decided not to use its GPS for directions to his rendezvous point with DoubleThink. Now he had to worry about the other hacker's safety as well. So he would have to do this the old-fashioned way. He would stop at a gas station and check a map once he had put more distance between himself and Granville. For now, he headed for the I-5 entrance ramp.

The brake lights of the cars ahead of him smeared into blurry blobs of color. Max blinked back tears. He could run from Granville, but he couldn't escape his memories of Evan, or missing his dad, Courtney, and the life he was leaving. He wasn't sure for how long.

Max switched on the radio and scanned for anything but the news. He couldn't handle listening to people conjecture about STOP and the debate anymore. He settled in for a long ride, splitting his attention between the uncertain road ahead and looking for flashing red and blue lights and black cars behind him.

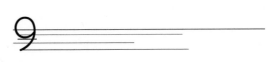

9

WAR TEXTING WAS EASIER THE SECOND TIME
around, when Max traded the Elantra for a green Nissan Cube
he found in the parking lot of the library in Redding, California. According to his map, he was about halfway to Roseburg.
He got back on the road just after eight p.m., confirmed he still
wasn't being tailed, and decided to chance a quick call home
on his burner phone.

Max was prepared to leave a voicemail because his dad
rarely heard the phone. But he picked it up on the first ring.

"Hello?" Bradley's voice was strained, the way it got when
he was stressed out about work.

"Dad, it's me."

"Oh, thank God. Where have you been, Champ? You
skipped school today?"

Max tightened his grip on the phone. He hated nicknames

like "Champ" and "Sport" and "Ace." Bradley only used them to tease Max.

Something was wrong. It was easy to imagine that the men following Max earlier were tapping the call, or maybe were even there at his house.

How long did it take to trace a phone call?

Max eased the car into the right lane and slowed down a little. "I couldn't go back there. I was too freaked out about what happened."

"I understand. But next time don't leave my car at the coffee shop."

Max sighed. His dad loved that car. He was probably legitimately pissed about that one. "Yeah, sorry. I just needed to run for a bit."

Bradley was quiet for a moment. "Where are you now? I'll come get you."

"No need. I'm just hanging with a friend. He'll give me a ride home," Max said.

"Who are you with?"

It wasn't like his dad to ask so many questions. Bradley Stein wasn't the stern, overprotective type, and he had always trusted Max.

Smart, Dad.

It was weird knowing that someone was eavesdropping on their call, but this was an opportunity to explain away Max's behavior today, if they played things right. But if they raised any suspicions, his dad could be arrested for interfering in their investigation.

"My friend Ming." Ming was a forward on Monte Vida's soccer team, and definitely not a friend. Max didn't even remember his last name.

"You're calling from his phone?" Bradley asked.

"Yeah. . . Why?"

"Because I have your phone right here."

"How'd you get it?" Max started to move into the left lane when a car zoomed past from his blind spot. He swerved back over to the right and a horn blared. He bet the FBI would realize he was on the road and would be analyzing that recording for clues to his whereabouts.

"A federal agent dropped it off after school since you weren't there to collect it today."

"Great. I was starting to go into withdrawal without it."

"I know what you're going to ask. It's working just fine," Bradley said.

That meant the Feds had what they needed from the phone. They wouldn't have returned it otherwise.

"Oh, and Courtney called the house looking for you. She sounded upset," Bradley said.

"Yeah, we argued after the debate. Maybe we need some time apart."

"That's probably a good idea, Sport."

So the Feds had gotten to her too.

"You sure you don't want me to pick you up?" Bradley asked.

"Yeah. Thanks though. Hey, I should let you go back to work."

"Well, it's a school night, so remember your curfew."

Max didn't have a curfew, and if he did, Dad would never notice if he kept to it or not.

"Of course." It felt like they'd been on the phone too long, but Max had one more important thing to say, and he wasn't sure when he'd have another chance. "I love you, Dad."

"You too, Ace. Be safe." Bradley clicked off.

That was that. There was no going back. He would have to face this head-on.

Max switched off the phone and pulled out the battery. He checked his map and made a quick change in plans: He would take a short detour away from his true destination and ditch the phone at a service station, in case the Feds had managed to get a fix on him.

What were they after? If they just wanted to talk to Max about the text message and his connection to Evan, they were going about it in a shady and aggressive way. Granted, Max running at the first sight of them had probably convinced them they had good reason to pursue him.

Unlike at Evan's place, the FBI wouldn't find a shred of evidence of Max's past as a hacker. It might be unusual for a teenager to own three laptops, but he was the son of a computer geek. There was nothing more incriminating in his room than porn and some pirated media on his hard drives. When Max made a clean break from hacking, he'd never looked back. Until now.

Max grabbed a quick bite and a replacement phone at the

next rest stop, then he pushed on, mulling over the call and the strange turn his life had taken the rest of the way to Roseburg.

He reached the Denny's several hours early for his meeting with DoubleThink, so he parked in the lot beside a row of cargo trucks and napped as best he could manage in the compact car—which wasn't well, even as exhausted as he was. He finally dragged himself into the restaurant at seven, in search of a more comfortable seat and a cup of coffee to wake him up.

The inside of the Roseburg Denny's looked exactly like the one in Granville, where Max and Evan had spent countless late nights eating pancakes and chicken fingers to fuel their online misadventures. Even the picture placemats were identical. The resemblance was oddly comforting; after driving north 450 miles, it felt like his home was still close-by, even though he'd never been farther from it. The restaurant was nearly empty aside from a few big guys who were older, hairier, and wearing way more plaid than Max. They didn't set off any alarm bells. He didn't think any of them were undercover government agents, but no one looked like a hacker, either. Max must have arrived before DoubleThink.

He squeaked into a slightly sticky booth by a wide window facing the parking lot where he would see everyone who arrived.

He yawned. God, he was exhausted. He was also famished. All he'd had on the road was a two-liter bottle of pop and a package of Twinkies. He might as well eat while he waited for DoubleThink.

He looked around for a waitress. There were two women in matching black blouses arguing by the register, a short woman with brown hair styled in a pageboy cut, and a blond girl with a ponytail. He couldn't hear them, but the brunette glanced over at Max not once but twice.

Why would they be talking about me?

Nervous now, Max pulled out his new phone and connected to the restaurant's free network. To his relief, his absence hadn't made the news yet, but he had missed a significant update during the night: All the media sites were buzzing that STOP had been identified as Evan Baxter.

Even though he'd known this was coming, it was still a shock. With this break in the story, more pieces would fall into place quickly. Max would have to keep moving, and he would have to keep looking over his shoulder.

"Good morning," a woman said. Max slapped his phone facedown on the kids' maze printed on his placemat. He looked up. The brown-haired waitress smiled at him—Jessica, according to her nametag.

"I'm Jess, and I'll be your server today." She handed him a wide plastic menu. "Can I get you started with a drink?"

"Coffee, as much as you can spare." Max returned the slimy menu. He was just going to get his usual. "And I'll have the Ultimate Omelette and the Lumberjack Slam with sausage, scrambled eggs, and wheat toast."

"An Ultimate and the Lumberjack with sausage, scrambled eggs, and wheat toast." She repeated it without writing it down.

"I'll put that order in and be right back with your coffee."

"Thanks."

Max waited until she had gone to the kitchen before picking up his phone. He wiped his hands on a napkin before scrolling through the top news article.

There wasn't much personal information about Evan yet, but that would certainly change. Right now, all they were talking about were basic facts: Evan had been a seventeen-year-old student at Granville High School, diagnosed with Asperger's syndrome. He was described as a computer wunderkind who kept to himself.

Max was more interested in the glaring omissions: how Evan had died, where his body had been found, and how the FBI had ultimately figured out his identity.

Jess came back with a mug and a coffee pot. She filled his cup and Max gulped the coffee black.

"Can you leave the pot?" Max asked.

"We aren't supposed to." She refilled his cup. "Just ask when you want more. Your food should be out in five minutes."

A rusty green pickup truck pulled into the lot outside. Max propped his elbows on the table and held his coffee cup up to hide the lower half of his face as he watched a man in his thirties with long, tangled hair approach the Denny's, a camo backpack with a broken strap slung over his right shoulder.

The man entered and shuffled past Max's booth to a table in the corner behind him. Max shifted to keep an eye on him.

The man pulled a battered laptop from his bag and plugged it into an outlet. DoubleThink?

The man started typing on his computer, paying no attention to Max or anyone else in the restaurant. When Jess tried to hand him a menu, he waved it off and ordered a coffee and cherry pie without looking away from his screen once.

The sky was turning gray. Distant clouds were tinged with a soft, rosy glow. Max stared out the window, searching the parking lot for anything out of the ordinary. But it looked exactly as it should: boring. Peaceful.

He kept looking at the man with the laptop in his reflection in the glass until Jess brought over his food. For the moment, Max was content to scarf down his meal and let DoubleThink approach him when he was ready.

By the time Max had polished off his second plate of breakfast and ordered a slice of cherry pie, the truckers had left and the local morning crowd was filtering in. A couple sat in the booth across from Max, holding hands and gazing into each other's eyes. Max turned away and kept watching the vehicles coming and going outside.

Jess brought over a thick wedge of cherry pie and a receipt.

"My shift's ending. Do you mind if I ring you out? You don't have to leave or anything. Lorraine will take care of you if you need anything else." Jess nodded toward an elderly woman with curly white hair.

"Thanks." Max's phone showed it was just before eight. He didn't know how long he should stick around. The man in the corner was still working intently on his computer, and none of the other customers seemed like hacker types. Maybe DoubleThink was a no-show.

Max paid his bill with a generous tip, mentally revising the amount of money he had left.

Just when Max was gathering his things to go, a young woman slid into the booth across from him. The first thing he noticed was her hot pink ski jacket, followed by the black knit cap pulled down low over her forehead, covering the tips of her ears. She wore a pair of those yellow-tinted glasses favored by programmers and gamers who spent a lot of time staring at screens.

"Good morning, sunshine," she said.

"Um," Max said. "Can I help you?"

"I'm here to help *you*." She turned her head to survey the parking lot.

"*You're* DoubleThink?" She looked about Max's age. She looked like a she.

"Bingo." Satisfied with what she saw—or didn't see—outside, she looked at Max.

He looked over her shoulder at the older guy still tapping away at his laptop, oblivious to everything around him.

"I thought he was DoubleThink," Max said.

"Nah. He's writing a screenplay." She sniffed. "It's terrible."

Max turned to the girl. "How do you know that?"

"I was curious, so I grabbed a copy. You know, public Wi-Fi. He's on page 223, with no sign of getting to any kind of point. And his Panjea password is 'mommy.' I can't make this crap up."

Max stared at her. She had dark circles under her eyes. Of course, she'd had a long overnight trip too.

"I can't believe it," he said. "You're. . . "

"A girl?"

"A teenager," Max said.

"So are you. So was Evan."

"Okay, yeah, now that you mention it, I'm surprised by the other thing."

"Why is it a surprise that I'm a girl? Did I seem particularly masculine online?"

"No, but. . . you didn't seem particularly feminine," Max said.

"What does that even mean?"

He massaged the corners of his eyes. "I don't know. Forget it."

"You didn't seem particularly sexist online, but here we are."

Lorraine swept over to their table and deposited a second coffee mug on the table in front of DoubleThink. The waitress filled her cup, refilled Max's, and left the pot between them.

"Thanks," DoubleThink said.

Lorraine winked at her and bustled off.

Max stared at the coffee pot.

"I'm sorry. Does the rest of Drama—" He lowered his voice. "The group know?"

"They never asked, I never volunteered. And why should I?

It's your problem if you automatically assume that I'm a man just because I don't say otherwise. And, let's face it, our crowd isn't big on sharing."

She wrapped her hands around her coffee cup. She was wearing frayed lavender fingerless gloves. Her fingernails were painted white with a black letter on each: A on her left pinky, followed by E, O, and U on her ring, middle and index fingers. Her right hand had H on her index finger, then T, N, and S. Her thumbnails had no letters.

Max smiled. Her nails were decorated with the home row keys from a Dvorak keyboard, which had a different layout from the more common QWERTY keyboard. When she rested her fingers on the home row, her fingers would line up with their corresponding keys.

"And maybe I was taking advantage of people's expectations," she went on, "but you can never be too careful online. Also: It's fun seeing people's reactions when they find out. Not that it happens often. Only ever once, actually." She sipped her coffee. "So shall we get to business, Maxwell? I don't have all day."

"It's Max," he said. "And you're. . . ?"

"DoubleThink is fine."

"It's weird using your handle in real life."

"Make it D.T. if you want."

"How about Deety?" Max asked.

She shrugged.

"You won't tell me your real name?" he asked.

"I wouldn't be showing you my face if wearing a mask in public didn't draw so much unwanted attention."

"You could have sent someone in your place."

"To pretend to be me?" Deety smiled. "Maybe I did. Maybe DoubleThink is really a guy after all, eh?"

Max glanced at the screenwriter.

"It's *not* him, okay? Let it go. Jeez," she said.

"I didn't see you come in. I was watching the door this whole time."

"Your eyes were closed a lot of the time," she said.

"No they. . . . You were watching me? How?" He looked around as if he could tell where she'd been hiding.

Deety picked up the coffee pot and refilled her cup. "I'm a master of disguise and subterfuge."

"Dressed like that?"

"I actually like pink. Is that too 'feminine' for you?"

He shook his head. "It just makes it hard to blend in, doesn't it?"

"If you ran into me on the street, are you more likely to remember my face or my coat?"

He studied her, wondering if this was a trap. She was cute, but the bright parka did draw his eyes more.

"Your coat," he admitted.

"You can't tell much about me under all this." She prodded the thick padding with her fingers. "And clothing is a lot easier to change than a face. But I can do that too."

"Master of disguise."

"Right. You're a good listener."

"I hear that a lot." He smiled.

"Like!" she said. "Anyway, I slipped in through the back door so I could see you before you saw me. I had to make sure you weren't a creeper, even if Evan vouched for you. And I wanted to be sure you weren't followed."

Said the girl who spied on *him* first.

"How do you know I'm really Max?" he said.

"I've seen your picture," she said. "It was several years old, but you look about the same."

"It doesn't seem fair that you have all this information on me and I don't even know your name."

"Get used to it. At least I won't use that information against you. Unless you try to screw me over."

Deety flagged down Lorraine.

"I'll have whatever that was," Deety said. She pointed at one of Max's empty plates.

"The Ultimate Omelette," Max said.

"That," Deety said.

"Sure thing, sweetie," Lorraine said. "Anything else for you?" she asked Max.

"Nothing, thanks."

"We going to be here a while?" Max asked after Lorraine was out of earshot.

"Not me. I didn't sleep either." She yawned.

He poured the last of the coffee for her. "Did you see the news?" he asked.

"Yeah. Now everyone knows about Evan, and of course they don't understand." She sighed. "But 0MN1 and the others trust you now. Your intel was good, and that's the most important thing to them."

"There's something you should know." Max folded then unfolded his hands. "I saw Evan die. I mean, I can't be one hundred percent positive what I saw on the video was real. But I believe it."

She lowered her eyes and stared intently into her mug. "Tell me," she said.

He described how Evan had delivered his cryptic message then pulled a gun. Max described the gunshot, how it had been so loud it scrambled the audio for a second, and then the spray of red. How everything was red, red, red, and Max's ears were ringing long after it was over.

The terrible memory turned Max's stomach. He bent his head and swallowed hard, then sucked in deep breaths until the nausea passed.

"I'm sorry," Deety said.

Max nodded. Deety's eyes glistened behind her glasses. That's when he decided he could trust her with everything.

"I still haven't found the whole video online," she said. "I can find pretty much anything on the internet, but it's like it didn't happen."

"They must have it locked down tight. I know someone who had a copy, but the investigators probably wiped it."

"If we can get it, Dramatis Personai will make sure everyone sees it," Deety said.

"I know it might contain another clue, but it's gruesome. I don't even want to see it again."

Lorraine delivered Deety's omelette and a fresh pot of coffee, along with a second slice of cherry pie for Max. He picked up his fork, but the shiny, bright red filling made him queasy. He pushed the plate away.

He watched Deety shovel massive forkfuls of omelette into her mouth."Deety, did Evan know that you're—"

"A girl?"

"That you have such cool nail polish is what I was going to say."

She eyed Max then unzipped the top of her parka and pulled a smartphone from an inner pocket. She thumbed in a lengthy passcode—Max counted at least twelve clicks of the keypad, which further won him over. She swiped at the screen and tilted it to face Max.

It was a picture of Evan next to a girl with shoulder-length blond hair with pink streaks, parted on the right and pinned back. She was several inches taller than him, which would make her around five-foot-eleven, the same height as Max.

It was summer, but Evan was wearing his signature black T-shirt and gray cargo pants, shoulders hunched and hands in his pockets. His red hoodie was draped over Deety's shoulders, like a superhero cape. She was wearing a green babydoll shirt with the chemical structure for caffeine on the front and faded denim shorts. Long legs with thigh-high black boots. Curvy figure. A tattoo of a red line wound down and around her right arm. She looked like a video game heroine, or a badass Little Red Riding Hood.

Max reached for the phone and she yanked it out of reach. "No one touches my stuff," she said.

"When was that taken?" Max asked.

"HGH."

Hackers Gonna Hack, the hacker conference. So this picture had been taken in August.

Stupidly, Max was jealous that Evan had other friends he hadn't known about—maybe even a girlfriend? He should be happy he'd been fine on his own. Knowing that alleviated some of the guilt Max had felt over spending time with the soccer team and Courtney instead of with Evan.

"I didn't let anyone in DP know I was there, and only Evan knew I'm DoubleThink," Deety said. "He was cool with it. He hated crowds as much as I do, so we hung out together a lot in Austin, whenever we weren't coding."

"I bet Evan thought it was a date." Max laughed.

Deety looked at the picture somberly. "It does look like one." She placed her phone on the table. "Tell me more about him."

"You knew him," Max said.

"We spent a few days together in meatspace. Evan didn't talk much in person. But online, he was funny. What was he really like?"

Max shook his head. "That was the real Evan online. In

person, he was always reserved. Thoughtful." Max picked at the crust of the cherry pie. Part of it crumbled between his fingers. "He was unsure of himself, except when he was hacking. Then, he thought he was invincible."

"Don't we all feel that way?" she said.

"Not me. I'm not as good as Evan was."

"Who is? Oh. But you don't like being second best. Is that why you quit?"

Was that it?

"No. I wasn't even second best. Hacking made me feel *more* vulnerable. I was taking chances I would never take in person, and honestly, it seemed dangerous. That's why I stopped. I was scared it would end. . . badly."

They fell silent again. But that felt okay, not like the awkward gaps in conversation that sometimes happened with Courtney. He would rack his brain for something to say, always trying to impress her and figure out who she wanted him to be.

"Look at us," Deety said. "We're a couple of sad sacks."

Her eyes flicked around the restaurant and to the window.

"Might as well get to it." She swept her arm across the table, pushing their plates aside. Deety reached inside her parka again and pulled out a slim, translucent plastic CD case. Pink. She weighed it in her hand, looking at it thoughtfully. She placed it on the table and slid it across to Max.

The disc inside was labeled "Music Mix" in black permanent ink in Evan's handwriting. The titles of fifteen of his favorite songs were scribbled around it, spiraling toward the center from the outer edge of the disc.

Evan had made a bunch of those for Max a long while back, when they first started hanging out; collections of his favorite selections from all the albums he'd downloaded that week. Max had asked him once why he didn't just share all the files with him online, and after that Evan had stopped making discs for him.

"He must have liked you. A lot," Max said.

Deety turned her head away and stuck her chin up. "It's camouflage, idiot."

"This is what you were talking about?" Max asked.

"What were you expecting?"

"I don't know. A thumb drive. An SD card. A roll of microfiche."

"Those are more conspicuous, and CDs are easy to destroy. Use a Sharpie, scratch the surface, break it into pieces."

"Put it in your microwave," Max said.

He and Evan once destroyed the Baxters' microwave by nuking CDs in it and recording videos on their phones. It was powerful magic, making lightning in a box at home. They'd been mesmerized by the crackling blue sparks that danced across the discs' surfaces. They burned up quickly, over in a literal flash, but it was so beautiful while it lasted.

"Exactly. Plus, it was a clever way to send me something in the mail without anyone getting suspicious. Chelsea Manning snuck all those files out of her army base on—"

"A Lady Gaga CD. Yeah."

Max glanced over the list of songs and, sure enough, Lady Gaga's "Telephone" was number seven. Outside of the pages of comic books, Evan's heroes had been brave people with conviction, who put their lives and freedom on the line, like Chelsea Manning, Daniel Ellsburg, Edward Snowden, Julian Assange, Glenn Greenwald, Laura Poitras, Aaron Swartz, and Michael Hastings.

"I'll just copy the files off," Max said.

"Take it. It's yours," she said. "That's the only physical copy. I wanted you to see it to prove it came from Evan."

"This is his handwriting," Max said.

"And the tracks are the key to the encryption he used. He likes—liked puzzles."

Max rotated the CD case to read the titles through the translucent front, reading the song titles: "Everything Has Changed" by Taylor Swift, "Team" by Lorde, "We Might As Well Be Strangers" by Keane, "All Kinds of Time" by Fountains of Wayne, "Counting Stars" by OneRepublic. He recognized many of them as Evan's favorites.

Evan listened to everything. While lots of people downloaded hundreds of gigs of music, movies, or books that they would never even use, Evan consumed everything. He hoarded, but he didn't keep anything he didn't have a use for.

"What's really on here?" Max asked.

"I found two files, but they're hidden and encrypted. The first one is called 'LinerNotes.txt.'"

"Let me guess: not liner notes?"

"Sort of. They're liner notes about *you*."

"Me? Evan doxxed me?"

"He couldn't help it. When Evan loves something—"

"He has to know everything about it."

Deety smiled wistfully. "He also left instructions to contact you if I didn't hear from him after the debate."

"All that's in one text file?" Max asked.

"It isn't a text file. Change the file extension to .odt once you copy it over. You have OpenOffice?"

"Not on my current machine, but I'll get it," Max said. "What's the password?"

Deety smiled. "Don't you want to figure it out for yourself?"

"Maybe when I'm not being chased by FBI agents," Max said.

"I work better under pressure. Anyway, not that you need to see the contents of that file, since it's all about you, but the password is pretty simple: the track number followed by the first word of each song title, working your way toward the center."

"I would have figured that out," Max said.

"That's the idea."

"It would have taken me a while though."

"We'd talked about different ways of encrypting files before. I got it on my fifth try. And that passphrase doesn't work for the second file."

"Which is. . . ?"

"The one labeled 'Discography.txt.' Not a discography, I bet. It's a huge file, but that's all I know about it, because encryption. You'll have to do a little cryptology of your own. Good luck with that."

"I may already have the password," he told her, referring to the text message Evan had sent him.

She shook her head. "He took a big chance."

"He's—he was always careful."

"I'm surprised he didn't work out something more secure with you beforehand, like with me."

Max looked down. Evan had been trying to reach him for weeks and he'd kept putting him off. He might have been able to send this data to Max directly without involving Deety, if only he'd made himself available. He might have been able to do something to help Evan sooner, so he didn't have to take his own life.

Max retrieved his laptop. "Well let's see what's on it," he said.

Deety put her hands on top of the computer to prevent him from opening it.

"Not here," she said. She snatched her hands back as if they'd been burned. "Sorry."

"It isn't mine," Max said. "And I'm not that sensitive about my equipment."

She raised an eyebrow. "And that's my cue to get going." She slid out of the booth.

"Don't you want to know what Evan died to protect?" he asked.

"Definitely no way. *I'm* not willing to die for it."

"He was your. . . friend."

"He was yours first. I barely knew him." She sighed. "Look. My life is complicated enough. I have responsibilities. I can't get involved."

"But you're already involved."

Her expression hardened. "My part is over. Don't kill the messenger, right? That's all I am. The messenger. Now you have whatever it is, the way Evan wanted. You decide what to do with it. I'm out."

He looked at the microwave mounted on the other side of the counter. He picked up the CD. She followed his glance.

"Do whatever you think is right," Deety said.

That's what Evan had said. But Max needed to see the big picture before he could make a decision like this, and he owed it to Evan to see what had been so important to his friend. Maybe it would help him and Evan's family understand why he had killed himself.

"I just want to go back to my old life," Max said.

"Too late for that," Deety said softly. "Those days are gone forever, along with Evan." She looked at the time on her phone. "I have to go. It's a long way home."

"Okay. Thanks," Max said. "How can I find you again?"

"You won't." Deety turned and walked away.

She went out the door, sending a blast of cold air into the restaurant, without glancing back or saying good-bye. And after Lorraine dropped off his second check and cleared their plates, he realized she hadn't paid for her meal either.

Lorraine brought Max change from his bill while he was transferring the contents of the CD—music tracks in .cda format and two hidden .txt files—to an encrypted folder on his laptop. Until he knew what he had, he wouldn't know what to do with it or where to go next.

"Aren't you going to be late, honey?" she said.

"Huh?" Max said. "For what?"

"School, dear."

He'd forgotten it was a school day.

The time on his computer said it was 8:18 a.m. He had planned on staying here to work, but that didn't seem to be an option. If he holed up in the library or a coffee shop in town, he would be challenged for not being in school, and that would lead to other questions.

He needed to go someplace where he wouldn't attract attention.

10

SCHOOLS MADE THEIR STUDENTS' SAFETY THEIR
top priority, yet they often left a wealth of unprotected information online. After a few minutes on the Roseburg High
School website, Max had a copy of the student handbook, the
bell schedule, and a campus map. The school's blog gave him
insight into student life there, and it was easy for him to mem-
orize the names of the administrators and faculty.

No one stopped him when he ran inside with his backpack
slung over one shoulder, mingling with the other students trying to beat the late bell.

Max figured that in a school with over fifteen hundred students, he wouldn't have any trouble going unnoticed for one
day. He took a quick moment to orient himself on the map on
his phone. He watched the flow of bustling strangers heading
for their first class.

Max turned right and headed straight for the Media Center, which contained the library and student computer lab. When he got there, a class was settling down, taking up all twenty computers. Slipping into the school without drawing attention was one thing, but a teacher and other students would know he'd never been to the class before.

He hurried to the back of the library, hoping no one would question him, then turned off the aisle and ducked down behind a bookshelf.

He crouched and pretended to be looking for a book on a low shelf, listening for someone to give the alarm. All he heard was the usual before-class chatter.

Still crouching, Max made his way along the bookshelf until he reached the far end. He moved to the corner and sat on the floor with his back against the wall. The dome security camera was directly above his head.

He picked out the other security cameras in the room, none of which had a clear line at him. He figured no one was actively monitoring each one of them all the time anyway. At Granville, they were mainly there to provide evidence if there were some kind of incident—and to foster a false sense of safety.

Max wondered how much trouble he could get into here if he were caught. He didn't have a weapon or anything, but he was trespassing. An arrest would notify the FBI of his where-abouts, and local law enforcement would hold Max until the Feds collected him.

He'd just have to make sure that didn't happen. If he were challenged, he would just pretend to be a new student considering a transfer, or a cousin visiting a student or something. Evan might have been better at behind-the-screen hacks, but whenever they had to talk their way around security measures in the real world, Max had taken the lead. If all else failed, he would run.

Max added this to his growing list of crimes, which paled in comparison to stealing two cars in one night—not to mention the file he was carrying, which could contain any amount of illegally procured information.

It was time to see what Evan had entrusted him with.

Max fired up his laptop and half-listened to the teacher, Mrs. Bradshaw. He had happened into an introductory programming class, where the kids were designing and coding basic computer games from scratch. Maybe one of these kids was a hacker too, or would soon enter that world, never suspecting things could end as grimly as they had for Evan.

He located the hidden folder and the encrypted files Deety had mentioned. As curious as he was about what Evan had written about him in the LinerNotes.txt file, Max was more interested in the mysterious Discography.txt file. He connected to the school's open Wi-Fi and downloaded Evan's favorite encryption program, NewCrypt, and OpenOffice. Evan had never trusted other people enough to rely on standard PGP encryption, claiming that "Pretty Good Privacy" wasn't good enough. NewCrypt scrambled the contents of a file, folder, or drive so only one passphrase could unlock it.

He installed the programs and launched NewCrypt. When he opened Evan's file with it, a password dialog box opened. So far, so good.

He typed the long string of alphanumeric characters into the password field. He placed his right index finger on the Enter key and held his breath.

He pushed down.

The colorful Apple beach ball swirled at the center of his screen for a moment, then NewCrypt spat out a decrypted file. So the text Evan had sent Max moments before he died had in fact been a key, and after two days of searching, Max had finally found the lock. He could hardly contain his excitement.

But then Max's ears perked up. The students in the class weren't talking about their projects anymore.

"He doesn't have many friends," a girl said.

"Nice try, Jordan," Mrs. Bradshaw said. "Sign out of Panjea."

"This is news. It's *relevant*," Jordan said.

"Really. What are you looking at?"

"Evan Baxter's profile."

Max gave them their full attention.

"That hacker from the news?" Mrs. Bradshaw said.

"They say he was part of Dramatis Personai," Jordan said.

Max opened a browser. The lead story on CNN had been updated from this morning. The FBI now revealed that Evan was connected to at least a dozen high-profile corporate hacks perpetrated by Dramatis Personai in the last year. They claimed he had been part of a long-term investigation into several members of the hacktivist group.

So they were already trying to spin a story around Evan that made him look like an unstable, amoral criminal, and the implication was clear: Evan had felt the noose tightening and killed himself rather than be arrested and questioned. But Max didn't see how the FBI could have known about Evan all along—he was just too careful. The only way they could have connected him to Dramatis Personai now was if someone else in the group had given them that information.

Although there was still no discussion of how he killed himself or what his possible motives were, apparently the FBI was actively pursuing a lead on a possible accomplice, a fellow student at Granville High who had disappeared after the debate.

A shiver went down Max's back. They had to be talking about him. And he still didn't know why they were so interested.

Max switched back to the text file from Evan and tried to open it, but all it displayed was gibberish. As with the other file DoubleThink had already cracked, Discography.txt wasn't really a text document—Evan had altered the file name to hide its contents.

Max examined the code, looking for a hint as to the type of file it was. Then he spotted a word he knew in the garbled sequence of characters: "Kill_Screen."

He started to see more names scattered among the weird characters: "PHYREWALL," "0MN1," "GroundSloth." He grew excited; this file had something to do with Dramatis Personai.

Following DoubleThink's steps, Max changed the file name to an .odt file, the extension for OpenOffice text documents. The computer warned him that this might render the file unusable.

It's already unusable, he thought.

OpenOffice didn't know what to do with the file either.

"But don't you think it's weird?" Jordan said. "Everyone is talking about Evan Baxter and 'the silence of six' online, except on Panjea. I'm not seeing anything about it in my news feed, and whenever I post about it no one comments on it."

"You shouldn't be on Panjea right now anyway, Jordan," Mrs. Bradshaw said.

That is *weird*, Max thought as he studied the troublesome file.

It was huge, much larger than most Word documents, even when they were loaded with graphics. It was almost like it contained multiple documents, or perhaps lots of large images. Evan had always taken pride in the thoroughness of his research, whether he was doxxing someone or studying the company he and Max were going to infiltrate next.

Max ran through all the file formats he knew, starting with common video files, in case Evan had made another recording. But there were dozens of file name extensions for dozens of formats, and checking each one by one was tedious business.

"Tooms has to be hiding something," another boy said.

"Why?" Jordan asked.

"He's the government. The government is always hiding something. Tooms resigned from the Senate Intelligence Committee last year. Maybe he did it over this 'silence of six' business."

"I think he's cute," Jordan said.

"The Senator?!" her friend replied.

"Evan Baxter," Jordan said.

Max smiled. Evan would have blushed furiously if he'd heard a girl call him cute. He never would have had the nerve to talk to her though, even if he knew she liked him. Not in person, anyway.

Then again, he'd managed very well with Deety. Max couldn't believe Evan had hung out with her. What had that been, anyway? A date? Was she his secret girlfriend?

It didn't matter anymore, except that this amazing thing had happened in Evan's life, and he'd never breathed a word to Max about it. Just like he'd never mentioned Dramatis Personai, but had that been for his—or Max's—protection?

Max considered the possibility that he was looking at many different files. How would Evan have made them look like one file?

Duh.

Max changed the file name to "Discography.zip." He opened the software that extracted zipped files and was rewarded when it gave him a file folder named "BABEL." Inside were more than a dozen files: OpenOffice documents with names, mostly hacker handles he recognized from Dramatis Personai, like Kill_Screen.odt. He opened that one and found a complete dossier on a twenty-one-year-old college student at MIT named Leroy Brown, complete with a photo and clippings of political cartoons he had drawn for his college newspaper.

Evan had doxxed his fellow members of Dramatis Personai. That's why the folder was named "Babel": One of Evan's all-time favorite comic books was *JLA: The Tower of Babel*, in which Batman revealed that he knew the secret identities of the other heroes in the Justice League and how to defeat them—part of his preparations in case one of them ever went rogue and he had to take them down.

That was Evan: always prepared. Just like the goddamn Batman.

Max closed Kill_Screen's file and scanned through the rest of the list. He hovered over DoubleThink.odt then moved on. There was a group of files at the bottom all sorted together in alphabetical order under the letter *X* with usernames he didn't know.

Six of them.

Max's pulse quickened as he opened the first one, X-1_ Miller.odt. The first page was a screenshot of a Panjea profile for Ariel Miller, a twenty-three-year-old systems administrator from San Jose, California. She had long brown hair, pale skin, freckles, and a self-conscious smile. She had taken a selfie with her cell phone in her bathroom mirror while wearing a bathing suit with a pattern of R2D2 from *Star Wars*.

The next page was a copy of an article from the *San Jose*

Mercury News where they had interviewed Ariel Miller, then age nineteen, for a story about people named after characters from pop culture. The reporter had asked if she liked *The Little Mermaid* because of her name, suggesting that the names parents give their children are self-fulfilling prophecies or attempts to influence their lives from birth. Ariel had said, "Well, it's a great movie. I can relate to Ariel's desire to be part of a world she isn't meant to be in."

The third page showed another photo of Ariel. She had dyed her hair red and wore torn burlap tied with rope as a dress.

The file ended with another news article. It showed Ariel's Panjea profile picture under the headline HIT AND RUN.

Max leaned closer to the screen, gripping the sides as he read: "Local authorities are on the lookout for a black SUV that struck and killed Ariel Miller, 23, of San Jose, at 7:23 p.m. while she was crossing Walnut Street on 4th Avenue in downtown San Bruno."

Death was a permanent way of silencing someone.

With growing dread, Max opened the next file in the list: X-2_Powers.odt. Another Panjea profile, showing a heavyset black guy named Geordie Powers, originally from North Carolina. Under Employer he had written, "I'd tell you, but I'd have to kill you." His location was listed as Arlington County, Virginia.

Geordie's file concluded with an article describing how the nineteen-year-old had been beaten and stabbed to death in an alleyway late at night. It was described as a mugging, but only his laptop had been taken from his backpack—he still had his wallet with all his money and cards inside. There were no witnesses and police had no suspects; although there was a security camera in the alley, the computer storing the footage had crashed and the files couldn't be recovered.

What a coincidence.

The next file: X-3_@sskicker.odt. This was one of the Dramatis Personai members who had "disappeared"!

Max skimmed a chat log of hackers discussing a target: a software company that was charging outrageous amounts for downloadable content for a big new game that had just come out. The company claimed they were providing new levels, but @sskicker had hacked into their e-mail server and found messages from the development team about levels they had decided to withhold at the last minute to make extra money. They were essentially forcing customers to pay for content that they should have had right from the beginning.

Words were highlighted throughout: references to stores and the time of day. Next to one of these, Evan had annotated "Arizona?"

Logging chats was not allowed specifically for this reason. It looked like Evan had been storing months worth of them and using them to piece together the identities of Dramatis Personai hackers.

The next page showed the Panjea profile of a thirteen-year-old boy named Sayid Fawaz, who was just old enough to have a

Panjea account. It was followed by an article about him being killed in a drive-by shooting while walking to a movie with his friend, Steven Oberkircher, in Phoenix, Arizona. Miraculously, Steven hadn't been injured.

Max closed his eyes. Sayid had been so young.

X-4_Infiltraitor, another of the missing hackers, was Ty Andrews, sixteen, from Fairbanks, Alaska. Max didn't read the article, just the headline: TEEN DROWNS IN LAKE NEAR FAIRBANKS.

By now, Max was feeling sick, but he had two more files to go. Max knew who X-5_Marks.odt referred to even before he opened it.

Everyone had heard about the bizarre death of Kyle Marks, a thirty-one-year-old who had died in a fire in his Brooklyn apartment two months earlier. Kyle had been a prominent tech reporter with a popular vlog called TangledWeb.

The fire had happened in the middle of the day while he was editing his show and chatting with a friend online. With no explanation, he had stopped responding, and moments later, fire trucks were responding to his address. The fire had supposedly been caused by faulty electrical wiring in the old building, but no one knew why Kyle hadn't been able to escape in time or ask his friend to call for help.

Max scrolled through the file. Evan had collected every report he could find about the story and every article Marks had ever written covering Panjea.

Max couldn't believe that Kyle Marks had been a victim of

this conspiracy, whatever it was.

The final file, X-6_L0NELYB0Y.odt, was for the third Dramatis Personai member who had gone offline. Max opened it and scanned through it quickly: Jeremy "Jem" Seers, age sixteen. . . no Panjea profile, no picture. He was also from Fairbanks, Alaska. Max wondered if Ty and Jem had been hacking buddies, like he and Evan had. The odds that two members of Dramatis Personai had lived in the same town and never met were slim. There was much less info on Jem, a lot of Evan's question marks around chat logs, and no cause of death—just a police report filed by his parents, an article about an Amber alert, and a missing persons poster. What horrible fate had he met if there wasn't even anything left of him for the police to find?

Max slowly closed his laptop. He couldn't look at any more. His hands shook.

What is the silence of six, and what are you going to do about it?

Evan wanted him to do something with all this, but what? Could he send these files to the police? There wasn't any hard evidence that the deaths were actually murders, or any clues to who was responsible. And Evan could have done that much himself. As for turning to reporters. . . . Well, maybe he had, and that's why Kyle Marks ended up dead. Having that on his conscience might have driven Evan to suicide.

Then why enlist Max if there was a good chance he would be in danger, too?

If Evan wanted him to warn the other members of

Dramatis Personai that someone had hunted three of them down, Evan could have just given DoubleThink the passphrase instead. Did that mean he didn't trust her with it? Or he was worried that this information would be used against everyone in Dramatis Personai?

Or maybe he thought someone in the group was involved with their deaths—perhaps the same person who had ID'd Evan as one of their own.

Quietly arranging the deaths of six people had to require serious resources: deep pockets and major connections. Since Evan had posed his question at a debate in front of presidential candidates, perhaps he had suspected their involvement. That was a frightening thought—one of them would be the next president of the United States.

Max jumped up. He walked off the pins and needles in his legs, pacing back and forth on the thin library carpet. The room was now empty and as quiet as a cemetery. He looked at the clock—he'd been here for three hours without realizing it.

He could approach the FBI with the little he knew. Hopefully his cooperation would get them off his back. But if the Feds were in on it—as it appeared they might be—Max might end up like Ariel, Geordie, Ty, Sayid, Kyle, and Jem.

So he had to keep investigating. Figure out what Evan had uncovered and find proof that people had died for it. Find out more about the people who had been murdered; if he could find any evidence that one of their deaths had been more than an accident, then he could reconsider approaching the authorities.

Why not start at the beginning? Ariel Miller had been the first to die, and of the six, she had lived closest to Max's current location. He looked up her former address in San Jose. He could be there by tonight.

The bell rang. He saw that students were allowed to go off school grounds for lunch, which made this the easiest time to sneak out and get back on the road. Max collected his laptop and bag and left the library, joining the crowd of students heading toward the cafeteria.

Max cut through the cafeteria, toward the doors at the back that led directly to the parking lot behind the school. He hadn't parked there, of course, but his stolen vehicle was just on the other side of it.

The smell of food set his mouth watering and he felt a pang of hunger. But he abruptly lost all interest in lunch when he saw two girls sitting across from each other at a table in the corner, hunched over back-to-back laptops like they were playing a high-tech game of Battleship.

The girl facing him was short with brown pigtails and oversized black eyeglasses. She tilted her head to the right and left as she tugged on each of her pigtails in turn—right, left, right—with focused concentration.

The girl with her back to him had her long blond hair in a ponytail. A crumpled Denny's bag sat on the table alongside two empty takeaway containers.

It couldn't be. . . .

The pigtail girl glanced up and her eyes widened in

recognition when she saw Max. How did she know him? She said something to her companion.

The girl facing her turned around and pulled off her yellow-tinted computer glasses. DoubleThink! She locked eyes with him.

Max made a beeline for their table.

"Are you following me?" DoubleThink and Max said at the same time.

He sat down next to her and glanced at her screen. He couldn't read it from this angle. She had a protective filter on it that rendered it a shimmery gold. Nice.

"What are you doing? You can't be here," Deety hissed.

She looked subtly different. It was only the absence of any makeup now that made him realize she'd been wearing it this morning. And now that Max saw her long hair, he realized she'd been the other waitress at Denny's that morning, the one who had been arguing with Jess. Maybe she had been coming up with an excuse for why she couldn't serve him.

DoubleThink had supposedly driven six hours from Seattle to meet him, but apparently she lived in Roseburg and went to school here.

"And you said I wouldn't be able to find you again." Max grinned.

Deety's eyes flicked to pigtail girl. Max turned to her. Up close, she looked like a younger version of Deety. She wore a baggy, blue plaid shirt buttoned over a purple T-shirt. Was this her sister?

"Hi, I'm Max," he said.

"I know," the girl said.

"Shh. Not so loud." Deety glanced at the tables around them, but it was so noisy in the cafeteria he doubted anyone could overhear them.

"I wasn't following you, Deety," Max said. "I just needed to get out of the open. This seemed like the perfect place to blend in. I didn't know it was your school. You said you lived in Seattle."

"You can't be surprised that a hacker lied to you," Deety said.

"I was just starting to trust you too," Max said.

"You *can* trust me," Deety said. "With the important stuff."

"Me too," the younger girl said.

"Stay out of this," Deety said. "You have to leave, Max."

"I was just about to," he said. "I looked at those files. There's something really big going on."

"I'm not interested. I don't want to know anything else," Deety said. "People are looking for you."

"I noticed. But how did you know?" Max asked.

Deety turned her computer around and Max saw his high school yearbook photo on the screen—on CNN.com.

He leaned closer. The caption read, "The FBI is on the look-out for Maxwell Stein, a known associate of Evan Baxter who hasn't been seen since Wednesday morning. He is considered a person of interest in their ongoing investigation of the hacking incident during Tuesday's presidential debate."

"Damn," Max said.

"We can't be seen with you. Please, Max. Just go. Now."

"Deety—or whatever your name is. Did you know Evan doxxed everyone in Dramatis Personai? Including you?"

The younger girl gasped.

Max glanced at her. "And the 'silence of six'? Six people have died under suspicious circumstances. Including hackers. Your friends. Infiltraitor. @sskicker. L0NELYB0Y. Who knows who'll be next?"

"I just have to make sure it isn't someone else I care about," Deety said.

"Like Evan? Like your sister?" Max glanced at the younger girl. "Deety, it's up to us to make sure no one else gets hurt. That's what Evan wanted us to do."

"You don't know what Evan wanted any more than I do. And we can't take any chances." Deety spread her hands and looked around. "This is our life."

"Don't I get any say?" her sister asked.

"No," Deety said. "You have this file with you, Max?"

He tapped his laptop. "Encrypted. It's still on the CD too."

"Destroy it. That's the only way out of this." She nodded to the side of the cafeteria. "There's a microwave. Burn it. Deny everything."

"Penny! We don't destroy information," her sister said.

"Penny?" Max asked. "That's much nicer than Deety."

"Risse—" Penny caught herself. She slapped the table in frustration.

"Risse is a nice name, too," Max said.

"It's short for Clarisse." The younger girl smiled.

"I thought you said Evan doxxed me," Penny said.

"He did, but it didn't feel right to read your file." Max had avoided looking at the file named DoubleThink.odt, out of a weird sense of respect for Evan's only other close friend—and maybe more than that. "I bet that sounds stupid, but. . . ."

"No. That's the first thing you've said that makes me interested in helping you," Penny said.

"Really?"

She sighed. "I'll at least look at what you've got. But I mean it. We can't be seen talking to each other. And you shouldn't be seen at all."

Penny handed him her black knit cap and computer glasses. "Put these on before someone else recognizes you. Start thinking like a fugitive."

Max pulled the hat low and slid on the glasses.

"Have you been on the run before?" Max asked.

"I just have common sense," she snapped.

Penny typed on her laptop. "I'm wiping the school's security footage from this morning. I bet you're all over it."

Max looked up. Another dome camera was positioned by the entrance, with a clear view of him. He ducked his head.

"You can do that?" Max asked.

"Already done." She hit the Enter key and closed her laptop. "Let's go. Lunch is the best time to sneak out. I'll take you somewhere that should be safe, but we have to stop at my house on the way."

Risse closed her laptop too.

"Nope. You're staying here," Penny said.

"What?" Risse asked.

"I don't want you involved."

"I'm already involved. We're a team."

Penny shook her head.

"If you're going home first, that means you're worried. Whatever you're planning, it'll go twice as fast with my help," Risse said.

"Not if I'm more worried about you," Penny said.

"You know I'm the smarter, better half of DoubleThink," Risse said.

"Facepalm," Penny muttered. "Damn it, Risse."

"I thought he knew about that already! You never tell me anything," Risse said.

"Because you'll just blab it to everyone!"

Risse was also DoubleThink?

Max snapped his fingers. "The other night, one of you was typing in the chat room, and the other was talking to me."

Mind. Blown.

"We make a pretty good team. Online, anyway. In the real world, Pen's a little bossy."

"Oh?" Max said.

"You can't tell anyone," Penny said. "Please, Max."

"That you're bossy?"

She just glared at him.

11

MAX DROVE, WITH PENNY GIVING HIM DIRECTIONS
from the passenger seat and Risse in the back watching out
the rear window to make sure they weren't being followed. He
parked a block away from their house on Luellen Drive and
the sisters walked to a weathered white split-level. The front
yard was overgrown with scraggly bushes and weeds among
patches of dirt. The rusted hull of an old pickup truck sat in
front of the driveway.

Max waited in the car while they went inside. They needed
to destroy evidence of their extracurricular activities as DoubleThink before leaving. Penny might be acting paranoid, but
better to be paranoid than foolish, he thought, and he was
already learning to trust her instincts.

After Max noticed the same gray SUV drive down the

street for the third time, he wondered if she had good cause for concern. The vehicle moved slowly, as if guided by an unfamiliar driver looking for a certain street number. The windows were tinted so he couldn't see its occupants, but when it parked directly across from Penny and Risse's house and no one got out, he felt his pulse quicken.

He had to warn the girls. If necessary, he'd find a way to lead these people away from the house to give them time to escape. He fumbled with his backpack and dumped his laptop onto the seat next to him. He opened it and sent the command to start the car and left the engine running. He glanced down the street. The mysterious visitors hadn't seemed to notice him yet.

He dialed Penny's phone number and waited impatiently while it rang.

"Hello?" a girl answered.

"Penny!" Max said.

"No, it's Risse. Max?"

Max heard Penny's voice in the background. "Give me that."

"It looks just like mine," Risse said.

"But it was in my bag," Penny said, then spoke directly into the phone. "Max? What's up?"

"Listen. Try not to freak out."

"I don't freak out," she said.

"There's a car outside your house. A gray SUV with tinted windows. It drove past twice."

"FBI?" She sounded frightened.

"They haven't exactly introduced themselves."

The driver and passenger side doors of the SUV opened in tandem. A dark-haired man in a light brown suit and a blond woman in a long flower-print dress got out of the car and walked toward the house, black books clutched to their chests in the crooks of their arms. Bibles?

For a moment Max doubted they were dangerous—which was an excellent reason for them to choose those particular disguises. He was sticking to the plan. If he was wrong, they could laugh about it later.

"You need to get out of there," he said.

"We're almost done," Penny said.

"It's too late. Bring whatever you can't erase with you. Do you have a back door?"

"Of course."

"I'll drive around the block. Go downstairs and lock your front door, then sneak out the back and lock that too. I'll pick you up on the next street."

"Risse, go lock the front door," Penny said.

"What's going on?" Risse asked in the background.

"Just do it. Hurry!" Penny said.

Max pulled the car away from the curb and prepared to turn it around.

"Go!" Max said. "I'll meet you two on the street behind your house."

He heard Penny fumble the phone and then the call was

disconnected. He turned the car around and circled the block to the house behind Penny's, forcing himself to drive slower than he wanted to. A dirt path to the right of the home led to a common cement-paved patio. Max parked right in front of the small road and got out to open the passenger doors. He watched the back door of Penny's house anxiously, rocking back and forth on his heels. There was nothing he could do but wait.

Thirty seconds later, the storm door and back door swung open and banged against the side of the house. Penny barreled out and made a beeline for Max. She was still wearing that bright pink jacket.

He admired her form, head up, arms pumping, knees high as she sprinted across the scraggly backyard. She was fast, even carrying a bulky black duffel over her shoulder. She would be great on the Granville track team.

Penny skidded to a stop next to his car. She threw her bag into the backseat and spun around to look back, breathing heavily.

"Risse?" Max asked.

"She was right behind me." Penny took a step toward her house. Max grabbed her arm to stop her.

"Get in the car. I'll be right back." Max darted down the dirt path. When he reached the patio he heard a crack from the front of Penny's house, and wood splintering. They were breaking in.

If he went inside to look for Risse, he would basically be turning himself in.

Max kept running.

The glass in the storm door was cracked and it was hanging from only its top hinge. The back door banged open again and Risse bolted out. She staggered into Max's arms and dropped her duffel bag.

He grabbed the bag from her and pushed her toward the car. "Keep moving!" he said.

He slung the bag across his chest and followed Risse. It felt like he was lugging bricks.

They ran toward the car. Penny was behind the wheel, craning her neck to watch them coming.

Max tossed Risse's duffel bag into the backseat. Risse tumbled in after it and Max slammed the door behind her before jumping into the passenger seat.

The car peeled away as Max pulled his door closed. In the rearview mirror, he spotted the man in the brown suit running into the street. The agent waved his hand, as if trying to flag down a taxi. Then he started chasing after them. He tugged something out of his suit jacket and pointed it at them. At first Max thought it was a walkie-talkie.

"Gun! Stay down." Max hunched forward.

Penny swerved the car from left to right on the street to make them a harder target. The agent with the gun stopped in the middle of the road, legs spread apart, and took aim. Max pulled his attention away from the mirror in time to see the light ahead turn red—and a pickup truck approaching from the left, perpendicular to their path.

"Penny!" he shouted.

She jerked her attention from the mirror to the road ahead.

They couldn't stop in time.

Max yanked the wheel to the right as Penny accelerated, then she pulled it back, hard, to the left. The chorus of shouts inside the car was joined by a honking horn and the horrible screech of tires.

The car swerved sharply around the truck and miraculously cleared it. Max was jolted up and down in his seat and his stomach lurched as the tires on the right side bounced over the corner of the sidewalk. Penny wrestled the vehicle back onto the road and slowed down to the speed limit.

The truck's horn continued to blare behind them. Max twisted around in his seat to look out the back window. The truck was stopped in the middle of the intersection at an angle, half-turned toward them. He hoped no one had been hurt; it looked empty except for the driver.

"Ev-everyone okay?" he asked.

Penny glanced in the mirror. "Risse?"

Risse's head popped up into view. She had fallen or rolled into the footwell.

"Ow." She rubbed her right elbow. "I'm okay. Were they really going to shoot at us?"

"I think so," Max said.

Risse settled into the seat behind Max and buckled in.

"That was close," Penny said. "Sorry."

"Did you hack the DMV to get your license?" Max asked.

"License?" Penny asked in a shaky voice.

Max looked in the rearview and saw the gray SUV pull around the stalled truck.

"Great," he said.

"Don't worry. I can lose them." Penny hunched forward over the wheel and pumped the gas.

Max steadied himself by grabbing on to the dashboard.

"Are we really doing this?" he asked.

"I practiced driving on these roads." She raced through an intersection as the light went from yellow to red then made a quick right. She seemed more in control of herself and the vehicle now.

Max pressed his back into his seat and watched the SUV in his mirror. Penny increased the distance between them by weaving through cars.

"Where are we going?" he asked.

"Now that they've seen the car we have to ditch it. I know a remote place where we can hide out a while, and then dump the car later."

She made a hard left. Another car honked. Penny waved an apology.

Max's pulse was racing as if he'd just played in a tough soccer match.

"Did those goons follow us from the school?" Penny asked.

"I don't think so. It looked like they had your address," Max said.

"How?" Penny asked. "Why?"

"I don't know."

"So it's just a coincidence they turned up the same day you did?"

"Maybe they made the connection between you and Evan."

"What about Mama?" Risse asked.

"She'll be fine. If they question her, they'll be lucky if she knows what day of the week it is," Penny said.

The gray SUV wasn't behind them anymore. Max looked ahead nervously, wondering if they were trying to head them off somehow. But there were fewer cars on this section of road.

Penny turned onto a side street. "I think we lost them," she said.

Max and Risse looked behind them. There were now no other cars in sight.

"Or they gave up for now," Max said. As Penny had pointed out, their pursuers now had a description of the car and probably its license plate number, so it would be easy to find them again until they got off the road.

Penny drove through a thick canopy of trees down a long, winding path that was just wide enough for their compact car. After a few minutes on bumpy back roads they reached an abandoned stone cabin in a small clearing. The front door was boarded up, covered in graffiti. A dead tree was leaning against the back wall.

"And here we are," Penny said. She parked the car out of sight of the road.

"Didn't I see this place in a horror movie?" Max asked.

"We're away from everything and everyone. You can't even get a cell signal out here," Penny said.

"Now that *is* scary," Max said.

12

THE FALLEN TREE BEHIND THE CABIN HAD KNOCKED out a chunk of the wall. The girls wriggled inside the small opening easily, and Max passed their bags through to them. His larger frame made it more difficult for him to squeeze between the scratchy bark and the crumbling stone, but he made it. He pulled his backpack inside after him then stood up and brushed dirt from his knees.

He took in the one-room living space. The only furniture was a rickety wooden table in the corner and an overturned chair with only three legs. The floor was littered with dry leaves, dirt, and twigs. It looked like an animal had assembled a nest out of mud and branches in the fireplace, which was also abandoned.

Cozy.

Penny set up her computer on the table. It was sleek and ultraportable, the kind that transformed into a tablet. Light, compact, and the latest model—nothing like the duct-taped one she'd had at school.

"Wages go up at Denny's?" Max asked.

"I get decent money from freelancing. The job at Denny's is just how I keep Mom from getting suspicious."

Max considered Risse's frayed purple Chucks and her worn jeans with their rolled-up cuffs. Hand-me-downs. He'd seen their rundown house, too. He didn't think their family had much cash to spare. "Freelancing? As a hacker?" he asked.

"Nothing illegal. Well, it isn't entirely legal when I start, but lots of companies pay bounties to reward hackers for finding security flaws," she said. "With your skills you could be making big money too."

"I never saw it that way." Max slid his laptop from his backpack.

"I didn't figure you for a Mac user," she said.

"This isn't mine," he said. "I borrowed it when my laptop was middle-manned."

Penny raised her eyebrows.

"They caught me by surprise. It won't happen again." Max opened the computer and looked around. "I guess there's no electricity out here either."

Penny fished out a battery the size and shape of a brick and set it on the table. The table creaked under its weight. "This should have enough power to run it."

Max plugged in and booted his computer up.

"Keep that computer offline permanently, which you should have been doing anyway since it's stolen," Penny said.

"I've been careful."

"Still. We should only look at Evan's files on air-gapped computers, isolated from the internet. You don't know who could be watching. That's why I wanted to meet here—no internet access for miles around," Penny said.

"I didn't think of that," Max said.

He logged in to his encrypted hard drive. He clicked on the file named X_Miller.odt. "Here we are. The first of the silenced six was Ariel Mil—"

"Hold on, I want to see his file on DoubleThink first," Penny said.

"Okay," Max said. He opened the DoubleThink.odt file and nudged his computer toward her. "I don't need to see it. Delete it when you're done."

"Evan sent it to you, so it's okay if you read it. You already know about us anyway. But thanks," Penny said.

Penny paged through the contents of the file while Max and Risse looked over her shoulder. There was astonishingly little information.

A Panjea page showed a picture of Penny, in which her blond hair had pink streaks. Her profile indicated she was a year older than Max, a senior at Roseburg High. It also listed her full name.

"Penny Polonsky?" He smirked. "What, are you a superhero or something?"

"That depends on who you ask," she said.

Underneath the profile, Evan had included Penny's contact information, right down to her phone number and the GPS coordinates for what he assumed was her house.

Yet there were no chat logs, article clippings, or any other personal details about her, like the ones Max had found in the other files on members of Dramatis Personai. But there was a special note on the last page:

"Penny is one of the most trustworthy people in the world."

When she got to the end, Penny pressed a hand against her mouth and her eyes teared up.

"Evan was the least trusting person in the world, so that's quite an endorsement," Max said.

Risse scrolled back through the file. "Is that all? There isn't anything about me!"

"That's good, right?" Max asked.

"I guess," Risse said.

"You didn't tell Evan about Risse?" Max asked Penny.

"I wanted to, but it wasn't my secret alone to tell," she said. "He didn't even know I have a sister."

Evan would have been shocked that Penny had withheld a secret this big from even him. He had prided himself on his ability to dig up the truth, obsessed with knowing everything that could be known. It felt like an honor to have learned something that had escaped his notice.

"I felt bad ignoring him when he tried to chat with Double Think when it was me logged in. Talk about mixed signals," Risse said. "At least it never got. . . weird." She blushed.

"It's possible he found out about you and decided not to put it in the report," Max said. "Evan had his own sense of honor."

Max dragged the file to the Trash then deleted it permanently. He called up a program to zero fill the space it had been in with garbage files. There was no way anyone could recover the file, not even the FBI with all their resources.

"You could have used that to blackmail me into helping you," Penny said. "That's actually why I agreed to meet. To talk you into destroying the report." She didn't sound remotely ashamed of her ulterior motives.

"That was the only copy." Max showed them the mix CD Evan had sent him and showed Penny that he had carefully colored in the data side with a black Sharpie.

"Now the only way we'll be in any danger is if we do something truly stupid. Like help you," Penny said.

"Why would you do that?" Max asked.

"Because Evan clearly wanted us to work together. It was practically his dying wish. He wouldn't have given you my digits otherwise, or told me how to reach you."

Max leaned against the rough stone wall and took a deep breath.

"I'm beginning to see why he thought so highly of you," Penny said. "We'll figure this out together."

"Thank you," he said.

"It might be a good idea to stay away from home for a little while anyway." Penny leaned over his computer. "What else have you got on Dramatis Personai and the six people?"

He pointed out the files marked with an *X*. Risse gasped and pointed to one of the files. "Powers. Geordie Powers?"

"That's right. Did you know him?" Max asked.

"I've talked to him." Risse started typing on her laptop. Max noticed she never used her laptop's touchpad—only keyboard shortcuts—and windows flew open and closed on her screen at an impressive speed. She was looking for something.

Penny clicked on Powers's file. "It says here that Powers was mugged, but only his laptop was taken. Maybe he was a hacker too?"

"Hold on, I'm checking my old chat logs from Dramatis Personai. . . " Risse said.

"Does everyone store chats when they're not supposed to?" Max asked.

"Of course," Penny said.

Max started to reply, but stopped when he heard a rustling sound from outside. He held up a hand in warning. Penny and Risse froze, lips pressed together and eyes wide.

Max slowly moved to the front of the cabin and wiped some of the grime off the window with his thumb, letting more light into the dark room.

It took him a moment to pick out the road they had followed there. It looked clear. He tilted his head to listen again.

"What is it?" Risse whispered.

"There's someone out there," Max said.

"I think that's *nature*," Penny said. "Hear those birds?"

Max nodded.

"If someone were outside, you wouldn't hear anything," she said.

"This place doesn't make you nervous?" he asked.

"We're all a little on edge," Penny said.

Risse nodded.

"Let's just make this quick. If someone finds us here, there's only one way out of the cabin," Max said. Even he would have a hard time fleeing on foot through the forest surrounding them.

He kept an eye on the window while the girls continued to work.

"Here it is," Risse said. "I found a request from Evan from earlier this year for help accessing a government e-mail server. I helped him get a login and password by social engineering some poor intern in a Washington field office."

"Geordie," Max said.

"Yup. All I gave Evan was his account information. I don't know what he did with it."

"And now Geordie's dead," Penny said.

Risse's triumphant expression turned to horror.

"It's not your fault," Max said. "Maybe he was up to something and that's why Evan wanted to check his e-mail."

"I remember him now. He sounded so young." Risse brushed her fingertips lightly over the laptop keys, staring at the screen. "I told him there was a serious computer virus infecting the servers that he had spread by forwarding a chain letter."

"And you needed to log in to his account in order to quarantine the virus," Max said.

Risse smiled.

"Classic," Max said.

"He was scared that he was going to get into trouble," Risse said. "Do you really think he was killed because of me?"

"Not because of you, sis." Penny leaned over and wrapped her arms around Risse. "Because of what Evan did. He must have used Geordie's login to get something from the government e-mail system. And it was tracked back to him, not Evan."

"That wouldn't have made Evan feel too good about this either." *That's two deaths he would have blamed himself for.* Max was beginning to see what could have driven Evan to the brink, then pushed him over it. "But what did he find? Whatever it was must have led to everything else."

Penny clicked through the rest of the files. Risse was clearly crushed to find out she'd played a small role in a chain of events that left someone dead, but Penny's face remained impassive. She didn't say a word as she skimmed the dossiers for five minutes. Finally she pushed the computer away.

"Evan had a hunch something bad had happened to those hackers, but the rest of Dramatis Personai figured they'd been arrested or were laying low." Penny ran her hands through her hair. "No one wanted to believe anything like this was possible. Amazing that he pieced together what happened to them, just from research."

"All this must have taken a lot of work," Max said.

"He didn't mind hard work when he was properly moti-vated. When Infiltraitor—Ty Andrews—disappeared, it hit him really hard. They worked together."

"*Where* did he work?" Max asked.

"Panjea," Penny said.

Panjea? Max was stunned.

He'd thought it was a big deal that Evan was in Dramatis Personai, but he also had been employed by one of the most powerful tech companies in the country, if not the world.

"I can't believe he worked for Panjea," Max said.

"They employ a lot of Dramatis Personai members. They have some kind of elite hacking group. Evan was supposed to put in a good word for me, but he changed his mind and brought Infiltraitor on instead." Her mouth tightened. "I was furious. He knew how much I needed the job, but I guess it was lucky for me. You really didn't know?"

"When did Evan start there?" Max asked.

"Last October. No, late September."

Max had already distanced himself from hacking and Evan by then. But now that he thought back, Evan hadn't put up any resistance. In fact, he had subtly encouraged Max's deci-sion, saying that it wouldn't change anything between them. Max now wondered whose idea it had been in the first place. He'd been moving in that direction for a while, but had Evan nudged him the rest of the way?

The thing about social engineering was that you used

people's own inclinations to get them to do what you wanted. You couldn't force them to do anything. They always have a choice.

Max leaned back and stretched his arms forward. A sore joint popped softly. "Evan never mentioned a job. He probably wanted to avoid paying back the thirty bucks he owed me. What did he do for the greatest social media service in the world?"

"He didn't talk about it much. He said he couldn't. But it had to be one of their biggest projects if he was on it. He's a brilliant programmer." She flinched. "He *was* the best."

Evan had been working for Panjea for over a year, and Max hadn't known about it at all. Had they been that out of touch? It wasn't like he had forgotten to update him on the news in passing; Evan had actively kept this from him, along with his activities with Dramatis Personai—and Penny.

"That reporter, Kyle Marks, had a tech vlog, right?" Risse said. "He did a lot of stories about Panjea."

"So you think Evan found something out about Panjea, and the government killed people to cover it up?" Risse said. "They would have been investigating it too."

"Maybe they were. Evan's question implied someone knew what he was talking about," Max said. "If he hadn't killed himself, I bet he would have been targeted next."

"We don't even know that their deaths *are* murders. We just have Evan's suspicions." Penny spread her hands, palms up. "Just playing devil's advocate."

"Maybe Evan was murdered too?" Risse asked quietly.

"I saw him shoot himself," Max said. "It didn't look fake to me, but I'm no expert. Maybe that's why the video is being suppressed?"

"Could someone have made Evan do it?" Penny said.

"How do you force someone to commit suicide in front of millions of people?" Max asked.

"Threaten someone they care about." Penny looked at Risse.

Max nodded. That would do it. Evan would have taken a bullet for his parents, or Max and his dad, and probably even Penny.

"If we could get the full video out there, people would start wondering why *his* death was being hidden," Penny said.

"Until we can get hold of it, we have to deal with what we do have. We think we know what 'the silence of six' is, but if those people were murdered, we don't know who killed them, or why," Max said.

"We should go through every one of these files thoroughly," Penny said. "Who knows what else we'll find? We've already established a link between at least three of the victims, four if you include Evan: Panjea."

"That's their slogan. 'Everyone's connected,'" Risse said.

Max opened Ariel Miller's file. "I want to find out more about Ariel. She was a sysadmin, but there has to be a reason her death captured Evan's interest. This file's named X-1, so she was the first one who died—six months ago. If her family remembers anything weird about her behavior leading up to her death, or if they remember anything unusual about the accident, it could help us build a case," Max said.

"Give me a copy of the files and I'll go through them while you do that," Risse said.

"That would be a huge help. The sooner we read them, the sooner we'll know what we're up against," he said.

Penny shook her head. "We don't want them, Risse."

"We'll be fine with encryptions, air-gapped machines, all that spy stuff you're good at. I need to do something. If we're right and the U.S. government is killing American citizens, we can't ignore that," Risse said. "We shouldn't let Max take all the risks."

"I don't know." Penny pursed her lips.

"Come with me," Max said.

"To San Jose," Penny said.

She and Risse exchanged a long glance.

"Okay," Penny said.

"Yeah?" Risse asked.

"But only as far as San Jose," Penny said. "If we don't find proof that something bad happened to Ariel, we're coming back home and you're on your own, Max."

"I'll take it. Thank you," Max said.

"This is why I joined Dramatis Personai in the first place. Besides, I have to see what Evan found out about the other members. I hate to think it's possible, but one of us must have tipped off the FBI about his involvement." Penny folded her arms. "I want to know who it is."

"That's what I figured too," Max said. "When can we leave?"

"As soon as we hike back to town and steal another car. We already have everything we need from our house," she said.

Risse unzipped her duffel bag and pulled out a series of items. "Spare laptops, chargers, backup batteries, burner phones, USB sticks, headphones." The last item was a pair of oversized vintage headphones that seemed out of place among the more modern tech. She lined everything up on the table.

She peered inside the bag. "Also hair dye, makeup, hats, sunglasses, a couple changes of clothes, snacks, five hundred dollars cash, toiletries, and. . . sundry. Oh, and socks. You can never have too many socks. These have toast on them." She held up a pair of socks decorated with cute cartoons of anthropomorphic toasted bread. "Everything a girl on the lam could ever need."

"'On the lam'?" Max said.

"She watches too much TV." Penny reached inside her sister's bag and pulled out a plush lavender unicorn. "You brought Thea too?"

Risse grabbed it from her. "Hey, I packed this when I was, like, thirteen."

"That was last year," Penny said.

"I'm both impressed and disturbed that you have go-bags," Max said. If he'd thought that far ahead, he wouldn't have had to steal and improvise once he was on the run. But he'd gotten out of hacking so he wouldn't have to worry about that kind of thing, or so he'd thought.

"That's what it means to be American in today's world. You're lucky we were so prepared." Penny looked Max up and down. "But we'll have to find you some new clothes, and see what we can do to foil facial recognition software."

Max frowned at the reminder that he was now a public fugitive. He had no right asking the two of them to travel with him when that meant putting themselves at risk of exposure and capture.

"Penny, maybe—" he began.

"Too late. We already said we'd come along. Don't worry, the Feds are looking for one teenager, not three," Penny said.

"We'll be part of your disguise," Risse said.

Penny put a hand on his shoulder. "It's gonna be okay."

Max smiled. It might not be true, but it felt good to hear the words, and even better to not be on his own anymore.

13

THE FIRST ORDER OF BUSINESS WAS GETTING new wheels. They walked back to a residential neighborhood, where Penny and Risse watched in admiration as Max war texted into an older model Volkswagen Jetta. Risse made him guide her through the steps until she got it.

San Jose was a straight shot down I-5 South. The first four hours of the drive went quickly, with Penny and Risse reviewing Evan's files on their friends in Dramatis Personai and shouting out the interesting information they discovered.

"There isn't much on 0MN1," Penny said from the front passenger seat. "Mainly a bunch of chat logs where Evan highlighted certain things 0MN1 mentioned: place names, comments about the weather, the time of day, phrases that might be particular to specific regions."

"Maybe he didn't have enough to go on," Max said.

"He had better luck with the others," Risse said from the backseat. "Get this. Edifice is a forty-year-old security guard in Wilmington, Delaware named Edward Swift."

"All he had on PHYREWALL was his first name: Matt. And the note 'Cleveland' with a question mark," Penny said.

"I'm compiling all this data into a spreadsheet. I'll put a copy on your thumb drive, Max. It's named TLDR." Too long, didn't read.

"Risse loves spreadsheets. She has a spreadsheet to keep track of her spreadsheets," Penny said.

"Is there something weird about that?" Risse asked.

"Good thinking, Risse. Thanks," Max said.

They stopped halfway to San Jose to pick up some takeout. When they got back on the road, Penny drove to let Max rest. But instead he tackled more of Evan's files—beginning with the one he had compiled on Max in the LinerNotes.odt file.

The information wasn't new to Max, of course, but it was by far the most complete profile Evan had prepared. Whereas the details about DoubleThink had been sparse, the profile on 503-ERROR seemed to have been written to impress the reader with Max's abilities and accomplishments. That made sense if Evan had written it to convince Penny that Max was worth trusting and helping.

Max scrolled back to the head of the lengthy document to look at the picture at the beginning. It showed a much scrawnier fourteen-year-old Max standing behind The Hidden Word, his and Evan's favorite bookstore, until it closed the year before.

"Why did he pick this photo?" Max mused aloud.

"It's a nice picture," Risse said, leaning forward from the back seat to look over Max's shoulder. "I thought we were the same age when I first saw it."

"Seat belt!" Penny said.

"I'm fine," Risse said.

"It's the law," Penny said.

Risse laughed. "We're in a stolen car." But she leaned back and buckled in again.

"The thing is, this photo's three years old. Every other profile has the most recent picture Evan could find, and he had plenty of pics of me," Max said.

Evan had snapped this with his DSLR camera when they were freshman. Back then they had been hanging out at the bookstore every day, reading everything they could find on computers and phone phreaks and hacking. The owner, Mr. Stenzler, hadn't minded stocking books he knew they wouldn't buy. Maybe that was one of the reasons the store had closed.

"Evan was sentimental," Penny said.

"Maybe he just liked it?" Risse said.

"Evan was big on nostalgia, but he didn't work that way. He couldn't help but be consistent with everything. It would have bugged him if this one profile picture was different from the others, unless he'd chosen it for a reason."

Something told Max this was significant, and whenever that happened, he was exactly like Evan—he couldn't let it go until he'd figured it out.

"He included your profile on the disc he wanted me to deliver to you. Maybe he wanted you to see it," Penny said.

"So he wanted to remind me of something? Our early days hacking?" Max stared at the image and thought back.

"That store was called The Hidden Word, so maybe there's a word hidden in the photo!" Risse said, leaning forward again.

"Seat belt," Penny said.

Risse sighed and flounced back. Her seat belt clicked back into place.

"Actually, there's a USB drive embedded in the wall of the bookstore," Max said. You could barely see it in the lower right corner of the image, even if you knew to look for it.

Max had read about people who embedded thumb drives in buildings for others to discover and had suggested that he and Evan do the same thing. Portable drives were cheap, and Max had a ton of them lying around the house that had been discarded by his dad's company.

Using Mr. Stein's workshop, they had fashioned a cement brick around a 500GB drive, and then swapped it for a loose one from the crumbling facade of The Hidden Word. Anyone who plugged into the portable drive could download thousands of free e-books Evan had mined online. Or they could add their own. But of course, only Max and Evan knew it was there in the first place, and as far as he knew, no one else had ever discovered it. Evan had installed a program that would execute on any computer plugged into the drive and let him know whenever files were copied or added.

"Are you saying he might have put something important on there?" Penny asked.

"It's possible. We installed a few of those drives around town. I haven't thought about them in a while," Max said.

"If there's something waiting for you back in Granville, then why didn't he send you that picture directly instead of sending it to me?" Penny said.

To bring us together, Max thought.

"Even though it's unlikely anyone else would figure it out, if he'd texted or e-mailed the pic to me as a hint, it would have drawn more attention to the store. The drive is hidden, but it isn't impossible to find—that's the whole point."

"What about playing around with the image itself? Alternating colored pixels, messing with the contrast and saturation, that kind of thing." Risse started typing on her laptop.

"That's smart, but Evan would have expected someone smart to think of it," Max said.

"So it doesn't have to be smart, it just has to be something *you* would think of?" Penny asked.

"Hey," Max said.

Risse giggled.

"I'm kind of being serious. Max, Evan must have picked that picture because it has a personal meaning for both of you."

Max nodded. "We had just gotten into hacking around this time. Really simple stuff. We tried phone phreaking, but that wasn't really our thing. I just liked messing with people and getting them to tell me stuff they didn't mean to, and Evan liked wandering around in systems where he didn't belong."

"That's the best!" Risse said.

"We were just getting into encryption, too. Evan thought it was important to respect the history of hacking, so we tried to recreate everything we read about, using those books as a primer on manipulating technology."

"What did you learn about manipulating images?" Risse asked.

"Lots. Hmm. . . ."

Max opened a window to display the hashCode behind the image. "There was a way to embed messages in the garbage code of an image file. It would never display as anything but noise in the picture, or it would be completely invisible, but by examining the code. . . ." Max whooped. "You were right. *Something's* been inserted here!"

"What is it?" Penny asked.

"I don't know. I was looking for a message, but this is more complex. Letters and numbers that don't belong there. . . ." He looked up. "It could be another passphrase, or even another file."

"How could he fit another file inside that one?" Penny asked.

"The file size isn't big enough to include another file, unless it's a very small one, like a short text file or a simple executable," Risse said.

"You have a copy of my file?" Max asked.

"Just the picture," Penny said.

Risse stuck her tongue out at her sister.

"I need a copy of the original so I can compare them for differences," Max said.

"Do you have it?" Penny asked.

"Sure. On my backup drive at home," Max said.

She groaned.

"But there'd be a copy of it in Evan's cloud. He kept everything." Max looked out the window at the dark trees whizzing by them as they sped down the Pacific Highway. "I need to get online."

"Isn't that too risky? What if the Feds have found his cloud already?"

"I just need to connect to it for thirty seconds," Max said.

"They would still have a record that someone had been there, and who else would have access to his account?" Penny said. "You'd be tipping them off that there's something important in there."

"So they'd find the original photo," Max said. "That won't help them. And maybe they'll waste resources looking through a couple terabytes of files for whatever it is they're after."

"I don't know," Penny said.

"We don't have a lot to go on. We have to chase down every lead, and I have a hunch about this," Max said.

"Okay. But we aren't stopping. Risse, give him the spare laptop."

Max copied the photo from his computer to a new SD

card and loaded it on the machine Risse handed him from her go-bag. They were serious about keeping everything separate and contained.

"I'm making a private wireless network with my phone," Risse said. "It's going to be kind of slow."

Max connected and pulled up the login page for Cloud-Source. Risse watched over his shoulder. She gave Penny a defiant look.

"That file structure doesn't make any kind of sense," Risse said.

"It does to me. Sort of," Max said. He clicked through folders rapidly to minimize the amount of time he was connected.

Evan had claimed his organization system was another layer of security, but Max just considered it an extra level of annoyance.

"If someone miraculously gets past my encryption, I don't have to make it easy for them to find what they're looking for," Evan had said when Max called him on it.

"So you're just being spiteful," Max had shot back.

"Hell, yeah. If someone's going through my files, I'm probably on my way to prison. This small revenge will be a solace to me."

Prison had always been the worst fate they could have imagined.

Max blinked a few times and kept drilling down in the folder structure.

"I thought you said it would only be thirty seconds," Penny said.

"This network is slooooooooow," he said.

"Seriously, it's a mess in there," Risse said. "It looks like he's clicking on random folders."

Max filtered the thousands of items in the folder he wanted by typing in 503, and came up with a few hundred results: all photos taken their freshman year of high school. He recalled the date and the GPS coordinates of The Hidden Word and narrowed it down to thirty. He clicked through the first five, not even waiting for the previews to load fully before moving on.

"Got it!" He made a local copy of the file and watched the progress meter fill.

"Great!" Risse said. "Um, did you mean to delete the rest of the files?"

"Shit," Max said. "What's happening?"

The number of files in the folder was going down.

"Someone else is in here right now, deleting the files." Photos were disappearing before his eyes, but since they were all large, shot in RAW format, it wasn't an instantaneous process.

"Disconnect!" Penny said.

"Not yet."

The file was almost done copying.

"Got it," Max said.

And then it was gone. The last of the files had been deleted. He clicked up a level and tried to open the folder again.

Folder not found.

"It's all gone." All those pictures from Evan's life. Evan had thought of the cloud as an extension of his brain; it was as if someone had killed him again by deleting that part of him. "Someone cleaned it out."

"Maybe you hit Delete by accident?" Penny asked.

"I'm going to pretend you didn't just suggest that," Max said.

Max logged out and Risse disconnected the computer.

"The government," Penny said.

"It would be a hell of a coincidence if a sysadmin just happened to discover files that have been sitting there for years, the very moment I accessed the folder."

"The timing's suspicious," Penny said.

"Little bit," Max said.

"Either they're after the same thing we are, or they don't want you to have it," Penny said. "I hope it was worth it."

"We'll find out soon." Max ran a program to compare the two photos and was rewarded with a plain text file that displayed a long alphanumeric sequence—all the characters Evan had added.

"Ding!" Max said.

"What was that?" Penny asked.

Max blushed. "I hear that in my head when my computer is done crunching a big file."

Risse was practically climbing into the front seat now. "That's code," she said. "We have to compile it."

Max handed the computer back to Risse and she settled back in her seat. She typed for a couple of minutes.

"Ding!" Risse said, making fun of him. Max twisted around

to look at her and she winked at him. "It's a torrent file."

"So we still need to use a BitTorrent program to download whatever it is," Max said.

"Yes, but not here. It'll take forever." Penny yawned. "We're almost in San Jose."

"Then after we talk to the Millers," Max said.

He leaned back in his seat and stared out at the road ahead. They were finally close to getting some answers.

14

MAX DROVE SLOWLY PAST THE MILLERS' SPLIT-LEVEL house in Willow Glen, San Jose. There were two cars parked in the driveway.

"Looks like they're home," Penny said.

"Where should I park?" Max asked.

"Go back around the block and park in front of their house. We don't have anything to hide from them," she said.

"Except for Max. Maybe he should be the one to stay with the car," Risse said.

"But I want to test his disguise," Penny said.

After they had reached San Jose last night and checked into adjoining rooms at a cheap motel, Penny had helped Max dye his hair. When he caught his reflection in the car mirrors, he was still surprised; it was strange to see himself with black hair instead of the mousy brown he'd inherited from his dad. Though Max's mom had left them a long time ago, he still vividly remembered her long, dark hair.

His next strongest memory of her was how much it had hurt when he'd realized she wasn't coming back. One of the reasons he'd gotten into hacking was to try to get in touch with his mother, but even Evan's skills hadn't been up to that task. Lianna Stein had vanished completely.

"They might not have seen the news about me," Max said.

"Unless they're living under a rock, everyone has seen you," Penny said.

Max pulled the car up and parked on the curb beside the Millers's driveway.

"That is definitely no rock," Penny stared at the house.

Max scratched his chin and felt the sting of broken skin.

"Max, stop that," she said.

"I shouldn't have shaved." Especially not with the cheap plastic razors and soap at the hotel. He'd nicked himself in three places. He now dabbed at the reopened wound with his thumb and it came away with a spot of blood.

"A beard would have made it obvious your hair is dyed. Beards don't do anything to prevent facial recognition anyway."

"Neither do glasses," Max said. He adjusted the clear Wayfarer glasses Risse had loaned him.

"No, but they can help fool *people*," Penny said. "Along with the makeup. Turn this way."

Max sighed and turned to Penny. She dusted his cheeks

with a soft brush. Through some theatrical trickery, she subtly altered the apparent shape of his face by applying shadows and highlights. It was very disconcerting to not fit his image of himself, and it forced him to consider how much he was changing inside as well.

It was becoming second nature to peer around every corner for government agents and police, especially now that they were about to question grieving parents about the potential murder of their only child. Even now, as Penny adjusted his makeup, he was looking around them and in the rearview mirrors for anything suspicious. This wasn't him.

"Okay. Are you ready?" Penny asked. She dabbed on some lip gloss and checked her own reflection in the visor mirror. She had put on what amounted to her own disguise: a plain white blouse and black slacks. She had pinned back her hair and put in small silver hoop earrings to resemble a young professional, like Ariel Miller had been.

"No, but let's do this." Max got out of the car.

"Good luck," Risse said from the backseat. "I'll text you two if I see anything that looks remotely federal."

Max and Penny approached the house. A curtain fluttered in one of the front windows as they moved up the walkway. They climbed the three steps to the porch and Penny rang the doorbell. Max brushed his hair away from his forehead self-consciously. It tickled.

"Stop," Penny hissed. She reached up and carefully rearranged his hair.

"Can I help you?" A woman's voice came from the other side of the door.

"Are you Ronni Miller?" Penny asked.

"That's right."

"We're. . . we were friends of Ariel," Max said.

"Oh." The door opened. A woman with shoulder-length brown hair wearing a gray business suit leaned against the jamb. The morning news droned inside the house. Her eyes flicked back and forth between Max and Penny. Was it his imagination, or did her attention linger on him a bit longer than necessary?

"Who are you?" Mrs. Miller asked.

"I'm Barry and this is Mel. We worked with Ariel." Max lowered his eyes and imagined he was talking about Evan. Tears welled up. "We're so sorry for your loss."

"Thank you." Mrs. Miller's chin trembled.

"Who is it?" a man called from upstairs.

"No one! Hurry up! You're going to be late!" Mrs. Miller hesitated then stepped outside and held the door closed behind her. "Her father took Ariel's death very hard. We both did, of course. But she was always his special girl."

"I understand," Penny said. "My dad's the same way."

Mrs. Miller nodded. "Your family's very lucky to still have you."

Penny looked startled.

"I know it's been almost seven months, but we wanted to talk to you about Ariel, if you have a few minutes," Max said.

"I appreciate you coming by, but we're finally moving on. You understand? I'm afraid. . . ." She glanced behind her and closed the door the rest of the way. "I don't want to upset Daryl."

"We only need a moment of your time. Was anything bothering Ariel before she died?" Max said.

Mrs. Miller frowned. "What do you mean?"

"Did she seem nervous or act unusual? Did she say anything that surprised you, maybe about her work? Did you see anyone around the house, or anything out of the ordinary?" Max asked.

"Ariel was killed in an accident. She was doing great, very successful. She was working a lot, but. . . ." Mrs. Miller pulled back. "You said you worked with her?"

Penny put a hand on Max's arm. "We're sorry to bring this all up again, but it could be important."

The door flew open behind her and Mrs. Miller jumped.

"Ronni?" A tall man with short gray hair and a thick beard appeared. He scrutinized Max and Penny. "What's going on?"

Mrs. Miller stepped back into the house and her husband wrapped an arm around her. "More people, asking about Ari." Her voice broke.

A pained look crossed Mr. Miller's face. "Why are you doing this to us?" he asked.

"I'm sorry," Max said. "We just need to be sure—"

"Please leave," Mr. Miller said.

"Sorry." Penny stepped backward.

"Leave us alone!" Mrs. Miller said. She moved back into the house, but Mr. Miller stood and watched them as they got back into the car.

"We're going," Penny said.

She and Max climbed back into the car. Max started it and drove away.

"That was awful," Penny said. "We shouldn't have come here."

"It was worth a shot," Max said. But he was unsettled too, thinking about the Baxters and how they were taking Evan's death. "I'm sorry to make them go through that again."

"We'll be helping them too if we find out the truth about how she died," Penny said.

"Will we?" Max asked. Finding out she had been murdered wouldn't bring Ariel back to her parents. Just like how if they completed their mission, Evan would still be gone.

Max, Penny, and Risse gazed across Walnut Street at the spot where Ariel Miller had been hit. Someone had arranged a candle and a small plush Flounder doll propped against the base of the street sign. The candle was out, but the toy looked new.

"She was killed on impact, according to eye witnesses," Risse said somberly.

Penny looked at her sister with concern.

"What are we expecting to find here? It's been six months," Penny said.

"I just wanted to see it," Max said. "We can still learn

plenty. This isn't exactly a busy intersection. It's a quiet residential street. Two-way traffic, no lights, but stop signs on every corner. Speed limit's what? Twenty-five?"

"An unlikely place for an accident," Penny said.

"Maybe it was a DUI. But they never found the driver, or the car. For once, security cameras would have been useful," Max said.

He stepped off the curb, staring down at the asphalt.

"Careful," Risse said.

He heard a car approaching from his left and looked up. A blue pickup truck rumbled up the street toward him, slowed, and rattled to a stop before it proceeded through the intersection. He had trouble imagining Ariel being surprised by an approaching vehicle, if it had been following all the proper traffic rules.

He looked both ways and walked into the middle of the intersection.

"If she was hit here, why aren't there any skid marks?"

"From May?" Penny asked.

"There was a hit-and-run back in Granville. The car tried to stop in time, and it skidded ten feet. Burned rubber the whole way. That was a year and a half ago, and the marks are still there," Max said.

"If someone was trying to kill her, they would have to know where she would be, or they were following her. What was she doing in San Bruno in the first place?" Penny asked.

"What's even around?" Max walked back to the sidewalk

and pulled out his phone.

He looked at the area on a map. "There are a couple of hotels down over on San Bruno Avenue. A coffee shop. If she was heading that way, maybe to meet someone, she must have been crossing south on Fourth Avenue." He turned around to look up the block. "And there's nothing back that way. The road ends." A yellow sign read NOT A THROUGH STREET.

"Maybe she was coming *from* meeting someone," Max said.

Risse opened her laptop and put it on the hood of their car. "I doxxed the three people interviewed in the news articles Evan collected. Two of them live around here. . . ." She nodded. "One of them said, 'Whenever I saw her, she always had a smile.' That was Gawain Wilson of 531 ½ Walnut Street."

Max picked out the small house a couple of doors down from them.

"Sounds like she was around the neighborhood a lot," Max said.

"If this was part of her routine, it would be easy to predict where she would be and when," Penny said.

"He also said, 'I heard a screeching sound that made me look out my window. Then I heard a scream and a horrible bump that I knew was a person. By the time I saw the body crumpled on the other side of the road, I knew she was already gone. The car that hit her was nowhere in sight,'" Risse said.

"I'm going to go see if Mr. Wilson is in." Penny straightened her blouse and set off. Max and Risse hung out by the car, keeping an eye on her. A man in a red baseball cap and a jean jacket came to the door when she knocked. Penny started talking and Wilson glanced over at them curiously.

"Hey, do you have any matches?" Max asked.

"Of course. In the bag." Risse didn't look up from the article on Ariel she was rereading.

Max rummaged around in their go-bag and came up with a waterproof box of matches. The girls really were prepared for anything.

Max crossed the street and crouched to relight the candle in the glass jar. He noticed a worn photograph of Ariel, the same one from her Panjea profile, in a picture frame secured to the signpost with wire.

He stood up and looked over to check on Penny. She was standing on the sidewalk half a block down from Wilson's house. She used her phone to snap several pictures of the road. She then held up her phone and walked sideways back toward the car, holding the phone steady, as if she were recording a movie up and down the length of the street.

Max got back across the street just ahead of her. Even from a distance, he could tell she was excited.

"Gawain heard the whole thing, just like he said in the paper. He was surprised that the police and the article kept calling it an 'accident,'" she said.

"He thinks she was hit intentionally?" Max asked.

Penny nodded. "I could tell he was nervous talking to me about it. But check this out. You were looking for skid marks?" Penny held up her phone and showed Max a photo of black tire marks on the dark pavement. She swiped through a couple of close-ups.

The marks looked like black crayon rubbed over the asphalt, stretching for about six feet.

"I'm no expert on forensics, but those look like acceleration marks," Max said. "I made those with our car when I was learning to drive and hit the gas a little too hard. I remember how loud the screeching was. My dad was so freaked out."

"This is how far they are from where Ariel was hit." Penny scrolled through a stitched-together panorama of the block-and-a-half of street between the skids and the point where Ariel was apparently struck, right where they stood.

"From what Gawain said, it seems like he heard the car when it was accelerating, and then it hit Ariel a moment later," Max said.

"She screamed, so she saw it coming, but she didn't have enough time to get out of its way," Risse said.

"And the driver didn't slow down or try to steer around her," Max said. "Did Gawain know Ariel?"

Penny nodded. "She lived near here. She rented a room in a house at the north end of Fourth Avenue."

Risse frowned. "The articles all said she was from San Jose, not San Bruno."

"Newspapers get details wrong all the time. Like calling murders accidents," Max said.

15

ARIEL'S ROOMMATE, LAUREN JOHNSON, WAS A
tall, friendly black woman with long braids down her back.
She brought out a tray with four glasses of water and set it on
the coffee table in front of the couch where Max, Penny, and
Risse were seated. Lauren sat in a chair across from them.

"Thanks for talking with us." Penny leaned forward, arms
resting on her knees.

Lauren intertwined her fingers nervously. "I want to know
what happened to Ari."

"Why are you so certain it wasn't an accident? Did you see
it happen?" Max asked.

"No, I was visiting my boyfriend in L.A. When Gawain
phoned me with the news, I *knew* she'd been murdered. Ariel
had been worried something might happen to her. She was
afraid of disappearing."

Max exchanged looks with Penny and Risse.

"What did she say?" Penny asked.

"That she had made a mistake and thought she was mixed up in something dangerous. She felt like she was being followed. That was the week before she died." Lauren rubbed absently at her right ear and looked lost in thought. "I know that isn't anything like proof, but if you'd seen how scared she was. . . . She was acting strange. Strange even for her. She was my girl, but she just wasn't right sometimes. Ari got all worked up over cell phones."

"What about cell phones?" Risse said, pausing whatever she was doing on her own phone.

"She was *paranoid*. She claimed someone was listening to us, watching us through them. We fought because one day she put both our phones in the refrigerator. I told her she could do whatever she wanted with her stuff, but don't mess with my phone," Lauren said.

"I know how you feel," Penny said, looking at her sister.

"I thought she'd gone off the deep end," Lauren said.

"She may have been right about someone monitoring her," Max said. "Edward Snowden used to ask people to put their phones in the refrigerator to block them from picking up sound."

"Really?" Lauren stared at her phone on the coffee table. For a moment, Max considered putting their own phones in the refrigerator.

"Um. The papers said Ariel was a systems administrator. Where did she work?" Risse asked.

Lauren rubbed her forehead. "I don't know."

"She didn't tell you?" Penny asked.

"All I knew was she did something with computers."

"That's true of most of the people in the Bay Area," Max said.

"She usually worked from home, but sometimes she took the train into the city. I figured she was sworn to secrecy or something so I didn't pry. The company must have been in an office building, because she had a badge. I saw it clipped to her bag once. But most of the time she sat in front of the TV with her laptop all day and all night."

Was Ariel a hacker too? Was that the connection? She'd gotten Evan's attention somehow, but he hadn't linked her to any of the members of Dramatis Personai. The only handle unaccounted for had been 0MN1, and Max had spoken to him a couple of days ago online.

"It was kind of annoying at first, having her around *all the damn time*. But it was also kind of comforting." Lauren sniffed. "I miss her."

"I'm sorry. I know how hard it is. . . . We just lost a close friend too." Max glanced at Penny.

Lauren pressed a hand to her mouth and nodded.

"I hate to ask, but is Ariel's laptop still around?" Max asked.

Lauren's eyes widened. "No, and that's another weird thing. I rushed home the morning after she died and found the back door unlocked. She never once left it open in two years. We've had some break-ins in the area, so we were both careful."

"Was anything missing?" Penny asked.

"Nothing of mine. The only thing of Ari's that I'm sure was missing was her laptop. It was usually right here on the coffee table or on her desk, and it wasn't with her when she died. Her badge from her mystery job was also gone; I looked for it specifically when I was packing up her things. I tried to tell her parents when they came for her stuff, but they didn't want to hear it. I can't blame them."

Max suppressed a groan. It was too much to hope that her things would still be there after half a year.

"Maybe it was just a robbery," Risse said.

"On the same night she died? Only in Ari's room?" Lauren shook her head, braids swinging out. "I don't believe in coincidences."

The night Evan died, his house was raided too, Max thought.

"Can we see her old room?" Max asked.

"There's a guy living there now. I still have to make the rent, y'know?" Lauren scowled. "Not that he ever pays it on time. *Musicians.*"

"It still might be helpful to see where she lived. Maybe she left something behind."

"I guess so. He's hardly ever home." She stood. "But just fair warning: Peyton is such a *dude.* No offense, Max."

The room looked like it had just been ransacked. Crumpled clothes were all over the floor and draped over the desk chair. A bong rested by a twin mattress on the floor. Dirty plates were piled up in a cardboard box under the window.

"I put those there whenever he leaves dishes in the sink too long. I don't think he's noticed," Lauren said.

Penny waved her hand in front of her nose. "It smells like a gym in here."

Risse was already poking around the outlet where the coaxial cable and phone lines emerged from the wall.

"Listen, don't touch any of his stuff, okay? I shouldn't let you in here without his permission." Lauren wrung her hands.

"No problem. I don't want to touch any of this crap," Penny said.

She checked between the desk and the wall while Max prodded the floor with his right foot, checking for loose floorboards.

"I don't think you'll find anything of Ari's. I had the room professionally cleaned before Peyton moved in. I shouldn't have bothered," Lauren said.

Risse checked the closet, paying extra attention to the ceiling. She ran her fingers up the inside of the doorjamb.

Max dragged over the desk chair and stood on it to peer inside the air vent.

"You guys are something," Lauren said.

"Did you discuss your concerns about Ariel's death with anyone else?" Max asked. His voice echoed in the empty air duct. The chair wobbled on uneven legs and he grabbed for the wall to regain his balance.

"The cops, but they laughed and told me to leave the investigation to professionals. I thought about going to journalists, but I never did."

"Worried they wouldn't believe you?" Max asked.

Lauren steadied Max's chair. "I. . . was afraid they would. I realized that if Ari was murdered, it might be a bad idea to let her killer know that I knew. Is that terrible?"

"You have to watch out for yourself first," Penny said, somewhat critically. She probed under the desk drawer with her finger then pulled it open. Pens rolled around inside it with a hollow sound. She looked at the drawer curiously.

Max hopped down from the chair and carried it back over to the desk.

Penny rapped the inside of the drawer. She wrestled with it for a moment before she freed it from its rollers.

"Hey!" Lauren said.

Penny looked around at the mess, shrugged, and dumped the contents onto the floor: three pens, a CD case, a strip of condoms, and three pennies. She turned the drawer back over and rested it on top of the desk. She felt around inside of it for a moment.

"Got something," Penny said.

"Really?" Lauren asked.

Something clicked and Penny pulled up a thin wooden square. "False bottom."

Max leaned over. "What's in it?"

Penny sighed. "Nothing."

"Nothing?!" Risse said. "Why have a false bottom if you don't hide anything in it?"

Max looked at the narrow space. It could easily fit SD

cards, DVDs, papers, pictures, or any other flat storage medium.

"Someone got here first," he said. Someone who thought just like they did.

"Crap," Penny said.

"You think Ari was killed for whatever she was hiding?" Lauren asked.

"We're only guessing right now, but her death may be linked to five other deaths," Max said.

"Five?" Lauren leaned against the wall by the desk. "How is that possible?"

"We're trying to figure that out."

"This is about that guy on the news! The computer hacker that killed himself at the debate." Lauren stared at Max and he saw the moment she realized who he was.

Max exchanged a glance with Penny. She was restoring the desk to the way she found it.

"He was your friend?" Lauren asked.

"My best friend," he said.

"I'm sorry."

"Thank you." Max looked around the room hopelessly. "Lauren, did Ariel give you anything before she died? Maybe a USB drive or an SD card?"

"Nothing like that." Lauren pushed her mouth to the side as she thought. "I almost forgot. She did give me something just before I left for L.A."

She led them back to the kitchen and pointed at a picture on the stainless steel refrigerator door: a printout of a photo of

Lauren and Ariel posing outside the Chinese Theatre.

"That's a nice picture," Max said.

"No, the magnet. I completely forgot about it as soon as she gave it to me. I didn't discover it in my purse until a couple of months ago," Lauren said.

The silver magnet holding up the photo was shaped like a rectangular jigsaw puzzle piece. It had two tabs on the left and right edges and slots cut into the top and bottom. The letter *A* was laser-etched in the center.

Max pulled the magnet free to study it more closely.

It was an eighth of an inch thick. The metal was smooth and cool and oddly concave, curving slightly outward. He turned it over but there were no other markings on the back. He passed it to Penny, who turned it over and over curiously.

"Does this have any significance to you, Lauren?" Max asked.

"It reminds me of her. She used to carry it around, like a lucky charm," Lauren said.

Risse looked at it quickly then handed it back to Max.

Max weighed it in his palm. "Could we borrow it?"

She hesitated. "Can it help you figure out what happened to her?"

"I don't know yet, but it might be important."

"Okay. I hope it helps." Lauren took back the picture that Max offered.

Max slipped the metal puzzle piece into his left pocket and curled his fingers around it.

"Me too," he said.

16

MAX, PENNY, AND RISSE WALKED BACK TO THEIR CAR in silence. Max kept looking around, expecting someone to jump out at them from behind a tree at any moment. The deeper he got into this, the less safe the world seemed to be.

Penny had promised to accompany him only as far as San Jose. Now that they were pretty sure Ariel had indeed been murdered, he couldn't blame her and Risse if they wanted to get out. He was already wanted, so he had no choice but to keep going. Maybe once he revealed the truth, whatever it was, to the world, the Feds would lose interest in him—or no longer be able to touch him.

Max pulled his laptop out and put it on top of the hood to start the ignition.

"So. . . " he began.

"I think now it's time to download that torrent file," Penny said.

Max smiled. "Yeah. But where should we go?"

She checked her phone. "The perfect place is nearby. Start the car. I'm driving."

"Why is this a good idea again?" Max asked as he followed Penny and Risse into the mall. They stood in front of the ground level entrance and watched the crowd of weekend shoppers bustling by.

"Crowds are your friend. It's easier to blend in," Penny said.

"I'm not going to blend in wearing *this*." Max adjusted the black eyepatch she had given him in the car. He was wearing Risse's glasses over it, and he was reasonably certain that he looked ridiculous.

"That's going to make sure you blend in as far as the security cameras are concerned. Facial recognition algorithms measure the distance between your eyes and your other features. That patch makes you invisible to them. Especially if you tilt your head more," Penny said.

"Aaaarrrr," Risse said.

"Thanks," Max said.

"We should split up. I'm going upstairs to Everything Electronic. Computer stores are great for wired internet with an anonymous IP address, as long as we're in and out fast. I'll download Evan's file while you find a new outfit with Risse. May I suggest a blouse with puffy sleeves and a tricorn hat?" Penny said.

"Ha-ha. Okay, we'll find you in the computer store when we're done," Max said.

"Be careful." Penny headed for the escalator.

Risse towed Max over to ThrifTee, where she picked out a faded "I Want YOU" T-shirt, where Uncle Sam was wearing glasses like Max's.

"Is this supposed to be ironic?" Max asked.

"Of course it is. It's hipster. But more importantly, and even more ironically, shirts like this confuse the hell out of Panjea's photo tagging. It focuses on the face printed on the front of your shirt instead of your own."

"Sold," Max said.

He accepted the reversible black-and-white hoodie she found for him too. He only resisted when she tried to get him to change his sneakers for purple Dr. Martens.

"I can't run in those," Max said.

"How about a mismatched pair of sneakers?" she asked. "That would look cool."

"I'm not giving up my shoes. These are already broken in," Max said.

"Fine. But if you get caught because they track you down by your footprints or something, I'm going to say I told you so. At least roll up the cuffs of your jeans."

Max rolled up the left cuff and sighed.

"The other one too."

He shook his fist in mock fury.

Max carried his old clothes out in a brown paper bag and

went with Risse to Everything Electronic. Penny was typing at a desktop computer at the end of a row of six display models. She cracked up when she saw Max.

"What?" he said. "You don't like my new threads?"

"Now you look like a patriotic pirate." Penny tugged at the sleeve of his hoodie, which he was currently wearing black-side-out. "This is nice, though."

"How's it going here?" he asked.

She resumed typing. Her yellow computer glasses dangled from the blouse under her unzipped pink parka. A lock of blond hair was sticking out of her knit cap. She twitched her nose whenever her hair tickled it. He was tempted to brush her hair out of the way, but it was kind of cute when she scrunched up her face like that.

"The download finished ten minutes ago." She showed him the thumb drive on a chain around her neck then tucked it back into her blouse. "I'm catching up on current events. I have good news and bad news."

Max took a deep breath. "Bad news first."

She lowered her voice. "They're stepping up the search for you. You're wanted for murder."

"Murder?" Max whispered. "Who did I supposedly kill?"

"Evan." Penny showed him an article on CNN. He skimmed it, fighting mounting panic. Withholding information that could help the federal investigation was bad, but being suspected of murder. . . .

The article mentioned that Bradley Stein had issued a

missing persons report for Max when he didn't come home after school on Wednesday:

"He never misses soccer practice," Mr. Stein said. "He's a good boy and I'm worried that something may have happened to him. I just want him to know that I trust him and I love him, no matter what, and I hope he can come home soon."

Max teared up.

It had been smart of his dad to file that report, so it wouldn't seem like he knew Max had gone on the run.

"This is stupid. There are over four hundred witnesses to his suicide," Max said.

"According to print*is*dead, the FBI are considering the possibility that Evan's video was prerecorded," Penny said.

Max noticed a chat window open with Dramatis Personai in another tab. Penny had been busy.

"Then someone would have had to post the video for Evan," Max said.

"Someone who was there when he died?" Risse asked.

"Or he wrote a script to post the video for him," he said.

"Dramatis Personai got hold of a scan of the police report. It says that Evan died that afternoon, a few hours before the debate began," Risse said.

Max opened tab after tab of news stories. The *New York Times* was running a series of interviews with kids from their class, as well as stories about Max's short soccer career and his friendship with Evan. They moved fast.

"Where are they getting this stuff?" Max asked. "I know

Evan was alive just before eight p.m. because he sent me that text."

"Like you said, anything can be automated. Max, where were you before the debate?" Penny asked.

"Seriously? I did soccer drills then went for a five-mile run."

"Alone?"

"Yeah."

"You could have killed him and set the video to play during the debate to serve as your own alibi. Which would be really clever."

"Penny!"

"I'm just saying: With the FBI choosing what information makes it to the public, and the media using it to paint a picture, they can make it look like anything they want."

"They could even fake a police report about his time of death," Max said. "Where did they find his body?"

Risse was typing at the computer next to them. She was also talking to Dramatis Personai. "Apparently 0MN1 and a couple of others analyzed the public portion of Evan's video. They enhanced the footage and turned down the contrast enough to see some empty book shelves behind him and part of a sign."

She turned the screen toward Max. He instantly recognized the abandoned store, even without the sign in the background.

"The Hidden Word," Max said.

"Where that picture in your dossier was taken," Risse said.

Max nodded numbly.

"Everyone in that auditorium saw the same thing I did. We saw him kill himself. I certainly know I didn't do it," Max said.

"People are susceptible to suggestion. It happened quickly. It was shocking and graphic. It would be understandable for anyone to doubt what they saw," Penny said.

"We need that video," Max said.

Penny smiled. "Ah. And that's the good news. Fawkes Rising released the full video this morning."

She switched to a new tab and a familiar blog opened. Full Cort Press.

"Courtney?" Max said.

She had embedded the video from Fawkes Rising, with a warning about its graphic subject matter. In the post, she shared her own experience from the debate and the actions taken by the FBI afterward.

"How did Fawkes get this?" Max asked. "The guy who runs it always seemed like nothing but a conspiracy nut to me."

"He offered a three thousand dollar reward for anyone who could get him a copy. He claims someone at your school leaked it. That nut did you a big favor: Now that Dramatis Personai has an unedited copy, no one will be able to remove it from the internet."

Max grabbed the mouse and pressed the Play button, but Penny instantly closed the tab using the keyboard.

"Hey!" he said.

"I already downloaded a copy." Penny patted the necklace

chain where it rested against her collarbone. "We should go."

Max nodded. She cleared the browser and covered her tracks on the computer.

They headed out as a group. Max felt high-strung, worried about the bogus murder charge that made him more of a target than ever, but excited that they finally had the video—and Evan's files. He felt like they were getting close to knowing what was going on, or at least everything Evan had known.

"Hey, guys?" Risse said. "Does that look suspicious to you?" She pointed to the ground level, three floors down.

There were five men in polo shirts, jeans, and windbreakers riding up to Level Two, looking around and scrutinizing the people riding past them on the down escalator. Each guy wore a badge around his neck. A sixth man in a T-shirt and cargo pants stood by the down escalator on the other side, where he also had a clear view of the elevator bank.

"Uh-oh," Penny said.

Max sneaked a peek over the railing and saw more agents on the way. One was stationed at every landing and by the elevators.

"Let's go," Penny said.

"Where?" Risse asked.

Max turned around to face the electronics store they had just left. He recalled the map of the mall he'd glimpsed on the way in. They were at the northeast corner of the third floor. The down escalator was on the opposite end of the floor. They would be noticed immediately if they went for it.

"How did they find us?" Risse asked.

"Maybe they picked up on the network activity? Can't be too many people in the area who are using Tor to mask their IP address or download massive files over a mall's ISP," Max said. "Or someone recognized me."

"It doesn't matter how they found us. They did, and they're going to *catch* us soon if we don't get moving," Penny said.

"The problem is we don't know how many agents they brought. If that's all there are, we may have a chance. Follow me," Max led them toward Macy's. "Macy's takes up two levels with their own set of stairs between them."

"Good thinking. That'll get us down to Level Two, but then what?" Penny said.

"We'll figure it out when we get there." Max pulled up his hood.

Penny snuck another quick glance over the railing as they moved away from it, trying to hurry without looking like it.

"They just left another guy on Level Two. The rest of them are moving for the up escalator."

Because of the mall layout, they would have to get from one end of the floor to the other to continue going up.

Max ducked into Macy's, with Penny and Risse behind him.

"Try to hide behind crowds," he murmured.

As they hurried toward the stairs, Penny stripped off her colorful parka and draped it on a rack of returns. She pulled off her knit hat too, letting her blond hair spill down to her shoulders. She pulled it back and knotted a loose ponytail as she power-walked.

Risse placed her purple parka around a mannequin's shoulders.

Max scoped out the stairs first to make sure there were no agents waiting for them. A woman in a red vest, a Macy's security guard, eyed them suspiciously as they rushed past and clattered down the stairs. Max held up a hand as they neared the bottom. He tiptoed down the rest of the way and peered around the corner.

"The coast is clear," he said.

From here, he could see the elevators directly across from them on the other side of the floor. To get to them, they would have to run all the way around, dodging shoppers and under the scrutiny of the agents above them.

The agent on Level Two was to their right, guarding the down escalator.

Max could see their play clearly, as if he were applying a strategy on the soccer field. He put down the shopping bag with his old clothes.

"So, I figure they have two guys on Level Three above us moving in on the electronics store, looking for whomever was using the computer. They probably don't even know they're after me, and they shouldn't know anything about you two. But if I start running, they'll follow," he said.

"You want to be a decoy? They actually want you," Penny said.

Just like they would with the player with the ball, the opposing team would converge on him, trying to chase him down or head him off before he could reach his goal.

"I can outrun them," Max said.

"Can you outrun bullets?" Penny asked.

"They won't fire in a public place. There's too much risk of hitting a bystander. Besides, they'll be surprised. They're probably expecting some computer nerd who's going to panic at the sight of government agents."

"They're trained professionals," Penny said.

"I've avoided guys like them before, and right now I'm highly motivated. And I have a plan."

"Let's hear it," Penny said.

"It looks like there's someone posted at the bottom of each of the down escalators, with about one hundred feet between them and the elevators. You two are going to walk out of the store and turn right then quickly make your way around the floor to the elevators opposite us. Those'll take you past the down escalator and the agent waiting there, but he shouldn't pay any attention to you. You get in the elevator and head down to the garage level, while I head for the up escalator."

"I tried running down an up escalator once. It didn't go well," Penny said.

"Slapstick city," Risse said.

"I'm fast," Max said.

"Anyway, they'll see you," Penny said.

"That's what I want. We don't have time to argue. You have to get yourself and Risse out of here, and this is how we do that. If you have another suggestion, I'm all for it."

Penny scowled. "Fine. We'll try it your way."

"Thanks. Don't worry, it'll work. I'll see you at the car in the parking lot."

"What if we don't?" Penny asked.

"If you make it and I don't, release Evan's files to the public. If you're about to be captured, ditch or destroy the USB drive."

Penny nodded.

Risse nodded at the elevators. "The one on the left is moving up from the ground floor now. I've been timing them. We should be able to catch it on the way down if we go now." The elevator shaft and doors were glass, showing the occupants peering down as they ascended.

"Go," Max said.

"Good luck," Risse said.

Penny and Risse headed out of the store and turned right. Max gave them a head start and watched them proceed along the floor while pretending to window shop.

Max tightened the straps of his backpack. Then he took off like a shot.

He flew across the floor, weaving between shoppers and pumping his arms hard, hands spread flat. He moved so fast he felt like his feet barely touched the floor.

The tiles were much more slippery than he expected: When he rounded the corner he slid and nearly fell. But he caught his balance and kept going toward the escalator. The moment he hit its first metal step, he heard the agents call out the alarm.

Despite his guarantees to Penny, he wasn't at all sure they

wouldn't fire at him. But on the escalator, he was pressed in close to other people and it would be difficult for them to get a bead on him with Max moving in the opposite direction of the flow.

He hurtled down the stairs two at a time and again stumbled. He grabbed on to the rubber railing and steadied himself before moving double-time, shoving his way past startled, then angry, shoppers.

"Sorry! Sorry, excuse me," Max said as he squeezed past a large man on his left.

"Dumbass!"

"You're going the wrong way!"

"You little shit."

"Stop him!" The agent on Level Two was pointing down at Max from the railing. Max grinned when the man rushed past Penny and Risse to head for the escalator. Then the agent turned around and ran after the girls.

"Crap," Max huffed. But he couldn't worry about them, because the agents heading up to Level Three were turning around and trying to make their way down their own rising escalator.

Max felt like he was barely moving, but the bottom of the escalator was gradually getting closer.

A man in a gray pea coat grabbed at Max's arm. Max felt himself being pulled backwards and up.

"Hold on there, kid," the man said.

Max stomped on the man's foot and yanked his arm free.

He jabbed his elbow in the man's back, forcing him to pitch forward with a grunt of pain.

"Nothing personal," Max said.

Max continued down, taking long strides, hyperaware of how precarious his position was. But he kept his knees high and his eyes on his goal.

He leaped down the last five steps, landed hard, slipped, and tumbled to his hands and knees painfully. A man about to climb on the escalator backpedaled out of the way and a woman with a stroller veered to the side.

Max rested there for a moment, trying to catch his breath. His right knee throbbed from his fall. Then he looked up and saw an agent running straight for him, gun drawn.

Max stood and glanced up at the elevators. Penny and Risse were riding down in an elevator *with the agent from their floor.* They didn't appear to be under arrest—he was ignoring them and watching Max intently. Max spun around and saw two more agents heading down an escalator, almost at the ground floor.

Max ran for the exit to the parking lot. As he passed a pillar, he darted into the bathroom entrance behind it, almost colliding with another teenage boy on his way out.

Max passed the three urinals and took a stall near the far wall. He locked the door and climbed onto the toilet seat.

He pulled off his hoodie and quickly reversed it so it was white with a black lining. He hung it on the door and grabbed handfuls of flimsy toilet paper to mop the sweat from his face and neck.

He pulled off his glasses and eye patch and slipped them into his back pocket. He dipped a hand into what he hoped was clean toilet water then slicked his hair back. Finally, he pulled on the white hoodie.

Max sauntered out of the men's room and turned to his right, walking slowly toward the exit and trying to control his breathing.

When Max was a kid, he used to think that if he didn't look at someone, then they couldn't see him either. He'd walked around for a while like that, imagining himself cloaked in invisibility. He did that now, forcing his eyes to look at his phone, pretending to text, pretending to be invisible.

As he approached the exit, he looked up. In the glass doors' reflection, he saw four agents standing by the pillar, watching the bathroom he had just exited. One of them was leaning against it, doubled over with his hands on his knees and panting.

Max smiled as the automatic doors parted for him. But even as he stepped outside, he steeled himself for another ambush.

No one accosted him. And he didn't spot any other agents. Max headed for the stolen car, wondering if an agent would pop out behind other parked vehicles. If he noticed anyone suspicious, he would just keep walking and lead them away from Penny and Risse.

The girls were already in the car. Penny was behind the

wheel, and Risse had her laptop on her lap. She unlocked the doors. Max glanced behind him one last time before opening the passenger door and scrambling into the back seat. He huddled in the footwell.

Risse started the car from her laptop and Penny drove slowly toward the exit.

"See? Told you we'd make it," Max huffed. He was drenched in sweat and trembling all over. He shrugged out of his backpack and pressed himself lower.

"That was way too close. Hold on, one of their cars is circling the lot." Ten seconds later: "Okay, we passed them. Stay down, Max," Penny said.

"Make a left," Risse said.

"One of the Feds actually rode in our elevator. I thought he had us for sure, but he got out on the ground floor without giving us a second glance," Penny said.

"We got lucky," Max said. If they hadn't left the computer store when they did, they would have been caught in the act and pinned down. They would have been in cuffs before they even knew what was happening. "Where are we going?"

"Go straight for a while. Look for Skyline Boulevard then make a right," Risse said.

"I want to take a look at those files. We certainly earned them," Penny said.

"I think we should get off the road and stay low for a while. I found a spot that should be fairly secluded this time of day and is listed as a cell phone dead spot," Risse said.

"That sounds perfect," Max said. "It's possible that some cameras caught me without my disguise."

"Max!" Penny said.

"It's not a big deal. We'll be out of the area soon. They'll figure out pretty soon you were in the mall today, but they don't know where you're going next," Risse said.

"Especially because we don't even know that yet," Max said.

17

RISSE'S SECLUDED SPOT ENDED UP BEING A SANDY beach at the base of a high cliff. Sure enough, they had zero cell reception or data coverage.

"This is beautiful," Max said. There was a warm, gentle breeze coming off the sea. He lay back on the hoodie he had spread over the cool sand and closed his eyes. He breathed in the salty air and felt like he could just rest here forever, listening to the waves wash in and out.

"My name is. . . STOP."

Max bolted up and looked around. Penny and Risse were sitting side by side on an outcropping of rock and working on their laptops. Risse tapped a key and glanced at Max.

"You don't need to watch this again," Penny said.

Max got to his feet and brushed off his pants. He shook

sand from his hoodie and sat down on Risse's other side so he could see her screen too.

"Play it," Max said.

Risse clicked back to the beginning of the video and pressed the spacebar. The picture was warped and out of proportion, stretched out on the edges from the convex lens and angled downward from the center. The top third of the screen on the stage in the Granville High School auditorium was out of frame, but Senator Tooms and Governor Lovett were visible on either side of it. They were in shadow, due to the bright video screen between them.

"Was this taken from Courtney's laptop?" Penny asked.

"No, she was on the other side of the auditorium, closer to the stage," Max said. "This looks like footage playing on a screen in the school's security office. Someone recorded a copy on their phone."

Max sucked in a breath and let it out slowly as Evan's grotesque white mask appeared onscreen.

"My name is STOP."

"What's going on?" Bennett Avery said.

"Do you really want to know?" Evan asked.

"There's your proof that this was transmitted live!" Risse said.

"I forgot about that," Max said.

"That's because the clips on the news were edited," she said.

"He answered me! Is this live?" Avery said. *"What do you mean you don't know where it's coming from?"*

Evan: *"Just listen. Please listen."*

Three high-pitched tones blasted from the speakers. Max winced.

"What was that music?" Risse asked.

"It sounded like feedback from the sound system," Max said.

Evan looked directly at the camera. *"What is the silence of six, and what are you going to do about it?"*

That was where the video clip online ended, where the broadcast had been cut off. No one but the people in the auditorium had seen what happened next.

Evan pulled his hood down and slowly raised his mask.

"Risse, look away," Penny said.

Risse shook her head and kept her eyes glued to the screen, jaw clenched.

This time Max saw it clearly as Evan reached off screen and picked up the gun. The video feed scrambled for a second, like a damaged video file, or a malfunctioning old school video game screen.

Penny gasped as Evan nestled the barrel of the gun in his mouth. Max balled his hands into fists.

"I'm sorry. I'm sorry. I'm sorry. I'm sorry. . . "

The background noise in the video blocked out Evan's voice until the muzzle of the gun flashed and a loud bang reverberated through the auditorium.

Penny looked away. This moment had been playing on repeat in Max's dreams, but he forced himself to watch it again. This was the truth.

Blood and bits sprayed from the back of Evan's head as it snapped back. His body convulsed once and slumped backward then fell off-screen as blood speckled the camera and splashed onto the bulb of his LED lamp, painting the scene red.

Watching this play out again on Risse's computer almost made it all seem like a special effect in a low-budget film. The gunshot sounded hollow. Unreal.

Lovett tucked her head down and plucked out her earpiece. Two agents ushered her quickly off the stage.

Risse let out a long breath. "God," she said.

The screen on the stage went black and the lights came up. The video went in and out of focus for a second. Risse paused it.

Max cleared his throat. "Well. That still sucks." He glanced at Penny. "Are you all right, Penny?"

"I'll be right back." Penny's voice was strangled. She jumped up and ran across the sand, toward the water. Max heard her sobbing over the sound of the crashing waves. His eyes stung with tears as he heard her ragged gasps, as if air was being torn from her chest and she was drowning while standing ten feet from the shoreline.

Risse watched her sister with concern.

"Should I talk to her?" Max asked.

"She needs some time alone. She'll be okay," Risse said. "Penny's the strongest person I know."

Risse opened a video editing program and fiddled with

it for a few minutes, looking up often to check on her sister. Finally, she tilted her computer so Max could see the screen better. It displayed both the public clip of the broadcast and the high-definition security camera footage of the auditorium side by side.

Penny returned drenched in seawater, cheeks flushed. She sat down next to Max as though nothing had happened. "What's up?"

"You okay?" he asked.

"Yeah." She avoided his eyes.

"I synced up the two videos. Watch what happens when Evan says 'Listen,'" Risse said.

"Please listen."

Max heard those same piercing tones from before. "Ow."

Risse paused the video and pointed to the footage of the auditorium. "Did you see what happened?"

"When those three tones played?" Max said.

"You only heard *three* tones?" Risse asked.

"Yeah. How many did you hear?" he said.

"Five. What about you, Penny?"

"Three." She swept her damp hair away from her face and stared out at the ocean.

"Hmm," Risse said. "I'll play it again. Look carefully at the audience."

She played through the tones again, pausing on the second note.

"What am I looking at?" Max asked.

"Focus on the students," she said.

"They're wincing. Some of them are starting to cover their ears."

"What a discovery!" Penny said. "Maybe they're doing that because it's annoying."

"But check out Tooms and Lovett. Look at Avery."

"They look fine," Max said. "Like they don't even hear the tones."

"Yes," Risse said.

"*Why* do they look fine?" Max asked. "They had earpieces piping in audio, so they must have heard them clearly. The tones were bad enough in the noisy auditorium. If I heard that screeching right in my ear, I'd pull the earpiece out. They didn't even blink. You sure the video is synced up?"

"Perfectly."

Max saw Risse had included the time code onscreen, which matched the clock in the lower third of the CNN video clip.

"They probably have an audio limiter on their earpieces," Penny said.

"Look. A couple of the teachers heard something, though." Max pointed at Mrs. Tanner and Mr. Lundberg.

"How old are they?" Risse asked.

"Mmm. Mrs. Tanner is twenty-four, I think. Mr. Lundberg is thirty-one."

"Thirty-one? What does he teach?"

"Band."

Risse smiled. "And you really only hear three tones? Max,

pause the video when you hear the first one."

"Is this a hearing test?"

"Kind of."

Max jumped the video back a few seconds and hit Play.

"*Listen*," Evan said. A beat later, Max heard the first tone start and he paused it.

"There," Max said.

"I hear two tones before that," Risse said. "Hit F5 and play it again."

Max did, and an audiometer popped up in the upper right corner of the video window. He saw it spike when Evan spoke, then twice more when he couldn't hear anything, and three more times for each of the tones.

"If you don't stop doing that, I'm going to throw your computer into the ocean," Penny said.

Risse looked aghast.

"What is it, Risse?" Max asked.

"Mosquito tones. Sounds pitched so high, usually only kids can hear them."

"Of course," Max said.

He hadn't messed with mosquito tones since junior high. They followed the same principal as dog whistles: When people are young, most can detect sounds up to twenty kilohertz or so. The older you are, the lower the range you can hear. Most teenagers can probably hear anything from seventeen to twenty kilohertz. Most adults: sixteen kilohertz or less.

"Some of our classmates used that as a ringtone. The

teachers couldn't tell when they were getting text messages." Max smacked the table. "It was Evan's idea. He distributed the ringtones."

"Was he a musician?" Risse asked.

"No, but he loved music. He messed around with sound sometimes. Did some remixes, liked sampling noises from the environment and uploading them to sound libraries. He just liked doing stuff with technology, it didn't matter what it was."

"So he might have had better hearing than your average teen. And because I'm a little younger than you two, I can still hear the higher ranges. I need some time to work with this."

Risse plugged in her oversized headphones and started working.

Max looked at Penny.

"Did you have any luck with that file we got back at the mall?" Max asked.

"I couldn't open it." She stared down at the sand between her toes for a moment before getting up and bringing her laptop over. She sat close to Max and balanced the computer on her knees.

"Okay. . . ." A terminal opened on her screen and she plugged in her USB flash drive. She typed some commands and a graphical interface appeared that showed one file in the directory, named mxyzptlk.txt. That was definitely from Evan.

"It's encrypted. At least Evan was consistent and meticulous in his paranoia." Penny tucked her damp hair behind her ear.

Max reached for the keyboard. "May I?"

Penny hesitated then nodded. He slid the computer onto his knees. Risse glanced over, splitting her attention between her screen and Penny's as she manipulated audio samples from Evan's video.

Max opened a plain text document and started typing the elaborate password Evan had sent him days ago. The wrong characters appeared. He looked at the keyboard and hit the D key then checked it on the screen: *E*.

"I forgot. You use Dvorak," he said.

"You can switch it back to QWERTY mode—"

Max shook his head. He highlighted the text he'd already typed, deleted it, and started over with the new keyboard mapping in mind.

He typed a little more slowly than usual at first, but he was equally fluent in both layouts. He and Evan had used Dvorak as a very simple cipher back in the day; it was a convenient substitution code that wouldn't occur to most people who had the old typewriter layout drilled into their heads.

"Like!" Penny said. "You're full of surprises. But I tried that password, and the one from the CD. Unless he left us another clue somewhere, we're out of luck. I might be able to crack it, but it could take months. We don't even know how many characters the password is."

"I don't think that'll be necessary," Max said. "Evan wanted us to have this file, and fast. The clue is right in front of us. Does this word mean anything to you?" He pointed at the file name.

"Mix. . . izip. . . . Mix-el-plik. . . ?"

"Mxyzptlk." Max pronounced it *mix-yez-pit-a-lick.* "It's from Superman. He's a magical imp from the fourth dimension."

"So?" she asked.

"He's Evan's favorite comic book character. Like, ever. He felt like he was a kindred spirit. He wanted it for his handle but someone else was already using it."

"I find that hard to believe," Penny said.

Max opened mxyzptlk.txt in NewCrypt. A password screen popped up. He waggled his fingers over the keyboard then started typing three letters at a time, referencing the password he had typed in the adjoining window.

"I told you, I already tried that," Penny said.

Max missed a letter, and paused. He had completely lost his place. He pressed his finger on the Backspace key and glared at Penny while the line of asterisks diminished.

"Sorry," she said.

He started over from the beginning, meticulously copying the characters into the password field. He hit Enter and a dialog box appeared showing a decryption progress meter.

Risse pulled the right cup of her headphones off her ear.

"How'd you do that?" she asked.

"That password definitely didn't work before. I tried it, like, three times." Penny leaned over to glare at the screen.

"The only way Superman can defeat Mr. Mxyzptlk and send him back to his dimension is to trick him into saying his name backwards. Kel-tip-yix-em," Max said. "K-L-T-P-Z-Y-X-M."

"That's awesome," Risse said, at the same time that Penny said, "That's dumb."

"You reversed the password he'd already given you," Penny said.

"We used to trade messages back and forth all the time, and we realized we could use the same password twice if we just switched it around," Max said. "So on the way out to Evan, he would use one password, and when he sent his reply, I would enter it backwards."

"You're Evan's ultimate encryption key, Max," Risse said.

"Which is why the FBI wants him so much," Penny said.

The progress meter showed only five percent of the file had been decrypted. Six percent.

"A watched progress meter never completes," Risse said. She covered her ear again and went back to work on her own computer.

Eight percent.

"Jeez," Max said.

"Come on, Jarvis," Penny said.

"Jarvis?" Max asked.

She patted her computer affectionately. "Jarvis is my laptop."

"I know it's a thing to name your electronics, but I've never done it. Not that it's weird or anything," he said.

"It's weird not to," Penny said.

Evan had gone through a succession of computers with

geeky names he'd selected in alphabetical order. When he and Max first met years ago, he was using one called Eddard. As of a few months ago, his primary laptop was Rorschach.

Now all those computers were in the hands of the FBI, or whoever had broken into Evan's house the day he died. Max wondered what Evan would have named his next laptop.

"Technically, this one's Jarvis Mark VII. I have way too many machines to give them all individual names," Penny said.

Max cleared his throat. "Computers are just tools. I try not to get too attached."

"I think that attachment helps us work together better," Penny said.

"Attachment can also be a liability."

"You may have a point." Penny's voice was low.

The progress meter was only at eleven percent. Max banged his fist against the rock in frustration.

"Ow." His hands were still sore from his fall during their escape from the mall.

"Are you okay, Max?" Penny asked.

"I'm fine." Max watched Risse click through some dialog boxes on her audio editing software.

"I'm glad one of us is. I'm not doing so well myself," Penny said.

"I'm sorry. I should have known... I mean, I didn't think...." Max faltered.

She scooped sand with the top of her feet and let it fall

through her toes. "It's okay. You didn't even know I existed until a couple of days ago."

"It's weird that we were both such important parts of his life, but we didn't even know about each other until after he was gone." Penny lowered her voice so Max had to lean closer to hear her over the surf.

"That was Evan. He compartmentalized everything in his life. You must miss him a lot," Max said.

"I do. We used to chat every day. But you knew him in real life a lot longer."

"Yeah. We used to hang out every day." Max covered his eyes with his hand and rubbed his face. "I still see him though. Whenever I try to sleep."

"Nightmares?"

"Just one. You just saw it on that video."

"That's awful, Max. I'm sorry."

His dreams played out as if he was there in front of Evan while he died. Not only would Max fail to stop Evan from pulling the trigger, but he handed him the gun. Over and over again.

"You have to stop blaming yourself," Penny said.

"Maybe I didn't kill him personally, but it'll be my fault if I can't figure out what he's trying to tell us." Max glanced at the computer again. Thirty-three percent.

Evan always used to say that good hacking required you to take your time and be patient while you researched, prepared, and waited for an opportunity. It was about positioning yourself to be where you needed to be, with the right tools, to act when the moment came.

Some of that philosophy applied to playing soccer too, but at least on the field Max was always in motion. At least he got to kick something. And he always knew where the goal was and how to get there.

"No, it'll be *our* fault." Penny locked eyes with him.

Max smiled.

"What?" she asked.

"I'm just glad you're helping me. I know trust doesn't come easily for you."

"Or at all. It's only been me and Risse for so long." She glanced past him to her little sister.

"You two are lucky to have each other. When I was little, I wanted a brother. Maybe that's why Evan and I were such good friends," Max said.

Penny tilted her head to the right. He wondered if Risse had gotten the gesture from her, or vice versa. "Would you believe Risse and I hated each other when we were little? I didn't like having to share my stuff with her. After our dad left, I used to hope he would come back just to take her with him." Penny glanced at Risse and lowered her voice. "I think she wanted that too. She was his favorite."

"So what changed?"

"We found something we had in common: computers. We must have gotten it from Dad, because Mama can't even send a text message. After the divorce, she kind of checked out, giving us plenty of time to mess around online. Dad's old computer taught us more than he ever did."

"I'm sorry," Max said. "Did you have any luck tracking him down?"

Penny blinked. "What makes you think we tried?"

"Because I've been trying to find my mother. I thought she might have gone back to France, but she has no internet trail," Max said.

"Right? How is that even possible? It's like Dad doesn't exist. It's pathetic how easy it is to get into the DMV and IRS systems."

"They may as well make them public databases," Max said. "What will you do when you track him down?"

"Not sure yet. Either get in touch or ruin his life. Maybe those aren't mutually exclusive."

"Fair," Max said.

Seventy-three percent.

They watched the progress meter silently for a while, and then they both spoke at the same time. "You remind me a bit of Evan."

They stared at each other.

"Weird. . ." Penny said.

Max looked away and focused on the computer screen. Still seventy-three percent.

It wasn't that Penny was anything like Evan, except that she was brilliant at computers and committed to finding the truth. But spending time with the only other person who had been close to Evan made him feel a little like his friend was still around.

She was also a constant reminder that he wasn't.

He knew what Evan had seen in her. She was intelligent and snarky and pretty and. . . and she had been his best friend's girl until a few days ago, so that was as far as he was going to take that line of thought. Especially now, when they were both grieving and had so many other things to worry about.

The decryption meter jumped to eighty-nine percent complete. Ninety-three. . . ninety-seven. . .

"And. . . we're in. Risse!" Penny waved to get her sister's attention.

18

PENNY OPENED A FOLDER AND A LONG LIST OF FILE names filled the screen. "No wonder it took so long. This is, like, a gig of e-mails." She tilted the screen back and leaned toward it as she tapped on the first file, nails clacking on the plastic keys.

Risse draped her headphones around her neck. "What are we looking at?" she asked.

"There are hundreds of e-mails in here. Most of them are from defense-dot-gov addresses. So that's U.S. government." Penny paged through them quickly. Each message came up for only a split second but she seemed to be reading them all.

"Penny, can you speed-read?" Max asked.

"It's my 'superpower,'" she said. "Almost as cool as a photographic memory, huh?" She slowed down then scrolled backwards. "Hey. . . there you are," she crooned to the screen.

She pointed at the address of the sender in one of the e-mails: Geordie.Powers@defense.gov.

"Geordie," Risse said. "What's the e-mail about?"

Penny opened an attachment, a scanned PDF with 150 pages of tiny text, illegible until she zoomed in.

"A contract. I don't read legalese, so I'm not sure what all this 'reps and warranties' and 'agreed-upon services' is referring to. This one's a renewal, so we have to dig deeper to see what it's referencing," Penny said.

"Look who it was sent to." Max pointed: 13255679001@panjea.co.

"Panjea," Max said. "Can we figure out which account it's linked to?"

"Only if you're logged in to Panjea and the sender is one of your Peers." Penny jumped through the rest of the document. "Who's Kevin Sharpe?"

"He's a technology consultant for political campaigns. Why?" Max asked.

"He signed this contract." She pointed out two electronic signatures on the last page: Victor Ignacio, CEO of Panjea, and Kevin Sharpe, President and Founder of Kevin Sharpe & Company.

Max scrolled backwards through the document. Penny didn't even react when he took over the keyboard in front of her. "This is outlining a workflow for 'mutual information exchange.' I guess Sharpe's company is helping Panjea manage its users' information?"

"Or Panjea's sharing its users' information with Sharpe," Penny said.

"Their whole 'thing' is they promise not to sell information to *anyone*. They specifically mention the government. Their promises about making the world's first truly safe and secure system and improving the internet are why they've been so successful."

"I always thought that was too good to be true," Penny said. "The loophole here seems to be that they aren't *selling* the information. They're giving it away."

"For nothing? Ignacio's supposed to be a savvy business-man," Max said.

Vic Ignacio was known as a visionary and something of a renegade who started a boutique internet café called Synth-werks in the Bay Area a few years ago and turned it into the social media giant that Panjea was today.

Penny kept reading, dipping into random e-mails and files, the expression on her face a mixture of fascination and abject horror.

"Here's a PowerPoint laying out the framework for stream-ing all user actions on-demand to a 'backup server.' Kind of a digital wiretap logging every action we take on Panjea."

"That's gotta be boring. 'Max Stein Amplified Penny Polonsky's note.'"

"That's gotta be so illegal. Why would Sharpe—or anyone— want that stuff?" Penny asked.

"They're consultants and data nerds, so they probably just

study it all day. The more data they're tracking the better: our habits, our interests, our—"

"Voting patterns," Penny said. She highlighted a file called Poll_Projections_Prelimv2.docx.

"That's it. That's the connection. Sharpe was at the debate!" Max said.

"He was at your school? What for?"

"He's doing work for Governor Lovett's campaign. Mostly related to. . . her social media presence. But that doesn't make sense. This goes way beyond monitoring metrics to see how their campaign is doing."

"It's predictive modeling. Look. This document is describing an algorithm that can figure out how people are going to vote based on their online habits. Not just on Panjea, but everywhere. If they're somehow tracking that stuff live, and their algorithm is any good, they may know more about us than we consciously do ourselves."

"That won't change anything," Max said.

"Oh? Let's think about it. They can get info on any person's account, any time they want. It's like Max TV, on-demand. They're watching your every user action, sometimes while it's happening. When you log in. Which profiles you look at. Who you send messages to. What those messages say. What your friends are posting. What they're *not* posting—look, they're even capturing Panjea notes that were abandoned or deleted! It's like it's setting up a live feed of a person's life."

"So what do you do with all that?" Max asked.

"If you know what someone does every day, you have a good shot at predicting what they're *going* to do in the future, maybe even before they do. And if you know that, maybe you can manipulate them into doing something else."

Max nodded. "You could write an algorithm that makes them only see Panjea notes that support Governor Lovett, or say negative things about Senator Tooms."

"Or send them the wrong information about their polling location. Or let them think that their candidate's victory is locked in so they don't bother to vote. Or divert their campaign funds without them realizing it." Penny's eyes widened, flicking back and forth as her imagination went wild. The problem was: If a hacker like her could imagine it, then it was very likely possible.

"That would be a very sophisticated algorithm," Max said.

"Nah," Penny said.

"I thought we were just talking about aggregating information and passing it on," he said.

"You wouldn't do that if you didn't intend to do something with it one day. It's possible they're trying to capture everything because they don't know what will be useful, but with the election coming up next month, Sharpe would need to act on it quickly. Even without an algorithm trying to influence you subtly, with enough information and access to other systems and infrastructure, you could interact with people in other ways. Maybe go old-school and try to affect people in the real world." Penny jumped to her feet and started pacing in front of her computer.

"Sharpe wouldn't kill Ariel and the others just because they discovered this," Max said. "It's not a big enough secret. There has to be more to it."

She scrolled through more files. "We have to review it all and figure out how the pieces fit. What is this?" she muttered. "'Direct access to the user environment,' 'unique opportunities to capture the population.'" She shook her head. "This is horrifying. Panjea's into some nasty business."

"I think I've got something too." Risse pulled her headphone plug out of her computer and turned up the volume. "I've isolated the tones from Evan's video."

"What does it sound like?" Max asked.

"I'm not sure." Risse played the tones again. "D, E, C, C-down an octave, G."

"For the love of God, stop playing that," Penny said.

"*Re Mi Do* Do *So*." Risse sang the notes. She had a nice voice.

"*That* sounds familiar. Really familiar. But I can't pin it down," Max said. "I can also only hear that last bit on the clip. Do *Do* So? Da daaaa da. Da daaaa da?"

"Da da da, daaaa da. I lowered the pitch on these to something you both can hear." Risse turned her computer to face them and bumped up the audio as high as it would go. She pressed play.

DUH DUH DUH DUHHH DUH
It couldn't be.

"Play it again?" Max said.

DUH DUH DUH DUHHH DUH

"So the notes are—" Risse began.

"I know what it is," Max and Penny said at the same time.

Max gestured to Penny.

"It's from 'Closer' by deadmau5. It was Evan's ringtone," she said.

"Good ear," Max said. "But it came from a movie first. *Close Encounters of the Third Kind*."

"Oh." Penny blushed.

"What?"

"Evan took me to see that. It was playing at an art house theater during HGH. I should have remembered that," she said.

"Didn't you say you didn't see much of the film?" Risse asked.

"Risse!" Penny said.

"Hmm." Max looked away.

He was jealous. *Crap.*

Despite everything, even with all the intrigue, and their mission, and Evan's death. . . .

Max was starting to fall for Penny.

Penny met his eyes. She opened her mouth, then turned back to her computer screen.

"So what does it mean?" Risse asked. "It was obviously meant for one of you."

"Or both of us," Penny said softly.

Max cleared his throat. "I've seen the movie dozens of

times. Those tones were a message scientists sent to an alien spacecraft to let them know that we're intelligent. It's a mathematical signal—"

"Using the critical tones of the major scale!" Risse said. "Aha! So aliens are behind this. I knew it."

"Ha," Penny said. "It's a message, but I don't know what it means."

"I do, but you aren't going to like it," Max said.

"Well?" Penny and Risse said.

"It means we have to go back to Granville."

19

THEY HACKED A BLACK 1994 HONDA ODYSSEY and drove north to Granville. Max knew he would be recognized once he got back to his hometown, so Penny took the wheel while he and Risse pored over Evan's files on their laptops, this time with Max ducked down in the backseat.

It was now evident that Panjea was up to no good, and considering how many of the social media company's own employees had died recently, their activities seemed to be connected to a bigger, more ominous picture.

"We should release these documents and call it done," Penny said.

"Where? Send them to WikiLeaks? Fawkes Rising? Evan could have done that, but he didn't," Max said. "What would that accomplish?"

"People would flip out," Risse said.

"Evan's death and his crime are already drawing attention to the wrong issues. Instead of getting angry about Panjea watching our every move and basically being like an arm of the government, the public will focus on another lone hacker taking justice into his own hands: breaking the law, stealing secrets, then killing himself over the guilt. And Evan isn't here to defend himself," Max said.

"We are," Penny said.

"Would you come forward?" Max asked.

"Nope. We'd be charged too," Penny said. "Look at Evan's heroes: they're all living in exile, or in prison, or dead. Aren't you worried that'll happen to you next?"

Max almost lied. He wanted to seem as noble as Evan. He wanted to act like the hero his friend clearly thought he was. But...

"That's why I want to do this the right way. These e-mails expose Panjea, but we know Panjea can get away with this. We need solid information that will convince the world to bring them down. That's not going to happen with a bunch of Power-Point slides. It won't be enough to have a journalist explain the e-mails' significance to laypeople. We have to make a big splash that wakes everyone up to what's going on."

Penny looked at Max in the rearview mirror.

"We can prove that Panjea's sharing our information with the government, but not that they murdered six people just to cover it up. And if we can tie it back to Lovett through her connection to Sharpe, it would change everything. That'll affect who gets elected as the next president. We have to take this all the way, on our own. And we have to do it before the election," Max said.

"We're still missing something important," Penny said. "If we follow the steps that led Evan to the debate, maybe we can figure this out."

"Okay. How did he learn all this was going on?" Max asked.

"When he started working for Panjea, he could have stumbled across something while poking around in their servers," Penny said.

"But why did he go to Panjea? Evan never wanted to use his skills that way, and he didn't need the money."

"We already know where it began: with the first person who was killed," Risse said. "I just found e-mails in here from Ariel Miller to Evan. Dated from long before he started working at Panjea. She found out that Panjea was working with the government and wanted to get the information out. She asked Dramatis Personai for help, claiming that Panjea was able to spy on its users with their computers and cell phones. Turn on the webcam, eavesdrop, log everything they type."

"That was Ariel?"

"She was a hacker who sometimes hung around the forums. She went by the handle dinglehopper."

"I remember her. She sounded paranoid." Penny's voice was defensive.

"That's what people thought about the NSA," Max said.

"This is worse. The NSA slurps up everything and stores it, but we know Panjea is actively monitoring its users' activity."

"This gives a new perspective to their 'Everyone Online' project," Risse said.

"No shit," Max said.

Panjea had made major headlines with an ambitious plan to make cheap tablets and computers available to anyone, anywhere and everywhere, and provide free Wi-Fi to cities all over the U.S. Now, instead of it being a generous act of charity, Everyone Online seemed to have an ulterior motive: to collect even more data and control more of the ways people use the internet.

"It looks like only Evan and 0MN1 took Ariel seriously," Risse said. "Evan has copies of those chat logs in here, and from their private conversations, she decided to trust Evan because 0MN1 was too pushy and scared her off. He kept asking her if she worked for Panjea, because that was the only way she could have had access to their files."

"That sounds like 0MN1," Penny said. "He has no boundaries."

"Evan never asked her for any personal details. As far as I can tell, he didn't know if she worked for Panjea and he didn't care. He just trusted the information she gave him. He must have put the pieces together only after Ariel's death," Risse said.

"Would they really kill six people to win an election? Or is something else going on?" Max asked. He felt like they were working with random pages from a playbook for a game he didn't know how to play. There was no way to score points, let alone win, when you couldn't grasp the rules.

"Something called 'Project SH1FT' is mentioned in a lot of these e-mails and slides, but nothing describes what it is," Risse said.

"SH1FT? As in, shifting the election?" Penny asked.

"I guess we just have to ask: What could Panjea do if it was connected to everyone in the world?" Max asked.

They thought for a while in somber silence. They all arrived at the same answer: *Anything it wants.* "I wish we could just ask Evan," Risse said.

"Me too," Max said. He would have some other things to say to him first, though. "But maybe he never got to the ultimate answer."

"Maybe we can do the next best thing," Penny said.

"What could be better than this?" Max asked as he opened what had to be his five-hundredth document.

"Something occurred to me. When 503-ERROR disappeared, no one knew what happened. We pestered Evan, but he wouldn't disclose anything about whether you had been arrested, or died, or just given up," Penny said.

"He was good that way," Max said.

"Right. So hear me out. What if all the silenced six aren't dead after all? What if one of them really did choose to disappear? Say, someone who knew he was a target."

"You mean L0NELYB0Y, a.k.a. Jeremy 'Jem' Seer," Max

said. "He was the only one without an article about his death."

Penny nodded. "What do we know about him?"

"Not much." Max opened the spreadsheet Risse had made with all the information they had on Dramatis Personai. "He was from Fairbanks, Alaska, same as Ty Andrews."

"They had to know each other," Penny said.

"They went to the same high school. They were the same age. It's a small place, so, yeah. I assume they were friends," Max said.

"Ooh! I noticed something weird before, but I didn't think it meant anything until now. Infiltraitor—Ty Andrews—and LONELYBOY were never logged in to the Dramatis Personai chat rooms at the same time," Risse said.

"You think they were the same person?" Max asked. "But Ty Andrews is dead. He was a real person."

"I don't mean that Ty Andrews didn't exist. I think Jeremy Seer was both Infiltraitor and LONELYBOY."

"Then who was Ty Andrews?!" Max couldn't keep the frustration out of his voice.

"Let's find out," Risse said.

She and Max switched to other computers and connected to the internet through Risse's phone to dox Ty Andrews and look for anything connecting him to Jem. Max and Risse worked well enough together, but not as quickly as she and Penny did. Max would offer a suggestion after Risse had already considered it and discounted it, or when she was already halfway done with the search query. Every now and then, one of them would discover something and say it aloud, adding to their knowledge of Ty and Jem, slowly stitching together their portraits of the two boys and their town.

Risse updated her spreadsheet, now working from two computers in the cramped space of the passenger seat.

"Ty was poor," Risse said. "He didn't have his own computer."

"Jem was friends with Ty on Panjea, but he never left any messages there until after Ty was dead. 'I'm so sorry.' That was an edited comment. I wonder what he wrote originally. I bet Panjea knows," Max said.

"Damn. Jem deleted his Panjea account," Risse said.

"Deactivated or deleted?"

"It's completely gone. He deactivated it the same day that Evan deactivated his," Risse said.

"So they both knew something. Maybe they were working on this together."

A little while later: "Here's a comment on another student's Panjea page where Ty mentioned he didn't know how to swim. So what was he doing at the lake?" Risse said.

"I think you were right, Penny," Max said. He'd been going through the chat logs Evan had collected from Dramatis Personai. "Infiltraitor generally logged in from around five p.m. to seven p.m."

"After school," Penny said.

"Then L0NELYB0Y would log in from nine at night until one or two in the morning. After Infiltraitor disappeared, guess when L0NELY B0Y logged in?"

"Five in the evening to one or two in the morning," she said.

Max tapped his nose. "Bingo! With a break for dinner. They were only both logged in once, way back when L0NE-LYB0Y first joined the group, and there was one short, but weird, exchange." He read it aloud:

0MN1: Anyone have twitter's new api? They changed it again!

L0NELYB0Y: but good luck cracking *their* servers

Edifice: Earn something for yourself for a change, 0MN1

Infiltraitor: I bet someone at panjea can get it

Penny laughed. "L0NELYB0Y responded to Infiltraitor's comment before he posted it."

"It's easy to miss if you aren't looking for it," Max said.

"Risse or I would have noticed it if we'd been logged in at the time. It's sloppy. We had to watch for that kind of thing all the time."

"You were two hackers posing as one, and Jem was one hacker posing as two," Max said.

"Not a bad idea to keep a backup handle in case you have to scrap one identity, instead of starting a new one from scratch. Jem had built-in history, so he was able to pick up where Infiltraitor left off," she said.

"His biggest mistake was planting clues that Ty Andrews was Infiltraitor's real life identity. He probably thought it would be harmless; if the Feds ever came after him, they would realize he'd been framed and wasn't a hacker. Who would have imagined Ty would be killed?" Max said.

"Dick move, Jem," Penny said.

"Even Evan was fooled. Jem's apparent death might have been what tipped him over the edge."

"And he just let Evan think he was dead? If I ever meet him, I'll kill him myself, " Penny said.

"I *would* love to find this guy. Maybe he knows something about all this," Max said.

"Good luck tracking down a ghost," Risse said.

"He could still be online, wherever he is. Maybe he has another handle. Has anyone new joined Dramatis Personai recently?"

"No, the group's gotten a little suspicious with all the disappearances. That's why we were so curious about you returning, though I knew why you were there," Penny said.

"He might still be checking some of his old accounts. What's your public encryption key?" Risse said.

Max told her.

She typed for a moment then hit Enter with a sense of finality. "I just sent a private message from DoubleThink to all Jem's known addresses, asking him to contact you. If he's alive and goes online, hopefully he'll get in touch."

"Okay, Max. We just crossed over into Granville. Time to lay low and stay low," Penny said.

Max peeked out the window before lying down in the backseat. After spending years wondering what it would be like to get away from Granville, it was still his home, and he'd feared he would never see it or his dad again.

"Go straight on State Route 4 for a while. Take the exit for Lone Tree Way then drive east. Look for a big parking lot on the right and pull in there," Max said.

He closed his laptop and held it to his chest. It might be dangerous for him to be here, but it felt right. Things were coming full circle, bringing him closer to Evan and to what had set everything in motion. He just hoped the answer was worth the risk.

20

PENNY PARKED BEHIND A ONE-STORY BRICK building on Lone Tree Way. In the display window, a female mannequin dressed as a sexy Ninja Turtle posed with a male mannequin dressed as Gandalf the Grey.

"Halloween City?" Risse said. "Is now the time to be thinking about your costume?"

Max sat up in the back seat and reached for his laptop bag. "It's only Halloween City in September and October. The rest of the time it's either a discount furniture store or a used book warehouse. Sometimes it sells wine. But five years ago, it was my favorite comic book store. It was called Close Encounters of the *Nerd* Kind."

Penny groaned. "No wonder you guys loved it so much."

They climbed out of the car.

"I'll go inside and keep an eye out for trouble. Let's keep a channel open." Penny popped her Bluetooth earpiece in and turned it on.

"Good idea." Risse used her burner phone to call Penny's and turned on the speaker.

Penny tapped her earpiece. "Hello?"

They heard her through the speaker on Risse's phone.

"We're good to go," Risse said.

Max led them around the side of the building into the alley that separated Halloween City from the neighboring Bean Up—the same alley he'd used to escape from the his first pursuers five nights before. Penny kept going and turned the corner.

"I bet you take all the ladies here," Risse said.

Max laughed.

"So this is what Evan's musical clue was leading us to?" she asked.

Max dragged a dumpster away from the wall, giving him about two feet of clearance to scoot behind it. He gestured Risse closer.

"Remember those USB dead drops I told you about? Evan and I placed four of them around Granville, one at each of our favorite places. The first was at The Hidden Word. This is where we installed the last one."

He gestured toward the wall. Risse studied it for a moment.

"Aha!" She crouched and pointed to the tip of a USB stick protruding from a brick low on the wall. "Neat. I never would have seen that if I hadn't been looking for it. Think it's still working after all this time?"

Max pointed up. "The overhang protects it from the rain. And it's just a chip, no moving parts. I think this one was thirty-two gigabytes."

"Pricey a few years ago, for something you just left out in the open," she said.

"You know how some families have a bowl of candy in the house? We have a bowl full of flash drives."

Max slid his laptop out of his bag and opened it. He knelt next to the wall and carefully lined up the USB connector with the port of his computer.

"How's it looking, Penny?" Risse asked.

"They have a sale on Halloween masks. Two for one!" Penny said.

"You aren't supposed to be shopping," Max said.

"It's part of my cover."

Risse put a hand on Max's shoulder and leaned over to get a better look at the screen. The drive mounted and Max clicked on it to see the file contents.

"So?" she asked.

"It's blank," he said.

"Look for hidden folders," Penny said.

"Duh." Max changed the setting to display hidden folders and found one named SH1FTv3.1.

"SH1FT!" Max said.

"Open it," Risse said.

"I *know*. Jeez. Don't be a backseat driver."

Risse reached down and clicked on it. A password dialog box opened.

"Argh!" Risse said.

"What is it?" Penny asked.

"Another password," Risse said.

"Oh, come on," Penny said.

Max grinned. "I think I know this one," he said.

He slowly quoted Evan's favorite line from *Close Encounters of the Third Kind* as he typed it: "This. . . means. . . something. This. . . is. . . important." Evan couldn't have been clearer this time.

The folder opened, filled with dozens of file names.

"Now let's see. . . ." Risse grabbed for Max's computer.

"Easy! The files are still copying over." He held his computer in place against the wall. He grimaced when the corner of the MacBook scraped against brick.

"Oh-em-gee. Do you know what this thing is?" Risse asked.

"Not a clue." There were hundreds of files, but they only added up to around twenty-five megabytes of data—a drop in the bucket in a thirty-two gigabyte drive.

Risse ran her finger down the screen, pointing out the file extensions. "Look at all these OCX files. I think this is a worm."

A worm is like a computer virus, but much worse. Worms also spread from computer to computer, but they're programmed to adapt over time, and can even behave differently according to the system they're infecting.

"What's it doing here?" Max asked.

"Evan obviously put it here. The question is: How did he get it?"

"He wrote it," Max said. "Or helped write it. These files. . . . Only Evan would name a text file 'gocappies.'"

At Risse's confused expression, he explained. "Our school mascot is a capybara."

"Oh. Capybaras are *so* cute," Risse said.

Max kept his computer plugged in to the USB port while he made another copy of the files on a portable USB drive. "I'm going to keep all the copies encrypted with the same password. Remember: 'This means something. This is important.' Including spaces, capitalization, and punctuation."

"I see Evan was a *Blade Runner* fan. pris.txt, batty.txt, deckard.txt," Risse said.

"Isn't everyone?" Penny asked.

Max's USB drive managed the files more quickly than the three-year-old one in the wall. He plucked it out of his computer and handed it to Risse.

"Okay, here you go. I'm gonna nuke the source. Encrypted or not, I don't want this thing out there where we can't control it," he said.

"Don't forget to zero fill it," Penny said.

"Already in progress," Max said.

Risse sat on an upended milk crate in the alley and popped the USB drive in to her laptop. "This is beautiful. It looks like he used Lua and C++. Probably inspired by the Flame worm."

"Can you tell what it does?" Max asked.

"Not without rolling up my sleeves and digging into the source code."

"Isn't there a faster way?"

"I could run it, see what it does."

"That's a terrible idea," Penny said. "That would be like a scientist in some movie injecting herself with an antivirus. Illogical and irresponsible."

"We don't have any time to mess around and make sure it's safe. We'll make sure whatever it is can't spread to any other computers. Do it, Risse. Use my laptop."

"Are you sure?" Risse asked.

"Everything important is on that USB, and the two of you have copies of it all too."

She handed the USB drive back to Max. He slipped its chain over his head and tucked the drive into the collar of his shirt.

"That's not the point. The files and operating system are just the brain. This is your computer. It has a personality."

"It's a machine," Max said.

"Shh." She covered the microphone of the laptop. "What do you want to call it?"

"I stole it five days ago. The FBI could steal it from me at any moment. I'm not that into it. I don't know. MaxBook?"

"That's stupid. You aren't taking this seriously." Risse stroked the top of Max's computer. "Her name is Mayfly. Thank you for your sacrifice, Mayfly."

"I'm coming out," Penny said. "I want to watch this."

A few minutes later, Penny showed up with a shopping bag.

"You actually bought something?" Max asked.

"We're in Dramatis Personai. We love masks."

"I hope you used cash at least."

"Nope. Stolen credit card. Can't be traced to me."

"Penny!" Max said.

"I'm a *hacker.* I'm on the run. They'll get the charges reverted. It's no big."

"Bad news," Risse said. "I can't run this. Some of the code is missing."

Max headed for the car. "Then we have three other stops to make. I bet the code is distributed across the other dead drops."

"Clever. Even if someone else figured out the clue in Evan's video, only you know about the other dead drops." Risse folded her laptop and stood, brushing off the back of her jeans.

"Let's just make it quick and get out of Dodge," Penny said.

Risse waited in the car poring over the SH1FT code while Penny and Max collected the rest of it from USB drives around Granville. Neither of them spoke when they visited The Hidden Word, the first dead drop Max and Evan had made together. The back door was crisscrossed with yellow police tape.

The third dead drop was a tree in the yard at the middle school, and the last USB drive was inside one of the men's rooms at the Cineplex, hidden behind a loose tile in a toilet stall.

Risse copied the last of the files over, her face showing how excited she was. They were in an abandoned lot on the edge of town that was far away from any surveillance cameras, was out of range of any Wi-Fi signals, and gave them a good view of all the roads. The sun was setting, and they sat on a low concrete wall together with Risse in the middle, balancing Max's computer on her knees.

"I'm running every diagnostic test I know to monitor what SH1FT does to your computer," she said.

"Hit it," Max said.

Code ran down the screen. "Okay, so far the worm is just scanning the system to see what's installed. Pretty standard."

A light blinked on the front of the laptop.

"The worm just turned on the wireless radio, but of course there's no network. I'm capturing all the data packets though. Guess what it's trying to access?"

"Panjea," Max said.

"Panjea! I don't know what it would do if it could get into your account. Oh, now it's looking for some folders on your system. Hey, someone installed Panjea on Mayfly."

"The owner, probably. But that's under a different profile."

"Doesn't matter. It found them. Oh, hey, it's deleting a bunch of things. I think. . . it's purging your system of the code Panjea uses to track users." Risse looked up.

"It's making it safer?" Penny asked. "That doesn't seem right."

"Evan clearly made some changes to it. Some drastic

changes," Risse said. "Now it's a helper worm."

"What was it designed to do originally?" Max asked.

"I don't know. But this is probably what they're chasing you for, Max," Risse said.

Penny walked back and forth in front of them. "Okay, so people inside Panjea realize that they're evil and using the service to actually track users and share private data with the government. But Panjea can't access every computer, so they make this worm that can spread itself over time, giving them the same access to any computer that's connected to the internet."

"And they work to make sure that any computer that can go online has access to the internet, so they can take in more data," Max said. "But this goes way beyond predicting U.S. election results and influencing votes. This could go *global*."

"It would infect any computer it came into contact with, so it's a safe bet they want it to spread around the world. Which means the original version of SH1FT could spy on users anywhere, including foreign governments," Risse said.

"The U.S. government would certainly be interested in that," Max said. "But if Senator Tooms is elected, he would shut it down. He supports cyber espionage on other nations, but not at the expense of Americans. Or so he says."

"So someone wants Governor Lovett in office. And Sharpe is working to make that happen, no matter what," Penny said.

"Has to be. Sharpe's already linked to Panjea and to Lovett. If she's elected, he also stands to gain a lot. She'd probably give him a pretty cushy job," Max said. "But if word got out that Panjea was working with the government, the backlash might cause Lovett to lose the election."

Risse smiled. "If they're after you, Max, this could be the only copy. Evan might have stolen it and then wiped their files to buy himself some time."

"Time for what?" Max asked.

"To rewrite it."

"Well, if they want it so bad, why don't we give it to them?" Max asked.

"Like," Penny said.

"Only trouble is, they would check it out thoroughly before implementing it. They would be more equipped than I am to realize that Evan modified it." Risse closed the laptop. "They might even be able to revert his changes."

"What if we infected a computer at Panjea with it?" Max asked.

"It would have to be a production server," Penny said. "They would be well protected against worms otherwise. They do have a bunch of hackers working for them."

"How do we get in there?" Max asked.

"We don't have time to apply for a job, and it's not easy to get hired there," Penny said.

Risse held up her phone. "Haxx0rade is tomorrow."

"Of course!" Penny said.

Max read from Risse's phone. "'Come to Haxx0rade. Join us in hacking the world.' At least they're honest about it."

"Panjea is even offering bounties for hackers who discover flaws in their security, starting at a million dollars for anything discovered in the first hour and going down every hour until the end of the event," Penny said. Max could practically see the dollar signs reflected in her glasses.

"That's perfect," Max said. "We'll have direct access to their servers for twenty-four hours, and we'll just be a few people out of hundreds attempting to hack them."

"Getting into Haxx0rade will be tricky. Registration is closed," Risse said.

"It also could be dangerous," Penny said. "They're certainly looking for Max, and we know they've killed people trying to keep this secret."

Risse swiped her phone screen with a finger. "It's a 'hacking masquerade'—masks are mandatory, with prizes for the best one."

"They won't stop chasing me until they have this thing, so let's stop running and go to them," Max said.

"It's also invite-only," Risse said. "Your admission has to be sponsored by a Panjea employee. How are we going to get into this little soiree?"

Penny cracked her knuckles. "Leave that to me."

Penny went to work on her phone. Max looked over her shoulder as she logged in to Panjea. Her profile picture showed Penny in a white scoop neck T-shirt under a gray suit jacket. The shirt was tight and sheer enough to show the lace bra beneath it. Her hair was pulled up and she wore a pair of cat eye glasses. She looked more mature in every way.

"Whoa," Max said.

"I took that photo," Risse said proudly.

"For what? A dating profile?" Max asked.

He noticed the name on the account.

"Who's Emmie Steed?" he asked.

"I am," Penny said. "She's one of my alternate online personas."

"She has over three thousand Panjea Peers?" Max asked. "That's way more than I have, and she isn't even real."

"They're mostly men in the tech and defense industries. Emmie is one of my more popular alter egos. She's one of the few women working in infosec. I claim a lot of my bounties under her handle." She pointed it out in her profile, which was under the name: ^venger Gurl.

Penny typed a note. A minute later, she clicked on an Events notification. "Well, that was easy. Someone just invited me to Haxx0rade. It starts tomorrow at noon."

21

MAX, PENNY, AND RISSE SAT ACROSS THE STREET from The Wherehouse, an old warehouse in San Francisco's SoMa district that had been converted into Panjea's corporate headquarters. Max had seen pictures of the building and studied the latest floor plans in detail, but it was impressive in person.

Most of the facade had been sliced off and replaced with plate glass, allowing everyone to see inside its three floors as if looking into a giant dollhouse. Community groups angry about Panjea taking it over and destroying the original architecture had dubbed the building in its new configuration "The Whore House."

The wide window on the top floor was decorated with a fifteen-foot-high rendition of Panjea's iconic logo, stacked green serif letters illuminated by the interior lighting of the tall loft:

PAN

JEA

As if that weren't striking enough, a glass globe topped the building, like a cherry added as a finishing touch to a sundae. Suspended inside the hollow sphere was a cutout of the Pangaea supercontinent that lent the site its name. The glass surface of the globe displayed "Welcome, HAXX0RS" as it rotated. From here, it was hard to tell whether the text or the sphere itself was moving.

Penny slipped on her mask and turned toward Max. It gave him a chill to see her like that. She had chosen the smiling white comedy mask, sister to weeping tragedy—traditional symbols of theater going back to ancient Greek times, most recently adopted by Dramatis Personai. The companion mask was in the Halloween City shopping bag in the middle divider.

"Wish me luck," Penny said.

"Good luck," Max said. "Remember. If you run into any trouble, just get out of there."

"I got this." Penny straightened her mask. In keeping with her Emmie Steed personality, she was wearing a blue scoop neck shirt, a cropped jacket, dark jeans, and flats. Max doubted many people would be paying attention to her mask. "You're taking the bigger risk. If you get caught and someone recognizes you. . . ."

"I can still go instead," Risse said.

"No," Max and Penny said together.

"Boo," Risse said.

Penny popped in her Bluetooth earpiece. "I'll keep you posted by text until I get settled, and I'll have my phone on standby. Don't call unless it's an emergency."

Max nodded and plugged his earbuds in to his phone. He looped the cord up through the bottom of his shirt and let them dangle from his collar. "See you later."

Penny climbed out of the car and strapped her computer bag across her chest. People participating in the hackathon had to bring their own rigs with them. They would be allowed to plug in to the network and use the internet, but they were on their own from there. Penny was bringing her second-best laptop: the Jarvis Mark VI, a sleek, professional ThinkPad that fit her infosec persona. It was prepped with fake personal information for Emmie Steed and loaded with anti-*everything*, in case Panjea tried hacking into its guests' machines. Not that they already hadn't, under the auspices of their proprietary app, but this was as much an opportunity for them to steal hacker secrets as the reverse.

Risse clambered out of the back of the car. The sisters hugged.

"I love you. Be careful," Risse said.

"Love you too. Keep an eye on Max," Penny said.

"The plan is to keep an eye on both of you."

"If things go south, you go back home and forget about all this."

"Yeah, right," Risse said. "I'm your insurance. If you two get caught, I'll make sure Panjea has to deal with a PR nightmare."

Penny looked both ways and hurried across the street.

Risse retrieved her laptop and moved to the front passenger seat. The two of them watched Penny enter the building and walk to the reception area.

The place was hopping; they could see all the people moving around inside. It was the world's largest ant farm. And if the workers were drones, that made Victor Ignacio the queen. He was scheduled to give his welcome speech at twelve-thirty, which would be the perfect time for Max to try to access a development computer—if he could even get into the building.

Risse pushed her seat all the way back so she could prop her legs on the dashboard and her computer on her shins. Max worried they'd look suspicious, but San Francisco was one of the few places where it was perfectly normal to be sitting in a parked car typing on a laptop.

Penny had picked a sporty black BMW for this adventure. It was basically camouflaged in the heart of the city, which attracted many highly successful tech companies.

"I guess this is actually happening," Max said.

"Nervous?"

"You bet. I know we have a plan, but our skills will only take us so far. Too much still relies on dumb luck."

"Too late to have second thoughts."

"I'm already on sixth thoughts. But it doesn't matter. We're doing this. We have to do this."

Max was psyching himself up the way Coach Kim did the team before a big game.

Risse clapped. "She's in!" She showed him the image Penny had just e-mailed her: a photo of her Haxx0rade badge, a computer chip cut into the irregular shape of Pangaea, the supercontinent, with "^venger Gurl" etched in gold circuitry. A P-code, Panjea's proprietary barcode, was printed in the corner.

"RFID?" Max asked. He pronounced it "arfid," the way Evan had when he explained the technology to him.

"Definitely," Risse said.

Radio frequency identification is basically a chip in almost everything these days, from your passport to groceries you purchased at the supermarket. Most of them are passive—they only transmit information when an RFID reader magnetizes it, providing just enough power to send a small amount of information. People even inject RFIDs the size of a grain of rice into pets, so if they get lost a shelter can identify the owners. Helpful.

The problem is, there are ways to steal information from RFIDs. A savvy hacker could build a device at home to read them, or even use a cell phone for some types of RFIDs. Worse still: *active* RFIDs are always broadcasting and could be used to monitor a person's location.

"I'd have to examine one of those badges to know for sure what kind of RFID it has, but you could fit a tiny power supply in there easily. Here, scan that code," Risse said.

Max opened the barcode app on his phone and aimed the

camera at the cluster of dots on Risse's screen. A moment later, he was prompted to authorize a software download.

"Should I?" he asked.

Risse studied the message and the list of requested permissions.

"Wow. It wants to control a lot. Practically everything. But we can block most of these if we have to," she said.

"It's okay. This phone doesn't have any personal info on it."

Max installed the program and, moments later, the Haxx-0rade splash page appeared on his screen. He opened the app, which was called HackerAid. It prompted him to scan his badge again to connect his complimentary account, but he was able to skip the step; he didn't want to register as Penny. He thumbed through the options.

"It's an electronic guide," Max said. "It has maps of the different locations being used for the hackathon on each floor."

"Let me see."

Max started to give her his phone, but she shook her head and handed him the end of a USB cable attached to her computer.

He plugged the cord in and switched it to data mode. She clicked around on her trackpad.

"I've got the source code. It looks pretty clean... pretty elegant. Okay, I'm jealous."

He checked the time on his phone. "The keynote address starts in ten minutes."

He took the tragedy mask from the Halloween City bag

and propped it on his head. He pulled off Risse's fake glasses and tucked them inside his secondhand Panjea messenger bag, purchased that morning. It was easy to find branded swag from different companies at thrift stores, and he'd been able to assemble the rest of his simple wardrobe there—a gray hoodie, black polo shirt, well-worn jeans, and flip-flops—for much more than used clothes should ever cost.

He was playing to a stereotype, but in this case that was the point: to look like a Panjea employee coming in to work. Weekends meant nothing in the tech industry, and he figured it would be all hands on deck during Haxx0rade.

He slid the keycard from Evan's room into his right sleeve.

"I hope that thing works. They might have deactivated it after Evan died," Risse said.

"That's why I have the mask as a backup." Max popped an earbud into his right ear. "Call me if anything looks suspicious out here."

Max unlocked the driver side door.

"Hold on." Risse put a hand on his right arm. He turned back and she gave him a quick peck on the cheek, startling him. "That's for good luck. Be careful."

He pulled down his mask, hoping she wouldn't notice him blushing. "Being careful, big part of the plan."

He climbed out of the car and walked toward Panjea. He looked up at the massive logo.

Hold on.

He fished around in his pocket and pulled out the metal

jigsaw puzzle piece that had been Ariel Miller's good luck charm. He held it at arm's length and closed his left eye. He lined the silver piece up with the A in "PAN." It was a perfect match. He'd just found the puzzle it belonged to. Now all he had to do was find out where it fit.

He squeezed the puzzle piece and pocketed it. He could use all the good luck he could get.

Max stepped through the sliding glass doors into the spacious lobby, which was more 1920s Art Deco than futuristic starship, which one might have expected from the Apple store aesthetic on the exterior.

But Max had seen it all before, so he didn't miss a step. One of the keys to infiltrating a building's security is to look like you belong there, and that requires research. Since Risse was the only one not trying to sneak into Panjea, she had scouted the lobby earlier and snapped some photos on the sly. That meant he didn't need to pause and get his bearings—a dead giveaway if you were pretending to be an employee who entered the building every day. He already knew that the security desk was on the right, staffed by one rent-a-cop.

There was a row of three electronic turnstiles straight ahead. They were just wood-paneled columns, about waist-high, without any barriers to prevent entry. In fact, you could actually go around them entirely, but someone would quickly try to stop you.

Max headed toward the turnstiles with purpose, as if he did

it every day, without even glancing over to see if the guard was paying attention. The elevator banks were just beyond them, to the left. The main auditorium where Vic Ignacio would be addressing three hundred hackers in mere minutes was on the right, hidden behind tinted glass windows that were lit with soft, shifting colors.

If Max were doing this on a weekday, he would try to "tailgate"—sneak in on the heels of another employee with a legitimate badge. But Max was on his own. He felt exposed.

He picked the turnstile in the middle. As he walked through, he reached up with his right hand and brushed the sleeve of his hoodie against the reader. He was still looking straight ahead, unconcerned. The mask blocked his peripheral vision, so he didn't know that the badge hadn't worked until he heard the angry beeps.

Max took another two steps beyond the turnstile and froze. He looked back at the turnstile in surprise, as if he hadn't even seen it. If the guard didn't say anything, he would turn and keep going.

The guard said something. "Can I see your ID, sir?"

Max looked at the guard: mid-forties, balding, thin and fit. He pegged him for a marathoner. Time for Plan B.

"I'm here for Haxx0rade." He made his voice falsetto and walked toward the desk, adjusting his mask. He wanted to look relaxed and cooperative. He controlled his breathing and ignored the sweat beading along his scalp.

"You have to sign in," the guard said.

"I don't want to miss the keynote." Max added a nasal whine to his voice. Stereotypes sucked, but they made social engineering easier, because he was playing to people's expectations.

"This'll just take a second. What's your handle?"

Max hesitated. Should he play the lost badge gambit? He could easily guess the handle of another hacker who was here—Risse said that most of Dramatis Personai had made the list. After all, how could he prove who he really was?

"503-ERROR." He leaned forward slightly. "Five-zero-three-dash, then 'error' all in capitals."

The guard typed it in painfully slowly. Max glanced toward the auditorium, so if he picked up on his anxiety, he would assume Max was just worried about missing Ignacio's speech.

"I may not be in the system yet." Max preempted. "I was a late registration. Had a friend pull some strings."

The guard bent to look at the screen more closely. "I'll say. 0MN1's sponsoring your admission."

What?

Fortunately the mask hid Max's shock.

The guard pointed to the auditorium doors. "Stop by the registration desk."

"Thanks!" Max hurried past the turnstiles.

He was in, but 0MN1 had somehow guessed that he would be there. That could be a very bad sign. But nothing ventured, nothing gained—and this could well be his chance to find out something useful about the most mysterious member of

Dramatis Personai. Just knowing he also worked at Panjea was valuable intel.

A woman at a folding table by the door looked up when Max approached. She had a bandit mask tied over her eyes, but otherwise she was dressed normally, with a baby doll Panjea T-shirt and jeans.

"Welcome to HaxxOrade! What's your name?" she asked.

She had two yellow legal envelopes in a bin.

"503-ERROR," Max said.

"Cool handle!" She handed him the envelope. He snuck a glance at the other envelope and felt like his heart skipped a beat. It was labeled L0NELYB0Y.

Whether the final missing hacker had registered for the hackathon or 0MN1 had simply gambled that he might show up, it meant he was alive.

"This packet contains your badge, a schedule of events and panels, and a list of hackathon rules. The cafeteria downstairs is open all weekend and your badge will get you free drinks and meals until tomorrow noon. Remember to take care of yourself. Stay hydrated!"

"Do you work here too?" Max asked.

"I do." She nodded. "I'm in marketing."

"Do you like it?"

"It's the best! I wish I could hack like you guys, but we all have our roles to play." She gestured to the doors. "When you go in, try to be quiet. I think Vic is starting the program." She smiled.

"Thank you." Max stepped toward the auditorium entrance and opened the envelope. He tipped the badge into his hand. It was heavier than it looked. He slid it around his neck.

Max took out his phone and ran HackerAid. This time when it prompted him to scan his badge, he did. A moment later, the app displayed a blinking red dot with "503-ERROR" floating over it. He zoomed in on the screen and saw lots of green and red dots in the room ahead of him. When he tapped on one, a name appeared with a location: "TheWalkingDude: Auditorium."

The app was tracking everyone in the building.

Max wasn't claustrophobic, but as he imagined this program as a microcosm of Panjea's grand scheme to track everyone on the planet through the Panjea app on their cell phones, he became uncomfortably warm and itchy. He was having a hard time breathing.

"Is there a problem?" the woman at the registration table asked.

Max didn't look up from his screen. "You have no idea."

He fired off a quick text to Penny and Risse: 0MN1 works at Panjea! He knows I'm here. HackerAid's tracking all the hackers. Going in.

He opened the door and watched his little red icon move into the auditorium as he stepped over the threshold.

22

PANJEA'S AUDITORIUM WAS A BIG WHITE ROOM WITH no seats, and a simple stage and podium on the far end. Grooves along the wall, floor, and ceiling suggested the space could be divided with temporary partitions, and he assumed they brought in seats for press conferences and product announcements. Right now, it was filled with hackers standing around impatiently. The energy in the room reminded Max of the anticipation preceding a concert, and for many of the people here, Victor Ignacio was a rock star.

Max hovered at the edges of the mass, glancing at the people in front of him and back to the swarming dots on his phone screen. He figured out that the green dots were Panjea employees and the red ones were the hackers they were sponsoring, but everyone was wearing a mask.

It was a carnival, with masks of all kinds adding much-needed color to the space: grotesque Mardi Gras masks, Halloween masks, an overwhelming number of Guy Fawkes masks—made popular by the hacktivist group Anonymous and the film *V for Vendetta.*

There were a lot of people with masks they had made themselves: elaborate Steampunk ironwork and things that flashed and glowed. Someone had made a mask of Rorschach from *Watchmen*, with Rorschach patterns that actually moved and swirled into new shapes: a butterfly, a crossbow, a valentine. Max marveled at the number of intricate papercraft masks, and felt grossly inadequate with his store-bought plastic one.

Some had taken it to full-on cosplay. He saw some people dressed as Iron Man, Cybermen, and a lot of Batmen. Some were just wearing face paint, others had covered only their eyes with masks like Green Lantern and Robin and the Teenage Mutant Ninja Turtles. He recognized a "No Face" from an anime film, Darth Vaders, and a cadre of Stormtroopers. He was relieved to see many people wearing tragedy and comedy masks like his and Penny's, which were favored by Dramatis Personai supporters—though it was odd to worry about blending into a group that was simultaneously showing off and hiding.

It was fun to study the other guests without being self-conscious about it. If he let his eyes linger too long—and he caught himself doing that plenty of times—it didn't carry the same sort of taboo as it might have if his face were visible.

The masks distanced people from each other as much as they freed them to become closer.

It was a relief to not worry about being recognized for the first time in days. But Max didn't allow himself to relax. He was still surrounded by danger—literally.

Men and women dressed in black and wearing shiny metal masks modeled after *Battlestar Galactica* Cylons—complete with red lights oscillating across their visors—circled the auditorium. As they scanned the crowd they moved like robots, in a calculated, inhuman, predatory, sort of way, with slow turns of their heads. Tasers were holstered on their belts.

These guards didn't show up on his HackerAid app.

"Hey, 503-ERROR!"

Max jerked his head up. Someone in a gold helmet that seemed to have a boomerang jutting from the top of it was rushing toward him. The person had on a brown leather jacket and was holding a cell phone up to eye level.

Max took a step back as the person landed in his personal space.

The figure spoke and Max decided it was a guy. "It's really you. I didn't know you were going to be here. It is so cool to meet you in person. How are—"

"Do I know you?" Max asked. He felt like he had to interrupt just so the speaker could pause to take a breath. Listening to him was exhausting.

"Oh, sorry. I'm print*is*dead. I mean, that's my handle, but it's kind of a mouthful, so you can call me Print if you want for short. Can I call you Five-Oh-Three? That sounds kind of badass, doesn't it? It's funny how hard it is to pronounce a lot of our handles. You don't think about that until you come to an event like this."

"This is my first one," Max said. "I like your helmet. What's it from?"

"I'm the Rocketeer!" Print struck a weird pose, one that Max supposed was meant to look like he was flying. "I wish I could say I made this myself, but I bought it. It's a collectible. So you want a job at Panjea? Everyone here does."

"Not really," Max said. "I hear the workload is killer."

The lights dimmed.

"Oh, it's finally starting," Print said.

A spotlight came up and a bald man walked onto the stage wearing a green T-shirt that said "Tectonics Rock," beige cargo shorts, and white sneakers with no socks. He was wearing the Phantom of the Opera's mask from the Broadway musical, but it was transparent so Max could see his face clearly, looking much the same as it had on the cover of *Wired* magazine. It was Victor Ignacio.

The crowd erupted into applause.

Victor spread his arms wide, accepting the praise. Then he brought his hands together in one loud clap that silenced the room. "Thank you. People wondered why I insisted there not be seats in here today. The answer is: I have always liked standing ovations."

The audience laughed.

Ignacio rubbed his hands together. "Welcome to Haxx-0rade! Let's make some cool shit this weekend. Yeah?"

"Yeah!" the crowd responded.

Ignacio tapped his mask. "People also wondered why I wanted to make this a masquerade."

"Because masks are cool!" someone shouted.

"Yes! Masks are cool. And I really like yours! *Power Rangers* fan? Me too. Wanna trade?" Ignacio pulled his mask off and extended it toward the audience member in the red helmet. After a prolonged moment, he withdrew his hand. "No? Interesting. Other than wanting to give everyone a chance to get creative with their masks this weekend, I was also curious how people would take it. I thought it would make it easier for some of you, since I know hackers thrive on anonymity."

He whirled his mask around in his hands and started pacing back and forth on the stage. This was starting to take on the atmosphere of a TED Talk. Max knew the event was being broadcast live online, even though he couldn't see the cameras. In fact, he hadn't noticed any cameras at all in the building, but he knew they had to be there.

As he had at the debates, Max scanned the wings of the stage. Kevin Sharpe was standing in almost the same position he'd been in at the Granville High auditorium stage. What was he doing here?

"I am not a hacker." Ignacio held the mask out, facing him, and looked at it. "But some of my best friends are."

More laughter. Max looked around. Was this auditorium

equipped with its own laugh track?

Max got a text message from Risse: I see you in the app. Shouldn't you get moving?

Max looked toward the doors. More guards in Cylon masks were blocking them, the red lights in their visors pulsing ominously in the dark. He wasn't going anywhere right now.

Ignacio put his mask back on. "Masks are one way to hide your identities, and privacy is important to hackers. I like hackers, I employ a lot of you, and you might say Panjea was founded on hackers. This company started as a little startup in San Jose called Synthwerks."

Scattered applause.

"Some of you remember it? That's great to hear, because it was only around for a hot minute."

"I miss it!" someone shouted.

"Miss it?" Ignacio said. "But it's here. It's all around us."

He spread his arms again and walked backwards across the stage, turning in a slow circle. "Synthwerks was the seed for Panjea. Piles of money helped that seed grow."

Laughter.

But where did that money come from? Max thought.

"It seemed like a stupid idea to open an internet café. Even a few years ago, every coffee shop was pretty much an internet café. But Synthwerks was different. I thought so, anyway."

Applause.

"Why do people go online?" Ignacio asked.

"Porn!" someone called.

Ignacio laughed. "Yes, but it has to be bigger than that."

"That's what she said!" the same voice shouted.

"I guess I walked into that one," Ignacio said.

"That's what she said!"

Ignacio smiled.

"Escape!" Print called next to Max. Ignacio looked straight at them, and even though Max was wearing a mask, he felt like the man could see right through it.

"Interesting. Porn is a form of escape, isn't it? That's a good point." Ignacio looked at the heckler. "If you say that joke again, you're out." His voice had a hard edge to it, and his smile only made it more malicious. Then, his lighter tone was back again. "Well, my theory was that people are seeking other people like them, and it's easier to find them on the internet.

"The media often suggests that people who spend too much time online are antisocial, but I don't think that's true. We are *very* social, but our concept of society has to change and expand to include online interactions.

"So Synthwerks was a place where people could go be online together. Everyone who signed in could message anyone else in the café, converse in a chat group. Over the intranet, you could see what people had on their screens, but monitors had privacy filters and partitions between work stations so your neighbors didn't know what you, personally, were looking at. Big displays around the room also cycled randomly through everyone's screens making it easy to find out what others were into.

"And it worked. We were so popular we were turning people away! It was a bold experiment in anonymous disclosure. Synthwerks was helping to connect people with common interests. If you saw someone watching *My Little Pony*—" Cheers and whoops drowned him out for a moment. He held up a hand and continued when they quieted down. "If you saw someone watching something you liked, you could contact them through the intranet. You could watch the same episode together. And then, when you were ready, you could meet in person and have a cup of coffee together.

"*Wired* called it a 'bizarre social experiment,' but they changed their tune last month when Panjea was the topic of their feature story, didn't they? Is there anyone from *Wired* here? No, don't raise your hands. I don't want to know. Or maybe I already know. . . ."

Nervous laughter. *If only he were kidding.*

"To those critics, I said, life is a bizarre social experiment. I used Synthwerks too, but no one knew I owned the place, that I had dreamed it up. But no one really cared who had created it, because it already belonged to everyone. And hackers might like getting attention, but they like not getting caught even more. Am I right?"

Enthusiastic clapping.

"So, working out in the open like that, but behind a kind of blind, allowed hackers like you to brag about your abilities publicly without being *too* public. And the best thing is, the network was stable and secure, so we were protected from outside hackers. I realized that having hackers around, who were invested in the system they worked with, was like having technical support engineers pay *me* to keep it running. Now that's a good business model.

"Synthwerks became more than I had imagined. It was organic; its own little ecosystem. It evolved into a hackerspace that members used to collaborate on projects in perfect anonymity. I had plans to franchise it, open similar places all over the country, carry on my vision. But then I had a better idea, to expand the Synthwerks philosophy to the internet, where it can reach everyone, everywhere, all at once. I want to unite hackers, and unite the world."

Unite it, or conquer it? If the hackers in this room learned that Panjea had been sending information about every user to the government—maybe even their current locations—it would be mutiny. Max was tempted to shout out the truth to everyone there, but he knew that wouldn't go well for him.

Ignacio paused expectantly. Print started clapping and others followed suit. Max joined in.

"That brings me back to the idea of privacy. These days, I know this topic is a big deal. We all want to share everything, yet share nothing. With Panjea, the way I imagine it, everyone can see everything any time."

"Especially Big Brother," Max muttered.

"The only important thing is information, and everyone should have it. The problem is that when a person is linked to information—the source, the creator, the user—people tend to want to limit it. Privacy is all well and good, but identity is also inextricably linked with ego. I know a lot about ego!"

He sure did.

"The masks are a way of stripping away ego. They aren't about protecting identity, they're about downplaying it. Who you are doesn't matter. These masks, they don't even matter. You think a piece of plastic can protect you if someone wants to know your secrets?" Ignacio's gaze was sweeping the room, but Max swore it lingered on him. Then Ignacio turned.

"So this is your chance. I invite anyone out there who is daring enough: Take off your mask!"

Ignacio took his off and rested it on the podium. He looked around the room.

The lights came up halfway and everyone looked at one another. As the moment stretched on, Ignacio straightened.

"No one?" He looked around. "Well, we have an exciting twenty-four hours ahead. I hope you're well-rested and well-caffeinated. We will be holding a number of workshops, panels, and discussions here in this auditorium, along with other activities in conference rooms and workspaces throughout the other floors. *Mi casa es su casa.* And at the end of it all, I'm going to ask again for volunteers to remove their masks, and we'll see if any of you have changed your minds. At the very least, you'll be sleep deprived and your judgment will be compromised." He smiled.

"A little housekeeping: Details about our challenge quests this weekend are all in your packets and in the HackerAid app,

but feel free to visit the registration desk or stop me or another
Panjea staff member if you have any questions. There are show-
ers in the gym downstairs, next to the cafeteria. *Use them.* And
we have a zero tolerance policy of harassment; if anyone makes
you feel uncomfortable, speak to one of the toasters and we
will handle it." He gestured to the Cylon guards by the doors.

Ignacio clapped his hands again. "Now go make awesome
stuff!"

This started off another flood of applause. Max glanced
behind him and saw the Cylons had opened the doors again.

"That was disturbing," Max said.

"You think so?" Print said. "I think it's all really exciting."

"Why didn't you take off your mask?" Max asked.

"Because this is the one place where people judge me for
what I can do instead of what I look like."

From Evan's file, he knew that print*is*dead's real name
was Timothy Hawson. His picture had shown a doughy face
covered in eczema.

"Can you point me to a workstation?" Max asked.

"Allow me, Max." The synthetic voice sent a chill down
Max's spine. Print backed away, waving and muttering an
excuse.

Max turned around.

"Evan?"

23

MAX SAW A FIGURE IN A FAMILIAR WHITE MASK, WITH large, evil eyes and a grimacing mouth. A red hoodie was pulled up over his head, with a black T-shirt underneath. Gray cargo pants.

"Evan?" Max asked again, his voice cracking.

"You like it? I wanted to pay a tribute to our dear friend STOP."

Then Max realized. "That's in poor taste," Max said.

Wearing a mask like Evan's, with that flat, robotic voice. . . he was straight out of Max's nightmares. But after the initial shock, Max noticed he was taller and broader-shouldered than Evan. His body language was completely different too. Evan had always been fidgety, constantly in motion when he wasn't behind a keyboard. But this guy was strangely, eerily still.

"You know who I am, but who are you?" Max asked.

"0MN1. Good to finally meet." He extended a hand to Max. Max hesitated before shaking it.

"How about a behind-the-scenes tour?" 0MN1 said. "I want you to meet some more of my friends upstairs."

"Great. Thanks for the sponsorship," Max said. "How did you know I was coming?"

"I was hoping you would, so we would have a chance to talk."

Max nodded. He wondered what 0MN1 wanted with him. If he played along, this could provide the opportunity he'd been hoping for to infiltrate Panjea's servers.

0MN1 guided him to an elevator and took him to the third floor. "This is the heart of Panjea. Programmers are up here, doing the real work, and all the business stuff is on the second floor. PR, marketing, graphics."

Max's phone buzzed. He snuck a peek at it. A text from Penny: looking for open conference room with a live jack

"Are all Panjea programmers hackers like us?" Max asked.

0MN1 led him past rows of cubicles, five-by-five spaces, each one identical but for a few indications of the personality of the occupant: action figures, comic books, printouts of celebrities. Photos of kids and dogs and spouses. One of them even had a replica of an axe from *The Lord of the Rings* balanced on a shelf, surrounded by hobbit figurines.

"Every company has an A-team. Here, those are the hackers. The grunt programmers handle basic maintenance, server expansion, software implementation, that kind of thing."

"STOP worked here, right?" Max asked.

"His station was over there." 0MN1 pointed to the center of the room. There was a pod with ten workstations facing each other in a circle. Only two of the stations were occupied. 0MN1 waved. "Hey guys! Look, it's 503-ERROR. I told you he'd show."

"What up." A twenty-year-old guy stood to greet Max. He was thin with a goatee and a too-large flannel shirt with the sleeves rolled up. He looked a lot like Shaggy from the *Scooby Doo* cartoons. His Panjea badge identified him as Nolan Harrison, but Max recognized him from the photo in PHYREWALL's file. His real name was Nat Hardy.

The hackers were using aliases IRL too. It seemed trust only went so far when you were routinely breaking the law and there was always the chance that a supposed friend was reporting back to the FBI.

The second hacker didn't stand. He spoke up in a soft, depressed voice that reminded Max of Eeyore. "Hey, Five-Oh-Three. I'm GroundSloth."

GroundSloth! Evan hadn't had a good photo of him, but he knew the heavyset man was thirty-three and named Oliver Morton, even though his badge identified him as Austin Rhodes.

PHYREWALL was from Cleveland, Ohio, and GroundSloth was from Syracuse, New York. Did they work here all the time, or were they just in town for Haxx0rade?

"It's weird to meet in person." Max shook their hands.

Sweat pooled on his upper lip and he felt his mask sliding down his forehead. He grabbed it from the bottom and started to lift. He paused, eyeing the others. There was no point in hiding his face here—they all knew who he really was, thanks to the news. Still, anticipation and anxiety over what he was about to do made his pulse quicken.

Max pulled off the mask. The cool air felt good on his bare face. He slicked his damp hair back.

He looked at 0MN1 expectantly, but his host made no move to follow suit.

"Pretty ballsy to come here, with everyone in the world after you," PHYREWALL said.

"If any place is safe for him, it's here," 0MN1 said. "We're all wanted by the Feds. We protect our own."

"Is that right? What about Infiltraitor, @sskicker, and L0NELYB0Y?" Max asked.

"No one knows what happened to them," 0MN1 said.

"L0NELYB0Y's holed up in the woods somewhere. Living off the land," PHYREWALL said.

0MN1 shot him a warning look.

"Well, that's what I heard," PHYREWALL said.

"Evan doxxed everyone in Dramatis Personai. Those guys aren't just 'offline.'" Max said. "They're dead."

PHYREWALL laughed.

"What's funny about that?" Max asked.

"He couldn't have doxxed everyone," PHYREWALL said.

"He doxxed you, *Nat*," Max said.

PHYREWALL froze.

"Nat?" GroundSloth chuckled.

"It's not as nice a name as Oliver, is it?"

GroundSloth's jaw went slack.

"Evan knew the identities of the other members of Dramatis Personai, and he found out about the ones that died under mysterious circumstances. Other people too. Did any of you know Ariel Miller? She was a hacker who worked here just like you, and coincidentally, she's dead too," Max said.

PHYREWALL turned to 0MN1. "Was she that cute redhead?"

"Panjea employs a lot of hackers," 0MN1 said.

PHYREWALL sat down at his computer and typed. "Damn. He's right."

PHYREWALL's screen showed the same article that Evan had copied into Ariel's file. But Max was much more interested in what was next to PHYREWALL's computer: a small silver globe mounted on a circular base.

He slowly moved to PHYREWALL's side, pretending to look at the article. The surface of the globe was covered in faint lines—broken into puzzle shapes. The word *PANJEA* was printed across it, but the piece marked with the *N* was missing. Max had to get a closer look at it. It might just be a paperweight, but he was willing to bet that Ariel had one just like it.

"Ariel was killed six months ago," PHYREWALL said.

"That hit-and-run was intentional. She was targeted," Max

said. "Murdered."

PHYREWALL was visibly shaken. He looked at 0MN1. "Did you know about this?"

"Max, can we talk somewhere more private?" 0MN1 gestured to a long conference table by the window, right below the last *A* in Panjea. Max nodded and followed him.

"Have a seat," 0MN1 said.

Max ignored him and headed for the window. He looked down to the street below and saw three black cars line up across from where Risse was parked. On cue, his phone buzzed in his pocket, but he couldn't look at it now. Instead, he studied 0MN1's reflection in the glass.

"Did STOP dox me too?" 0MN1 asked.

"No, but I can make an educated guess. You're the only member of Dramatis Personai he didn't identify, and you're also the one who has been acting like he's in charge—even though the group isn't supposed to have a leader. Considering DP's stance against big corporations, namely Panjea's competitors, I'm willing to bet you're the person in charge here. Victor."

0MN1 tilted his head. Then he pulled off his mask. Victor Ignacio took a deep breath. "Why don't we start again? Hi, Max. I'm Vic Ignacio. It's good to meet face-to-face."

Max felt a little lightheaded. He'd been pretty sure that Vic Ignacio and 0MN1 were the same person, but it had still felt like a gamble, which had paid off. 0MN1 could have kept his mask on and laughed it off, so why had he finally revealed himself?

"Did you mean all that stuff you said in your speech?" Max asked.

"Did I sound like I meant it?"

"Yes."

"That's what matters." Vic pushed his hood back and rubbed the top of his bald head. "You might be surprised to hear this, but I'm glad you figured out who I am."

"Why?"

"I hate wearing masks. You can't speak in these things." Vic laughed.

Max allowed a thin smile, humoring Vic.

"Truthfully? I like surrounding myself with smart people. It's how I've become so successful." Vic winked. "Our little secret."

"Online you were very interested in knowing if Evan had sent me anything before he died," Max said.

Vic had taken off his mask, but it was like he was still wearing one. Max knew what a strain it was to put up a front for others, in order to get people to like you or help you. That pasted-on smile never left the CEO's face, but his eyes betrayed that Max had his attention.

"Maybe you were worried about some e-mails about your selling Panjea data to Kevin Sharpe, and that you're basically working for the government?"

Vic blinked. "Max, you have it wrong." He sounded almost disappointed.

"You're a big fan of transparency. Let's see what happens

when I release those files and we let the public decide," Max said.

Max's phone vibrated again, twice in quick succession. He could feel the urgency behind the messages, but Penny and Risse were on their own for now.

"That's not what I'm interested in," Vic said.

"What about SH1FT?" Max said.

Vic paused, calculating. Then he came to a decision.

"You have the code?" Vic asked.

"I know where it is."

"It's stolen property."

"Come on. That means nothing to a hacker. The theft didn't harm anyone, and information belongs to everyone, right? And so does the truth."

"I wouldn't say *no one* was harmed by its loss," Vic said.

Max felt a chill. "Are you admitting murder?"

"I didn't kill anyone," Vic said.

"But you knew people were being killed."

"That's ridiculous."

"You knew Ariel's death wasn't an accident. Maybe you were even the one who sent the order to remove evidence of her employment with Panjea. But whoever you sent missed something." Max flashed the puzzle piece. Vic's mask finally slipped and he showed genuine surprise.

"Whether you killed them or just let it happen, it's all the same result. My friend is gone, and six others are dead."

"Evan's death was his own choice. I didn't pull that trigger.

But I'll make you the same offer I made him, and I hope things will turn out differently this time."

Vic put his hand inside the pocket of his hoodie. Max readied himself to fight or bolt.

Vic removed his hand and showed. . . a phone.

He held it up and pointed it at Max, as if he knew what he was thinking.

"These days this can be much more powerful and devastating than a gun." Vic turned and aimed his phone at the fifty-inch monitor on the wall. He pressed a button and the screen lit up. A series of video windows appeared. The first one showed Max's dad talking on his phone. The second showed Courtney in her bedroom walking past the camera in a bathrobe. The third showed Lianna Stein in an office, typing.

Mom?

Max took a step forward. He hadn't seen his mother since he was five years old, but he recognized her immediately. Her black hair was shoulder length now and she was wearing glasses, but it was her. The woman who had virtually disappeared. How had Vic tracked her down, when Max and even Evan had failed to?

The images froze.

"When I ask you about SH1FT again, I want you to think about your friends and family, Max," Vic said.

Max tore his eyes away from the video image of his mother. If Vic knew how important it was for Max to find her, he would make Max a deal he might not be able to refuse.

Max looked out the window again. Four FBI agents in

black vests were hurrying from their cars toward the building. At least they didn't seem to notice the car Risse was waiting in.

Max's heart was pounding. He wasn't sure which fate was worse: getting picked up by the Feds, or being stuck here with Vic.

The CEO switched the screen to a security feed from the Panjea lobby. The agents were walking inside.

"Right now, this is the safest place you could be. If you help me recover the software Evan stole, I'll consider you a temporary employee of Panjea, with all the protection that offers. When I have what I need, I'll do what I can to clear your name and send you home to the people you love, safe and sound."

"And if I don't help?"

"I could let those agents take you. They have a lot of questions about Evan and your history as 503-ERROR." Vic put his phone away. "Sabotaging private websites through DDoS attacks is very illegal. I'll get what I want. One way or another."

"I'll think about it," Max said.

"Think quickly."

Max heard a phone buzz, but this time it wasn't his. Vic pulled his phone out again and answered.

"Keep her there. I'll be right down," Vic said.

Penny.

"Don't go anywhere, Max. I'll be right back to hear your answer." Vic pointed at the screen then grabbed his mask and hurried away, leaving one of his Cylon guards behind to watch Max.

24

MAX PRESSED HIS FACE AGAINST THE GLASS AND looked down onto Folsom Street, three stories down. Three 25-foot stories. Even if he could get this window open, that was too far a drop to work as an escape route, no matter how desperate he was.

Max opened HackerAid on his phone. He searched for Penny's handle, ^vengerGurl. She was still in the basement.

Max headed back towards the workstations. The guard didn't try to stop him; he just trailed a few steps behind so Max knew he was there. Max spun around and stared him down. Hard to tell with the visor, but the guard seemed startled. He gave Max a little more space, but he held his hand on his holstered Taser.

Max doubted the guard would let him leave the floor, or sit

down at an empty computer and upload the modified SH1FT program. Max had to figure out how to shake him and complete his mission.

There was a stairwell past the workstations in the far corner of the floor, but that door was being watched too—not by a Haxx0rade Cylon, but by a man built like a linebacker and dressed as a Secret Service agent, minus the official lapel pin. Another equally large man in a matching suit was stationed in front of the elevator.

Vic had his own security goons?

PHYREWALL and GroundSloth were still working at their desks. Max had a copy of SH1FT on the USB drive around his neck, but he didn't think he could convince them to install it on the server. Despite their doubts, they seemed loyal to Vic and Panjea, and they didn't have any reason to trust Max.

He had to change that.

He approached the hackers, unsure of what they were going to say or do. They eyed him warily.

"So. Vic's 0MN1," Max said. "I didn't see that coming."

"Isn't he great?" GroundSloth said.

"Meh. He's a script kiddie," PHYREWALL said.

Interesting. Not everyone liked Vic after all.

"You mean he isn't really a hacker?" Max asked.

"He thinks he is, but he's not a very good one," PHYRE-WALL said. "He's great at recruiting though. He may not be able to code on his own, but he knows how to get the best to work for Panjea. STOP was a good guy. You'd be a good addition to the team."

"Not sure he wants me for the team, or that I want to join. Does Vic always keep a guard on you?" Max asked.

"I thought they were here for you," GroundSloth said. "What happened over there?"

"Vic gave me his best sales pitch. I'm still trying to make up my mind. Panjea has a great salary and benefits, but there's that tiny chance of being murdered," Max said.

"What are you talking about?" PHYREWALL said.

"If Vic didn't order the death of Ariel and your Dramatis Personai friends, then he helped set them up. He's the only person other than Evan who knew who they all were in real life, and the only one with any power. If he wants to stop them from telling the world that Panjea's crooked, he knows people in high places who can make that happen."

"I don't believe it. Vic's not like that," PHYREWALL said.

"Hey, what's that thing?" Max pointed at the silver globe on PHYREWALL's desk.

"Why do you care?" GroundSloth said, an edge in his voice.

"It would make a great souvenir. Does the gift shop have them? Does Panjea have a gift shop?" Max asked.

"PHYREWALL," GroundSloth said.

PHYREWALL picked up the globe and put it in his desk drawer.

"What about this?" Max asked. He held up Ariel's puzzle piece. PHYREWALL's eyebrows shot up and he frantically patted his pocket. He pulled out another puzzle piece and relaxed for a moment.

"Where did you get that?" GroundSloth reached for it, but Max yanked his hand back.

"Ariel had it," Max said.

"She couldn't have. Vic only gives these to. . . well, us." PHYREWALL exchanged a glance with GroundSloth. "If Ariel had one, she must have been working on something important. Something we don't know about." He looked like he was going to be sick.

"And if she betrayed his trust by revealing something about Panjea. . . ?" Max said.

"Vic wouldn't take it well," said PHYREWALL.

Max pocketed Ariel's puzzle piece. He caught GroundSloth watching him closely.

"Ariel wasn't in Dramatis Personai, but she turned to the group for help, six months ago. She logged in to the forum as 'dinglehopper,'" Max said. "Two weeks later, she was dead."

"Oh shit," PHYREWALL said. "That was her?"

"She didn't know 0MN1 was her boss, but he obviously figured out who she was. You said he recruits lots of hackers. He—"

A loud alarm started ringing. Strobe lights flashed.

"What's that?" asked Max.

PHYREWALL groaned. "Fire alarm."

"Again? I'm just going to stay here and keep working," GroundSloth said.

"Does this happen often?" Max asked.

"Like once a month. It's an old building. We have to evacuate," PHYREWALL said.

"Fine." GroundSloth heaved himself out of his chair with a long sigh. He held onto his desk unsteadily.

Max followed them to the emergency stairs. The faux-Secret Service agents waited until he had gone through the door, then followed him down.

Shoot, Max thought. Now he had three guards following him. He had to get away from these guys.

He got his chance when they went down the stairs and people from the second floor jammed into the stairwell. The stream of hackers pushed their way in, oblivious to the people around them because their masks were limiting their vision, or maybe because they just cared about saving themselves. Within seconds, Max was cut off from the others.

Now or never.

He pulled off his badge, tucked it into the hood of someone ahead of him, ducked down and curled into a ball near the wall. People kicked him on their way down, shoved and cursed at him.

He waited until he thought PHYREWALL and Ground-Sloth and the guards had passed him. Then he popped up and elbowed his way back up the stairs.

After he passed the second floor landing, the stairs were clear. He kept going up, stumbling over his flip-flops until he finally kicked them off and went barefoot. He burst back on to the third floor and bolted down the side aisle.

He slid to a halt when he found the cubicle with the axe. He grabbed it. The prop felt solid and real. It wasn't sharp, but it could do some damage. He grabbed the red fire warden hat as well and put it on.

Max looked at the computer terminals in the center of the floor. This was his chance to install SH1FT. But the distraction of the fire alarm wouldn't go on for much longer. If Penny was in trouble, he had to find her and get them both out of there and past the FBI. But he wasn't going to leave empty-handed.

Max hurried to PHYREWALL's desk and tried the drawer. Unlocked. He slid it open, nabbed the globe, then jammed the fist-sized object into his messenger bag. It was lighter than it looked, like it was hollow.

As he slid the drawer closed, he caught a glimpse of silver at the bottom. He reached in and came up with another puzzle piece that had been stuck to the inside of the metal drawer. This one was marked with an *N* where the piece had been removed from the globe.

Max dropped the puzzle piece into his pocket. He felt it click and latch with Ariel's.

Finally, he checked HackerAid on his phone. Most of the dots, hackers and staff alike, were moving toward the exits around the main floor—including the one labeled as him. He thumbed down to the lower level and saw a red dot in a basement conference room. ^venger Gurl. Penny.

Max glanced at the computers one last time then ran back

to the stairway and clattered down the steps. He flew down to the second floor. Everyone must have already evacuated. He hit the first floor landing and started squeezing past some people coming up from the basement.

"Excuse me! Sorry, coming through!" He raised his axe above their heads and they got out of the way.

Max jumped the last few steps to the basement landing and hit the ground running. He ignored the pain in his feet.

"Penny!" Max shouted. He ran past the cafeteria. There was another row of conference rooms down here. The fire alarm was more muffled, but lights flashed up and down the hallway.

"Penny?"

Max heard a thumping sound on the far end. And a familiar voice. "Let me out!"

There she was.

The room Penny was in was named Thunderdome. Max jiggled the handle. Locked. Penny pounded at the door.

"Hello? Help!" she called. "I'm trapped in here."

"Penny, it's me," he said.

"Max! The door locked while I was trying to hack into the server. Then the alarm went off."

"The building's surrounded by FBI agents."

"I tried to pick the lock with a paper clip—" Penny said.

"You can do that?"

"Apparently not."

He looked around. The floor was clear. The last few people

were trickling into a stairwell on the other end of the floor. They would have to hurry if they wanted to blend in with the crowd.

"Stand back from the door. I'm going to hack in."

"Max, no offense, but even I couldn't hack it."

"Penny, just get back!"

Max stood with his legs apart and tested the weight of the axe again. He cocked it behind his shoulder and took a slow practice swing at the door handle.

"On three! One. Two. Three!"

He took a real swing and sliced through the metal doorknob like it was butter. *Bashed* more than sliced with the blunt edge, but it got the job done. The metal frame around the knob shattered and clattered to the floor.

Penny pushed the door open with a stunned expression. She had lost her mask too.

"You have a hatchet," she said.

"Battle axe," he growled. He grinned and leaned it against the door.

"Sometimes the best tech—" Penny began.

"Is low tech," Max finished. He'd heard Evan say that dozens of times.

Max held out a hand. "You ready to go?"

"Beyond ready."

She took his hand.

"Run!" he said.

They ran. He led her to the stairs and they hurried to catch up with the tail end of the crowd of employees ascending to the first floor.

"The FBI agents waiting outside are checking everyone as they exit," he said.

"Is there another exit?" Penny asked.

Max checked the HackerAid map. "Auditorium. Probably also guarded," Max said. "We have to assume they're at all the exits. They're really serious this time. They know I'm here."

"We should split up," Penny said.

"Not again," Max said. He squeezed her hand. "Any ideas?"

"We could hide somewhere," Penny said.

"It'll just get harder to sneak out when it's full of people again."

"Get new masks?" Penny asked.

"They're checking everyone."

"I bet that's going over well."

Max stopped walking. "Wait. They're looking for me."

"Max. No," Penny said. "That already worked once. They won't fall for it again."

"I can turn myself in. While they're busy with me, you and Risse can drive away."

"We'll think of something else," Penny said.

"It's too late." They were nearly at the doors. Max handed her the USB drive with SH1FT on it. She might not get another chance to install it, but they could keep it out of Panjea's hands and add it to the rest of the evidence of what they were planning. He also handed her Ariel's puzzle piece and explained what it was.

"One more thing, and this is a big one: Vic Ignacio is 0MN1."

"What?" Penny said. Her surprise quickly turned to anger. "Evan said he couldn't be trusted."

"Think he knew about it?"

"Evan would have found a way to warn me. It would have been in his files. 0MN1 must have kept his identity from him too. God, and we came right to Vic."

They were just about to step outside.

"It's time," Max said. "You hang back and get ready to run."

He lowered his head and studied the crowd, still looking for a path to escape as he came through the doors, Penny just behind him, still holding his hand.

His whole body was tense, ready to spring into action. He raised his head slowly. Vic was standing in the middle of the street, watching everyone who exited. Vic locked eyes with Max for a long moment then murmured something to a tall man standing beside him. A man in a gray turtleneck, with his arms crossed.

Kevin Sharpe.

Max almost lost his nerve when Sharpe turned and faced him.

Max dropped Penny's hand.

Sharpe leaned toward Vic and whispered in his ear. Vic shrugged, and Sharpe walked away. He quickly disappeared into the crowd.

Max raised his hand to the brim of his hat. He was about to pull it off and step forward when Vic shouted.

"There he is!" Vic turned and pointed. Across the street—in the opposite direction from where Max was standing. A figure bolted down the sidewalk, his flannel shirt flapping behind him. It looked like PHYREWALL, but why was Vic sending the FBI after his own employee? Five agents chased after him.

"What?" Max lowered his hat again and Penny pulled him to the right, to where Risse was waiting in the idling BMW.

"No, no." Max yanked his arm away from her. "We should split up to be safe. Meet me at Fisherman's Wharf, near the big sign."

"Max, come on. You aren't even wearing shoes," Penny said.

He grinned. "I've always wanted to try running barefoot." He nudged Penny along and pushed off into the mass of people.

He was bumped and jostled as he squeezed through the tightly packed clusters of hackers. Most of them had replaced their masks and had their phones out, posting pictures and updates *about* Panjea *to* Panjea, while moving slowly away from the building. He heard them speculating about the fire alarm and the presence of the FBI, wondering if this was some kind of trap.

"Now what do we do?" someone whined.

"We have twenty-four hours in San Francisco. Let's do everything!"

"What about the million dollar prize?"

"Like you would have won anyway."

"I knew I shouldn't have come."

"If Feds are here, there must have been a high value target," one girl said. "I know some Personai members were supposed to be coming."

"Vic Ignacio wouldn't sell out hackers to the FBI," a boy replied.

If you only knew, Max thought as he pressed between them and worked his way to the head of the crowd. He was making halting progress, but every painful step was taking him farther away from Vic and his minions.

Max flinched when someone stamped on the toes of his right foot. Someone kicked his shin and he sucked in a breath. Fortunately the crowd was moving roughly in the direction he wanted, but he needed to split off from the main group soon. Penny and Risse would be waiting.

"Watch it!" someone said.

Max glanced behind him and saw there were three guards in Cylon masks pushing toward him. The guys he'd given the slip to earlier? Two more guards were converging on him from either side, Tasers in their hands. They were only about twenty feet away and having better luck moving through the crowd, seemingly without a care to who they elbowed, shoved, and knocked down to get to him.

Angry shouts were rippling through the group now, and Max felt a shift in attitude as people shoved back.

Max shielded his face when someone pointed a phone at him, camera facing out, to get a recording of the approaching guards.

"Sorry, man," the guy said.

Max shrugged and sidestepped him. If people posted complaints about being stomped by guards dressed as Cylons, Vic was going to have a PR situation on his hands.

He was now on the edge of the crowd, which had stopped moving and seemed to be turning in on itself. The Cylons were stuck, swarmed on all sides by angry hackers blocking them with their arms, grabbing onto their clothes, flashing photos and taking video. Someone grabbed one of their masks and held it up like a trophy, whooping.

Max backed away. This was turning ugly.

Red flashed in Max's eyes. He blinked and looked down as a red dot traveled down his chest.

Shit.

He heard a loud pop, from somewhere in the middle of the crowd. A teenaged boy on Max's left stiffened and fell backward with a garbled cry.

Max hopped away as the kid arched his back and convulsed with a plastic wire attached to his right arm. A sizzling sound filled the air. Then people screamed.

Max turned and ran. He heard another pop behind him, the buzz of electricity from a stun gun, more screaming. Someone yanked on his shirt, but he pulled free. He kept going and left the crowds behind him.

Max reached 8th and Hyde just as an F Line streetcar was pulling away. He hopped on and fell into an open seat, looking back toward the sound of sirens in the direction from which he'd come. His feet burned. Their soles were raw, and his calves ached. But he was pretty sure he hadn't been followed.

25

MAX HEARD A TONE IN HIS EARS. IT WAS RISSE calling. He'd forgotten he was still wearing his earbuds. He answered the phone.

"You're a stubborn ass," Penny said.

"You and Risse are safe?" he asked. He steadied his breathing. The adrenaline high was finally wearing off, and fatigue was setting in.

"What's taking you so long? Pier 39 is super crowded."

"Good." He picked a tiny piece of glass from the ball of his right foot. He squeezed his eyes shut and clenched his teeth from the pain. He wiped his bloody fingers on his pants. "I'll be there in twenty minutes."

Max was relieved to see Penny and Risse. They were lingering near the Fisherman's Wharf sign, people-watching and eating cupcakes. He limped up to them.

"Max!" Penny said. "You made it."

She hugged him.

"I'm glad you two are all right," he said. "Where's the car?"

"In the garage," Risse said.

They walked there together. Risse gave him half of her cupcake.

"Whew," Penny said. "That was way too close."

"Tell me about it," Max said.

"What happened? Were you really going to turn yourself in?" Risse asked.

"I was. But Vic saw me and it seems like he set up a distraction of his own so the FBI wouldn't get me." He explained how he thought PHYREWALL had been sent to divert the agents, giving Max and Penny time to escape.

"He let you go?" Risse asked.

"Vic doesn't let things go. He sent his own people after me, but I managed to get away. He wants SH1FT, and for now, he thinks he has a better chance of getting it without involving the FBI. It looked like he was taking orders from Sharpe."

"So he doesn't want the FBI to have SH1FT," Penny said.

"I thought the government was working with Panjea?" Risse said.

"Sometimes the right hand doesn't know what the left is doing," Max said. "Sharpe and his team are with the government, but they're as much on the wrong side of the law as Panjea is. Maybe the FBI doesn't know and is working against them too. Better to keep SH1FT in our hands than see me get arrested, have it fall into the hands of the FBI and risk public exposure.

"I think PHYREWALL doesn't like Vic much. And GroundSloth could be persuaded to our side," Max continued. "Did you get anywhere with the server?"

"No." Penny scowled. "It's like the production servers aren't even in the building, or they're so locked down I couldn't see them. Did you have any luck?"

"All I got was this, but it could be something." Max handed them the globe he'd stolen from PHYREWALL.

"It's a 3–D puzzle," Risse said. She turned it over. "Look at this." She pointed out a small LCD display embedded in the bottom of the base. Max passed her PHYREWALL's puzzle piece, and she slotted it into its matching shape on the globe, completing the puzzle. As soon as it clicked into place, six numbers appeared on the LCD screen.

"A security token," Penny said.

Max's dad had a security token for work, but it was just an app on his phone. It generated a number that would authenticate a remote user on a system. As Max watched the Panjea token, the code scrambled and changed.

"Why would they need this at Panjea, where they should have direct access to all the systems?" Max took the device back and examined it.

"Extra security?" Risse said.

It would make sense for Ariel to have one of these devices if she needed to access Panjea's server from home. Max removed the piece with the first *A* in Panjea. The numbers disappeared from the LCD display.

The piece was identical to Ariel's, and when he inserted her magnetic puzzle piece instead, the numbers reappeared. The completed 3–D puzzle must close a circuit and turn on the display.

"Maybe the servers are located somewhere else, like you suggested," Max said. "Penny?"

She seemed preoccupied. He couldn't blame her. She'd been locked in a room, closer than she had ever been to being arrested.

"So this was a waste of time," Penny said. "We shouldn't have risked it."

"We got some good information," Max said. And now he knew for certain that his mother was out there somewhere, and it was possible to find her.

"We also got this." Risse pressed a button on her phone. Its speaker played and Max heard Vic's voice.

"When I ask you about SH1FT again, I want you to think about your friends and family, Max."

A shiver ran down his back. "Risse, you hacked my phone?" Max asked.

"It's easy when you can get your hands on it," Risse said.

Max reached into his pocket but his phone wasn't there. Risse smiled and handed it to him.

"You're a pickpocket," he said.

"It's a gift," she said.

"You got our whole conversation?"

She nodded. "Not entirely a confession, but he doesn't sound innocent, either."

Penny looked distraught.

"He gave Evan the same ultimatum," Max said. "And it worked, but not the way he was expecting. It looks like our next stop is to find Panjea's servers."

Penny put a hand on his arm to slow him down. She let Risse get several feet ahead of them.

Penny took a deep breath. "Max. . . ."

"Uh-oh," he said, sensing what was coming.

"We can't do this anymore. We're done," Penny said.

"You're leaving?" Max asked.

"We have to. I'm sorry. I know you've given up everything to see Evan's mission through, but I'm not prepared to do that. For her." Her eyes flicked to Risse, who was looking around happily at the stores along the pier.

"I understand," Max said.

"You do?"

"I would do the same thing. You have to think about Risse, and your mom. Look, I tried to get out too, because it was dangerous. I totally get it. I really appreciate what you two have done. I couldn't have gotten this far without you."

"That's what I'm worried about. Are you going to be okay?"

Max shrugged. "I'll figure something out."

"You're good at that. I. . . . Thank you for saving me back there."

"Whatever."

"Max, it's only going to get worse for you," Penny said.

"Your pep talks are almost as good as Coach Kim's. I know it sounds weird, but Vic's threat made me more committed to seeing this through." He didn't mention that Vic now had something that Max wanted: means to find his mom. "The only path out of this is finding a way to get the altered version of SH1FT online and getting the truth out there."

"Max, you can't." She held up her hands. "Sorry. That's not my call to make. You have to do what you have to do."

"You're right. You two need to go. In fact, I insist on it. They'll catch up to me sooner or later, and I don't want either of you to get dragged into this any further. They'll use our friendship against me. That's what they do."

When they got to the car in the garage, Max pulled on his sneakers and collected his things in his backpack. Risse eyed him warily.

"What are you up to?" she asked.

"This is where we part ways," he said.

"What? No! We're in this together, to the end."

"It's time to go home, Risse. We have to get back to our real lives," Penny said.

"You're that anxious to go back to school and your job and. . . Mama?"

"She's going to miss us if we're gone much longer," Penny said.

"No, she won't."

"School then. We can cover for some of the time we've missed, but if we're gone too long, it'll invite more questions. They'll figure out what we've been up to."

"But we're doing something. Finally! We've always talked about the good we were doing with Dramatis Personai, but that was just talk. Now here we are, fighting a real goddamn conspiracy. On the run from Men in Black. Exposing international crimes!"

"When you put it that way, it sounds kind of exciting," Penny said.

"It is!"

"It's also deadly, and you aren't taking it seriously. This isn't a game. Max and I might have disappeared today. We were lucky. We aren't cut out for this spy stuff."

"She's right." Max hated himself for saying it. "You've done enough already. I've got to handle this on my own from here. You guys have been amazing."

Risse started crying. "What did I do?"

"Oh, honey." Penny put her hand on Risse's shoulder. Risse jerked away.

"We can't give up. We're so close," Risse said.

"You're not giving up. You're my security. If something happens to me, you'll still have the information and you can release it. It's stupid for all of us to risk ourselves like this. We're the only ones who know the truth," Max said.

"It's time to go home," Penny said again.

"Penny, I know you're scared, but I'm not," Risse said.

"That's fine. I'm afraid enough for both of us."

"If I could go home too, I would," Max said.

Risse folded her arms and lowered her head. "This is wrong. We have a responsibility. This is way bigger than us."

"*You're* my responsibility," Penny said. "You're the only thing I care about. All of this. . . . It's *too* big for us. It'll sort itself out."

Max didn't believe that any more than Penny did, but he supported her lie.

"I couldn't have come this far without you," Max said.

Risse's lower lip jutted forward. It was easy to forget she was still a kid, because she was so smart and capable. But this was the right thing to do.

She grabbed Max in a hug. Then she leaned up on her toes.

"I'm not giving up. I'm going to keep working on this. You stay in touch and let me know if you need me," she whispered in his ear.

Max smiled. "You'll know."

Penny walked up to Max. "I'm glad we met," she said.

"Me too. I wish we'd met sooner, under better circumstances."

"I wish we'll meet again. Under better circumstances." She offered Max her hand. He shook it. He held on a moment longer than he needed to.

She rolled her eyes then leaned in. She kissed him on the cheek. She pressed her face against his shoulder.

Risse honked the horn in the car.

Penny stepped back. "Suddenly she's in a hurry to get out of here."

"Watch yourself," Max said.

"Good luck, Max."

Penny got into the car and drove off.

Max looked around the garage.

"Now what?" he said.

26

MAX SAT IN THE DARK AT HIS MOTEL ROOM DESK, trying to decide what to do now that he was on his own. In front of him were his open laptop, the keycard Evan had left Max, Ariel's 3-D puzzle piece, and the USB drive containing SH1FT.

He had spent the night researching 0MN1. Now that Max knew 0MN1 was Vic Ignacio, there was a lot more information to be found on him. It didn't seem possible that 0MN1 could have kept his secret from Evan, but apparently Evan had missed a number of things in his investigation.

Most of the information Max found was about Vic's old company, Synthwerks, which he had talked about in such idealistic terms at Haxx0rade. It wasn't often that you heard a visionary express sentimentality for their old failures at the height of success, but to Max it had sounded like Vic missed those days, or hadn't completely given up on his original dream.

In a way, he hadn't: Synthwerks was literally and figuratively the foundation for Panjea. The small internet café had been converted into a server farm that supported Panjea's services. It was about an hour away from the Wherehouse, back in San Jose, close to where Ariel had lived.

Max stared at the dot representing Synthwerks on the map. *Could it be?* Penny had said it looked like the production servers weren't on-site in San Francisco. Ariel had had an authentication device that would give her remote access to a server.

Max turned the keycard over and over in his hand. If the card hadn't been configured for Panjea's main headquarters, maybe it could get him into the satellite office.

Well, it was worth a look.

Max got up and stretched the kinks out of his neck. He had been sitting in that chair all night, barely moving. He leaned over his computer and checked his e-mail again, hoping to hear from Penny or Risse. They should have gotten home hours ago. Maybe Penny had been serious about distancing herself, but Risse would have let Max know they'd gotten back to Roseburg safely.

The only new message was from his dad. It must be important if he'd tried to reach out to Max with a full-blown manhunt going on.

Max decrypted it with his private key and opened the e-mail. There was no message, just an attached file. Max clicked on it and a scanned page appeared. The upper right quadrant bore the blue word "Telegram". It had been sent priority to Max's home address.

Who still sent telegrams?

The only text in the body of the telegram was "38.504778, 122.973956."

Latitude and longitude.

"Okay, I'll bite." Max sat back down and copied the strings of numbers into an online map. He held his breath while the image re-centered around a forest, the thick leaves obscuring the satellite view. The coordinates matched a campground in Guerneville, California.

So that's where the middle of nowhere is.

Max would have ignored it and headed straight for the Synthwerks data center, but for the word "STOP" at the end of the line. It looked like a signature or part of the message, rather than its traditional telegram usage, to indicate punctuation.

Evan? Could he be alive after all?

The campsite was only ninety minutes away from his motel.

What the hell. It wasn't like he was going to be able to get any sleep tonight. If there was even the slightest possibility that this was Evan trying to reach him, he had to see it through.

Those ninety minutes by car didn't take into account the hour-long hike, in moonlight, to reach the precise location according to his phone's GPS.

As he neared the coordinates, Max moved more slowly,

taking light, careful steps and pausing frequently to listen for other footsteps in the woods around him. Over the course of his walk there, he had convinced himself that everything about this situation screamed *trap*. This could be Vic or his people trying to lure Max out alone, using his feelings about Evan against him.

Stupid, Max, he thought.

He had come this far already, and he didn't want to turn back without at least checking things out. Maybe if he was quiet enough he could get a look at the person waiting for him before he was noticed.

Max almost missed the tent, but when he stepped into a clearing, it suddenly appeared on an outcropping just above him. It glowed with a soft yellow light from within. His host was awake, at least.

Max crept toward the tent softly—and tripped a string tied with cans that made a terrible racket. The light inside the tent was instantly extinguished.

Max froze and pressed his lips together. The slightest movement would disturb the cans wrapped around his ankles.

The silence stretched out, making him more and more uncomfortable. He felt like eyes were watching all around him. His skin crawled.

He couldn't take it anymore.

"Um. Hello? I got your telegram," Max called.

"Yo," a voice said behind Max. He jumped then tried to take a step backward. His feet got even more tangled, and he fell on his ass.

"Is that a phone?" The figure was cast in shadows. Max squinted up at him.

Max glanced at the phone in his hand stupidly. "Yeah."

"You can't bring that here, man. What's wrong with you?"

"I needed the GPS to find you," Max said.

The man sighed. "Turn it off now. Take the battery out. Bury it under that rock."

"You want me to bury my phone?"

"Yeah, man."

Max switched his phone off and pulled out the battery. He dug a loose grave for his phone, nestled it in the earth, then pushed soil back over it. He crawled over to a rock and rolled it over his phone so he could hopefully find it later. "Okay. Will you help me up now?"

The man crouched and cut the string binding Max's feet with a scary-looking hunting knife Max hadn't noticed him holding. He suppressed a shudder. The man walked toward his tent and went around the back. A moment later, the light switched back on and the zipper came down. A flap fell open, revealing the man sitting cross-legged inside, backlit by an electric lantern.

"Can I come in?" Max asked.

The man opened his arms wide.

Max ducked down and entered the tent. He leaned down to zip it up behind him, then turned around.

"Whoa," Max said.

There were stacks of computer printouts on every square

inch of the tiny tent's floor. There was an actual bed made out of reams of paper, with a blanket and pillow on top of it. The pages were printed on those old, continuous feed pages.

Max coughed. The tent reeked of pot.

"You must be Max." The guy was about Max's age, dressed in a wrinkled, white linen shirt, the underarms stained yellow, and hemp pants. He hadn't shaved in months or brushed his bird's nest of hair, so he looked like a castaway on a desert island.

"Jeremy Seer? L0NELYB0Y?" Max asked.

"Correctamundo. Call me Jem."

"You're Infiltraitor too, aren't you?"

Jem frowned. "Want some tea?"

"No, thank you."

Max looked around for someplace to sit and decided to settle on one of the piles of paper. He picked up the ream on top of the stack in front of him and paged through it. He'd seen it before. It was a printout of e-mails from Evan's BitTorrent file.

"Thanks for contacting me." Max didn't see anything electronic in the small tent. Just paper, and Jem, and more paper.

"I got the message DoubleThink sent. I only replied because you're a friend of Baxter's. What do you want?"

Where to begin?

"You faked your death," Max said. "What happened?"

"I saw an opportunity and I took it. By the time I found out they were coming after me, after Ty, it was too late. I'm sorry about that."

"So you decided to take off," Max said.

"I was ashamed. I had to leave. I wanted to find the people responsible." He looked around helplessly at the towers of paper surrounding him.

"Must be hard without a computer," Max said.

"It's easier for them to find you with your computer than for you to find them," Jem said.

"Evan thought you—L0NELYB0Y, I mean—was dead too."

"That couldn't be helped. That identity was next on the hit list. I thought it was better to disappear myself completely before someone else did."

"Is there an actual list?" Max asked.

"You bet. I have a scan of Sharpe's directive, with his signature. It's my insurance policy: If anything happens to me, it'll be e-mailed to every major newspaper, TV station, and blog. That's the only reason I saw your attempts to contact me; I have to go online once a week to reset it."

Max felt a jolt of excitement. It was the same feeling he had when he broke through a difficult encryption, or kicked the ball and knew it would go in the goal. A kill order was the evidence they had been looking for.

"Why haven't you released it already?" Max asked. "They wouldn't be able to touch you once it's out there."

"I thought about it. But I want to do more than just save myself. I know you agree. If you know about Sharpe, you also know about SH1FT."

Max nodded. "How did you get involved in all this?" he asked.

"I was in charge of designing Panjea's CDN. A content

delivery network is supposed to be a fail-safe system; if something brings down the main site, it would automatically switch to a backup server."

"Is that at Synthwerks?"

"Bingo, buddy! You've got all the answers."

"Let's see if I do." Max brought Jem up to speed on everything he had learned so far about Panjea and SH1FT.

"You're only half right," Jem said. "SH1FT is a two-phase operation. Phase One is proliferation, spreading to computer systems around the world via Panjea. Phase Two involves using the back door to infect SCADA systems with malware."

"SCADA?" Max asked.

"Supervisory control and data acquisition," Jem said. "Sensitive systems that manage national infrastructure."

"How does the government contract a private company to do that?" Max asked.

Jem laughed. "Panjea doesn't work *for* the government. It is the government. They bought Synthwerks and Vic Ignacio built Panjea for them."

It took a moment for all the terrifying implications to sink in.

"So Panjea's claim that it won't sell private data to anyone, even the government, is true. The government technically owns all the data on the site." Max massaged his forehead. "The government's new surveillance program is a social media service. Holy shit. We aren't going to let them get away with this."

"Evan was working on reprogramming SH1FT to take them down," Jem said.

"He did it. The only problem is, we can't get it onto Panjea's servers," Max said.

"That's very tricky. The worm has to be placed in a certain area of the CDN. Then the entire network has to be restarted so it can run during a maintenance cycle." Jem faltered.

Suddenly it all fell into place. "That was your job, wasn't it? Before you disappeared," Max said.

Jem didn't say anything.

Max's voice rose. "When Evan thought you were gone, he thought he couldn't deliver the worm."

With his family threatened and Jem supposedly dead, Evan had been alone and unable to complete his mission on his own. He hadn't just crumbled under the pressure—he had turned his death into a second chance. By killing himself publicly, he had hoped to highlight what Panjea had done, stop the killing, and give Max and Penny the resources they needed to hold the corporation accountable.

Max had caught up to Evan and now found himself in the same situation. He was alone, with no idea how to get the modified worm into distribution on a wide scale. Maybe he could give Jem a second chance too.

"Will you come back with me and install it on their server?" Max asked.

"No can do, man."

Jem's dismissive tone sparked Max's temper. "How could

you sit back and do nothing? You're only alive right now because someone else died in your place!"

"I didn't say I wouldn't help. Look, I can code a script for you that will place it in the right area of the CDN, if you can plug it directly into a production server. Provided they haven't altered the architecture. And you'll have to force a restart for the changes to take effect, before they discover it on one of their routine security checks. Running a maintenance cycle ought to do it."

"I'll take it." Max said.

"Listen, I'm sorry it went down this way. I feel partially responsible."

Max bit back his reply. "There's enough blame for all of us. We all let Evan down. But we can still make it right."

When Max turned his phone back on outside of Jem's tent, the sun was rising, filtering through the trees. He hurried back toward the main road. As soon as his phone picked up a signal, it beeped: He had missed four calls from Risse.

He rang her back.

"Max! Penny's gone!" Risse said.

"What?" Max walked faster.

"We got back home last night and the Feds were waiting for us."

Risse told him how they'd ditched their stolen car and walked home from Denny's. As soon as they'd reached their driveway they were surrounded by armed agents. Their front door had been kicked in and their house raided. Their mom was freaking out.

"I'm sorry. This is my fault," Max said. Vic had warned him. Now he was going after Penny and Risse.

"No, it isn't. They found her through the mail. They had a photo of the package Evan sent her with that CD. They were just following up, but because of our escape at the mall, all on security video, they have something to charge her with. At least they didn't find anything in our house—we cleaned it out pretty well. But they took our computers too."

Risse choked back a sob.

"Can you get access to another computer?" Max asked.

"Of course. I'll steal one if I have to."

"Get it, then get somewhere safe where you can work. You'll need to be online."

"What are we going to do?" she asked.

"Text me when you're set up." By then, he hoped he would have figured it out. "Make sure you aren't followed. They still might be watching your house. Vic has probably figured out who Penny is by now, but they still don't know about you, and I'd like to keep it that way."

Penny would never forgive Max if he let anything happen to her sister. He wouldn't forgive himself.

And he would not let Penny become another one of the silenced. Someone was going to live through this, damn it. And Sharpe and Panjea were going to pay.

27

FROM BEHIND HIS MASK, MAX STARED INTO THE bright light above his laptop screen. He looked at the webcam and watched his mirror image in the tiny window. This was the last thing Evan had seen: his own reflection on a monitor. And now Max was filming his own video for the same reasons, before potentially committing suicide.

He started recording.

"Hello, I'm Dramatis Personai. Life is theater. Watch. Laugh. Weep. The curtain is rising." Max pulled off his mask.

"I'm 503-ERROR." He paused. "My name is Max Stein. I'm here to answer a question: What is the silence of six?

"This is Ariel Miller. She was a twenty-three-year-old system administrator, but she was also a hacker—for Panjea. You know Panjea, right?"

Risse would edit in a picture of Ariel from Evan's file. Max introduced the rest of those who had been killed: Geordie, Sayid, Ty, and Kyle. He ended with Evan.

Since L0NELYB0Y wasn't actually dead, Evan had become the sixth who was silenced—but he had given his life while speaking out. He would not be silenced any longer.

"We have hundreds of e-mails proving that Panjea was created by the government, as a way of getting people to offer their personal information up willingly. Victor Ignacio, the hacker known as 0MN1, and Kevin Sharpe are using that data and Panjea to manipulate the elections in favor of Democratic nominee Governor Lovett. But you don't have to take my word for it. Read all about it in the attached files.

"Finally, I have a question for you. Now that you know about the silence of six, what are you going to do about it?"

Max let the question hang for a moment. "You're welcome."

He stopped the recording and output it, then uploaded it to Risse.

It was time to end this, one way or another.

Just after eight a.m., Max walked up to the two-story redbrick building at 715 Morse Street in San Jose. He wasn't wearing a mask, not even Risse's glasses. All he carried was his phone, a USB drive, and a keycard.

Though the building looked abandoned, the front entrance had a very new-looking security camera pointed at it, and another was set up down the short walkway from the street.

Max was sure whoever was monitoring it had gotten a good look at him, and security people were probably scrambling inside to intercept him.

Max slapped the keycard against the reader. The light flashed green and the door unlatched. He walked inside.

He had studied pictures of Synthwerks online, but the layout had completely changed. The counters once loaded with PCs had been ripped out and replaced by five long rows of shoulder-high network servers.

Max headed down one aisle to the far end of the room, wondering which of these servers was the best one to plug the worm into.

"Hold it," a voice said on his left.

Max turned.

"503-ERROR?" the boy said.

Max searched his memory for the name that matched the long-haired kid in front of him. "Edifice." Max raised his hands non-threateningly.

Strong arms clamped around Max from behind, pinning his arms to his sides. He struggled and broke free, darting around a server and racing down the aisle. Another guard appeared ahead of him, dressed in a black sweater and black jeans. Max cut to the right and slid between two humming servers. He reached the aisle, pivoted right, and ran for the opposite end. He made it halfway across the room before another guard jumped in front of him.

This time, Max kept going. He threw all his weight at the guard, knocking him down. Max kicked his gun away and turned to run, but the man grabbed Max's foot. He fell—hard. The floor was cement. His shoulder felt like it had been dislocated.

The guard pulled Max up and patted him down. He came up with his cell phone, the USB drive, and his keycard.

"Take him to the room." Edifice gave Max a curious look. "I'm calling Vic."

The room turned out to be the size of Max's bedroom at home, outfitted with a computer terminal, a large screen on the wall, and a telephone. A wide window in the wall provided a view of the larger server room outside it. This must be the supervisor's office.

The guard stayed inside with Max, one hand on the gun holstered at his hip. Edifice watched them from outside, and others gradually joined him. Max recognized PHYREWALL and GroundSloth—who actually waved. He saw a few other faces from Evan's files: ZeroKal, Kill_Screen, Plan(et)9. This was a who's who of Dramatis Personai.

The door opened and Vic entered with another guard. Were these Panjea's hired assassins? "Max. I hope this means you've decided to help."

Max looked at the hackers lined up outside the window. He grimaced with pain from his shoulder.

"Do you know that Vic helped murder your friends?" Max looked at each of the other members of Dramatis Personai. "@sskicker and Infiltraitor died to expose what Panjea is doing."

The hackers exchanged uncomfortable looks. Max didn't

know which of them had known and sided with Vic anyway. There had probably been rumors though. Some of them had to care.

PHYREWALL met his eyes.

Vic put Max's phone down next to the keycard and held up the USB drive by its chain, watching it spin around. "Is this what I think it is?"

"I return SH1FT, you leave my friends and family alone," Max said. "That was the deal?"

"That's the deal. Obviously that doesn't apply to you, or your girlfriend," Vic said.

"You have Courtney?" Max asked in alarm.

Vic blinked. "I was referring to DoubleThink."

"Where is she?" Max asked.

Vic gestured to the hackers. PHYREWALL walked in. Vic handed him the USB drive. "Check it out. Make sure it has what we need."

PHYREWALL sat down at the terminal and plugged the drive into the computer tower.

"What are you going to do with us?" Max asked. "Are we just going to disappear? Or maybe you'll let us go, and one day I'll get hit by a car, like Ariel Miller, the hacker who tipped Evan off about Panjea. Or my house will burn down, like what happened to Kyle Marks, the journalist who was going to report on Panjea. Weird. Seems like there's a pattern here," Max said. He looked at the hackers. "Panjea's about collecting data, analyzing it, looking at patterns. Information is useless if you never act on it. Are you programmers, or just part of the programming?"

Max heard the hackers outside muttering to each other. Vic shot them a cool look that quieted them down.

"You don't have any idea what's going on, Max," Vic said.

"Maybe I don't understand some things," Max said. "But how much does Kevin Sharpe keep you in the loop, Vic?"

"*I'm* Panjea," Vic said. "This is all my vision. We're demonstrating that technology is the most powerful force for good there is. We're bringing the planet together."

"And all you had to do was sell it out first," Max said.

"How are we doing with that drive, PHYRE?" Vic asked.

"It's encrypted," PHYREWALL said.

"What's the password, Max?" Vic asked.

Max smiled. "I'll only tell your boss."

"I'm the boss here," Vic said.

"You have some of the best hackers in the world working for you." Max glanced at the observation window. "See if they can crack it. Better yet, show us what you've got, *OMNI*."

Vic glanced behind him. "Max, you aren't holding up your end of our deal."

Max turned to the members of Dramatis Personai. "Did you know Vic asked Evan to dox all of you?"

"Is that true?" Edifice asked.

Max looked at each of the Personai members in turn. "Nat, Oliver, Leroy, Edward, Timothy, Yanni, Alex."

"How does he know our real names?" Kill_Screen—Leroy—demanded.

"Calm down," Vic said. "Why would I have you doxxed when you already work for me? You don't need to share your identities to do great work. He's lying to confuse you."

"Someone's lying." PHYREWALL folded his arms. "I'm not sure it's him. You made me distract the FBI agents the other day so Five-Oh-Three and DoubleThink could escape. I had a long time alone in their interrogation room to wonder why."

"You're free now, and they didn't press any charges," Vic said. "We protect our own. I'm watching out for you."

"Thanks, but that's the other thing I've been thinking about: Why did the FBI let me go? They know who I am, too— my real name, not my company identity. I've seen you meeting with that Kevin Sharpe guy. Given the government's feelings about hackers, you must have pulled some important strings to get me out."

"Explain that, Vic," Kill_Screen said.

"All right, all right. I will, but first give us some space, will you?" Vic said.

The hackers didn't move. Vic lowered the blinds on the window. "Now it's just us. Max, let's talk about this, okay?"

"Depends. Are you ready to make a deal or not?" Max asked.

"We already have an agreement."

"I'm renegotiating."

"What do you want?"

"You have SH1FT. I'll give you the password to unlock it if you let DoubleThink go in addition to leaving my friends and family alone."

Vic moved to look over PHYREWALL's shoulder. "Once we verify that SH1FT is on this drive, I'll consider it."

"Fair." Max looked straight at PHYREWALL. "The password is: 'This means something. This is important.'" He enunciated every word carefully, willing PHYREWALL to understand him.

PHYREWALL exchanged a look with Vic.

"Go ahead," Vic said.

"Full sentences, with regular capitalization and punctuation: 'This means something. This is important,'" Max said.

He hoped PHYREWALL would notice the executable he'd buried on the drive: L0NELYB0Y.exe, and its explanatory text file. If he ran it, he would run the script Jem had worked out that would spread the worm to Panjea's servers and prime them to be distributed to all users worldwide.

"It's, uh, more complete than the older build we've been working on. Why did STOP steal it if he was just going to finish coding it?" PHYREWALL asked. He clicked on a couple of other files. "The save date is October twenty-first," PHYREWALL said.

"The day Evan died." Vic shook his head. "That was a real shame."

To Max's surprise, he sounded sincere.

"We have e-mails that you sent to Sharpe asking people to be taken care of, including Evan," Max said. "When all this gets out, who do you think is going to take the fall? The guy who's the public face of Panjea, who's been lying to everyone who uses it? Or the shadowy government operative who can count on plausible deniability and his friends in Congress? Maybe even the new president, thanks to you."

Vic lowered his voice. "I didn't know how far they were willing to go until it was too late."

PHYREWALL glanced at Vic in shock. Then he turned back to his screen, stared at it for a moment, then clicked on a file. He looked at Max.

"Uh. I think I accidentally launched SH1FT," PHYRE-WALL said.

Vic spun around. "What? I didn't tell you to do that," he snapped.

"Sorry? I was just trying to pull up the code to study it, and it started running on its own." PHYREWALL said.

Vic shoved him aside to get at the keyboard. "That's fine. Then we're just a little ahead of schedule. Sharpe will be thrilled," he muttered. Panic was creeping into his voice—a contrast to his usually smooth air of charm and control.

"So you do work for Kevin Sharpe," Max said. "The question is: Who does Sharpe work for?"

"This isn't doing what it's supposed to do," Vic said. "PHYREWALL?"

"Oh, I may have neglected to mention: Evan made a few tweaks to SH1FT. He was never able to stop himself from tinkering with code," Max said.

Vic frowned. "What have you done?"

What hath God wrought? Max thought.

"The worm is going to infiltrate the entire Panjea network and reverse the damage it's done. It'll shut down the SH1FT surveillance and, eventually, it's going to brick your servers." Max looked around at the computers networked around them. "In fact, the program is so fundamentally different, we're calling it by a new name. ST0P. That's spelled with a zero."

Vic's left eye twitched. "I can still purge it from the servers before it gets out. It won't activate until after a maintenance cycle." He opened a web browser and typed in panjea.co. It loaded on the giant monitor mounted on the wall.

The browser circle spun and spun and spun, trying to load the page. Finally it displayed a message: HTTP ERROR 503: SERVICE UNAVAILABLE.

Vic groaned and started typing furiously. "What do I do?" he asked PHYREWALL. "Help me."

"Learn to code," PHYREWALL said. He walked over to the observation window, and while Vic was preoccupied, he opened the blinds. The members of Dramatis Personai were watching the proceedings silently and solemnly.

"I didn't earn my handle for nothing. Enough of my old botnets are still running to take down a site the size of Panjea," Max said.

Risse had helped him coordinate the DDoS attack on Panjea, and she had reached out to other hackers she trusted outside of Dramatis Personai to launch the biggest takedown ever in the history of the internet.

"We have failovers for that." Vic's voice betrayed his stress.

"The CDN? I'm counting on it. Your backups have been rerouted to *these* servers," Max said.

"Impossible."

"They call Kevin Sharpe the Architect? Well I know the guy who designed your network in the first place."

"Infiltraitor? He's dead," Vic said.

The phone on the desk rang. Vic stared at it for a long moment before answering. "Yes, sir. I'm aware. I'm on it."

Vic hung up. His face was pale.

"You didn't tell him about the worm," Max said.

"He'll figure it out soon enough, and I'm not going to be here when he does." Vic glanced at his screen. "The server's rebooting now. Sharpe isn't going to get a chance to silence *me*." Vic glanced at the guards. "Keep an eye on him. Both of them. *Everyone*." He opened the door and walked out, right past his hacker team. They all watched him go with expressions of disgust.

"Shouldn't we stop him?" PHYREWALL asked.

"Once we expose Sharpe and Panjea, he won't have anywhere to go," Max said.

Edifice poked his head inside the room. One of the guards swiveled and pulled a gun on him.

"Easy there, hoss. I just wanted to tell you there seems to be a large situation outside."

PHYREWALL pressed a button on a remote and the screen switched to a view from a security camera outside. About two hundred people in masks were protesting in front of Synthwerks. They were carrying signs that said "Panjea: Everyone is *Collected*." A Channel 7 news van was parked on the street behind them.

The guards glanced at each other.

Max grinned. In his video, he had appealed to the attendees of Haxx0rade to protest Panjea's shady practices at Synthwerks. Apparently the small excerpt he'd provided from Evan's files had been enough to convince them to mobilize, and they had come through just in time. He doubted Vic would be able to get around that crowd without attracting their attention and anger.

The guards rushed out of the office.

Max switched the monitor back to the browser. The other hackers filtered into the room and watched with them as Panjea came back online.

They were still logged in to Vic's account. His Panjea Peers were all posting confused and annoyed comments about the site being down for so long. As far as Max knew, it was the first time it had ever been down for more than thirty seconds. But a few minutes was pretty good for it to turn into an all-new, truly transparent Panjea.

"They have no idea anything is different," Max said.

The first news report about it would be going online now at Full Cort Press. Max had given Courtney a great story, along with Evan's video, Max's video, all the files, and an exclusive interview with Jem.

The desk phone rang again.

"Should we answer that?" PHYREWALL raised his eyebrows.

Max switched on the speaker.

"Hello," Max said.

"Who is this? What's going on over there?" a man barked.

"This is 503-ERROR," Max said. "My friends and I just took down Panjea. You're welcome."

The other members of Dramatis Personai snickered.

"I assume this is Kevin Sharpe?" Max asked.

A short silence. "Where's Vic?"

"He seemed to be in a hurry to leave," Max said. "You wanted SH1FT, you got it. We were just returning stolen property, in better shape than we found it in, like good citizens."

"You don't know what you're getting yourself involved in." Did Sharpe actually sound worried?

"You're the one who had Ariel, Geordie, Sayid, Kyle, and Ty killed. And now it's time to answer for your crimes." Max swallowed. His blood pounded in his ears and he felt his muscles tighten with tension.

"I know who you are," Sharpe said.

"Tell Governor Lovett she doesn't have my support anymore."

Sharpe hung up.

"Five-Oh-Three, what's going on with Panjea?" Ground-Sloth nodded at the screen.

A new note had appeared on Vic's feed—from Evan Baxter:

"When you buy the silence of six, everyone pays the price.

For shame, Kevin Sharpe. http://small.panjea.truth."

"What the hell?" PHYREWALL said.

L0NELYB0Y had made a little tweak to the code for ST0P that would post a message like that to every Panjea user's page. When they clicked on it, it would run the ST0P worm and take them to a site Courtney had set up to publish the e-mail archives Evan had collected. It also included a link to Evan's full video on Fawkes Rising.

"Oh, it just made another update," Edifice said.

Ariel Miller says, "I was murdered by Kevin Sharpe and Panjea. http://small.panjea.truth."

A few minutes later: *Geordie Powers says, "I was murdered by Kevin Sharpe. The U.S. government owns Panjea, and it owns your personal information. ST0P government surveillance. http://small.panjea.truth."*

Max sat down in the desk chair as all the nervous energy that had kept him going suddenly left him. He felt shaky and exhausted. His shoulder had a dull ache. He wanted to sleep for a week.

Max's cell phone rang. Plan(et)9 handed it to him. Max sighed with relief: It was Penny.

28

MAX STUDIED PENNY FROM THE CORNER OF HIS eye as he drove them to Granville Cemetery in his dad's Impala. After a week of driving a series of unfamiliar stolen cars—which had all fortunately made it back to their owners, who were generous enough to not press charges—it felt great to be behind the wheel of a car he knew well.

Penny had been quiet since he'd picked her up from the train station half an hour ago. He couldn't blame her—this was a somber occasion. But he hated to think they didn't have anything to talk about now that Panjea and Sharpe were slowly slipping from front-page headlines to filler. Courtney was continuing to cover all the latest developments on her blog, which was now drawing national attention and keeping her busy.

Yesterday, Kevin Sharpe had been indicted on five counts of murder, conspiracy, and a range of other charges related to his illicit activities as the head of Sharpe & Company. Governor Angela Lovett—President-elect Lovett—had severed all ties with him as soon as his crimes came to light. That had been enough to drop her in the polls until she and Senator Tooms were neck and neck, but she managed to hold back the effects of the scandal, and won on Election Day anyway. Max still couldn't believe it: The bad guy had become president.

The FBI was looking for Victor Ignacio.

Max and Penny hadn't been charged with any crimes. Public sentiment was in their favor, but they were told in no uncertain terms that the FBI would be watching them more closely from there on out. Max couldn't stop looking over his shoulder, expecting to see an unmarked car tailing him.

That hadn't stopped him from doing the media circuit, granting TV interviews, trying to carry on what Evan had started and get the truth out. It was ironic that he had all but given up his own privacy in order to discuss it, but he was eager to return to a normal life.

Max was glad to be home, but even though he was back at school, he didn't have his old life back. He didn't think he ever would.

Instead, his life had become a very strange charade of pretending he was the same old Max. He and Courtney were no longer one of the school's star couples, but they found they were even better as friends. Max had missed the end of the soccer season due to his shoulder injury, and while Isaac and Walter and the other guys tried to include him, the connection was missing. He couldn't shake the feeling that despite everything he'd done, they didn't trust him anymore.

Max had never felt more alone—even when he was on the run—and he'd been finding himself spending more time online, chatting with Risse and the tattered remains of Dramatis Personai, which seemed ready to embrace Max as 0MN1's replacement.

The real difference, and the one thing he couldn't do anything about, was that Evan was gone. No matter how much he hoped, no matter how many times he dreamed that Evan was still alive—better than the nightmares about him dying—his friend wasn't coming back. People kept calling Max a hero, but Evan was the real hero. Even after making the ultimate sacrifice, people weren't giving him the attention and praise he deserved.

Max still struggled to understand why Evan had chosen to deliver his message the way he had instead of fighting on. For all the theories he could come up with, he would probably never have the full answer. The only person who knew what had gone through Evan's head in those final days and minutes was Evan.

And so bitterness mixed with Max's grief. That's why he had invited Penny to Granville. That, and he'd wanted to see her again. But she acted like she couldn't even stand to look at him.

Max guided the car up the long driveway to the Granville Cemetery. He switched off the car and they sat in silence, listening to the click of the engine as it cooled.

"Is everything okay?" Max asked.

Penny turned her head slowly. "'Everything.' Everything will not ever be okay."

"Fair. I mean with you."

She pursed her lips. "We haven't changed anything. Lovett is President. People are still using Panjea. After the controversy over the data leaks, they lost about ten million customers, but that's only ten million out of two hundred million—and they're slowly coming back."

"I know. People think just because it has a new CEO that it's safe to use it again. Just like with the NSA, they complained online, they made jokes and T-shirts about it, but then most of them didn't want to change their habits. At least this time the people who tried to do something weren't punished."

"Except for the ones who died."

"Yeah. But they'll get justice."

"We'll see," Penny said.

"I think we did a good job. Evan couldn't have asked for better. Technology isn't inherently dangerous. It only becomes that way when people misuse it. Panjea was a major threat, but then we turned it against itself to fix the problem. Think about what else it's capable of."

"You're starting to get into this Dramatis Personai thing."

"I'm not doing anything."

"What do you want, Max?" Penny met his eyes.

He couldn't tell her what he really wanted. Not yet.

"I want to go to school, and hang out with my friends, and screw up and get in trouble, and graduate. I want to take. . . someone to prom. I want to do all the things we're supposed to do when we're young, because we're going to grow up too soon as it is."

"I think it's already too late," Penny said.

"You're probably right."

"You've said you don't fit with that life though. You fit with me. With *us*. You're a hacker, Max."

"I still have some things to figure out. I can't go back to my old life, I know that. But I'm not ready to dive into this new one either." Max glanced at the street behind them. There'd been a car there a second ago, but it was gone now. "I'm thinking I might try to go abroad next year, take a break from all this. Start over."

"Where?" Penny said.

"Granville High has an exchange program with France."

"Isn't that where your mom lives?"

"I don't know, but now I know she's out there. I need to find her." If Vic Ignacio knew where Lianna Stein was, Max had missed his chance to ask him. And Max had done a thorough job of disabling the only tool that might have led him to his mother when he took down Panjea's surveillance capability.

"They have internet in France," Penny said.

"They do. It's even better than ours. Except for it being in French."

She smiled. "I know Dramatis Personai won't be the same. Some things don't recover from a blow like the one this group's been through. Its own members working for the government, stealing information and working against other citizens, and even against themselves. Then there are the deaths. . . . Hacking isn't supposed to endanger your life.

"I don't blame them for not trusting each other. Sharing information and maintaining anonymity aren't compatible anymore. But if anyone can make them a force for good again, it's you. I'm just going to try working in the open for a while, as Penny Polonsky instead of DoubleThink. See how that goes."

She flashed her fingertips at him. Her nails had a fresh coat of paint: Panjea-green with red letters. B-E-Y-O-U-R-S-E-L-F.

"Be yourself," Max read.

She waggled her fingers. "Good advice for all of us."

"What about Risse?"

"She can be DoubleThink without me. I might start a sort of side business. Infosec consulting," Penny said. "It may not be entirely legal. Don't tell Cort."

"Uh oh," Max said.

"Want me to keep you posted?"

Maybe he didn't have to give up hacking, or try to keep his two worlds separate anymore. That would be impossible now anyway, with everyone aware of his past. He would like to keep using his skills to do something meaningful and positive, to help people more openly. To try to change the world the way Evan had.

"Yes," he said.

"Look for an invitation from +g00d," Penny said.

They looked out the windshield at the same time.

"I guess we should do this," Max said.

"I guess so."

They got out of the car and followed the directions Courtney had given him. Max soon found the grave they were looking for. EVAN BAXTER, BELOVED SON, JANUARY 11, 1997–OCTOBER 21, 2014.

"Hey, Evan." Max breathed heavily, his breath puffing up in front of his face.

He glanced at Penny, but she was looking resolutely ahead at Evan's headstone.

He wasn't good at this kind of thing. He didn't believe in an afterlife, and even if he was wrong about that, he doubted his friend's spirit was hanging around his grave.

Evan lived on as electronic bits scattered across the internet. He lived in Max's and Penny's memory, and in his legacy as STOP, a worm that even now was still working its way through computer systems all over the world. Those parts of Evan would never die, and the digital world had always mattered more to him than his physical one.

But it would be rude not to say hello, just in case.

"Sorry it's taken me a while to get here. Sorry for. . . everything. Uh, how's it going?" He sighed. "This is stupid. I don't know what I'm doing here."

"Just say good-bye. And thank you," Penny said.

He nodded. "I wish I'd had a chance to tell you this in

person. Evan, you're a freaking hero. Oh, um. . . also, thanks for introducing me to Penny. She's great."

The sun broke through the cloud cover and weak beams of afternoon light fell across Max and the gravestone.

Max looked up. "Is this for real?"

Penny giggled. And just like that, it wasn't somber anymore. Instead of dwelling on the days he'd missed with Evan, he found himself remembering the good times they'd had. All the things they'd done together that had made Max the person he was and led him here, to this moment, with Penny beside him.

Max noticed something on the side of the rectangular headstone, shining silver in the sun. He walked closer to examine it, then hopped off the grave.

"Sorry!" he said.

"I don't think he minds." But Penny skirted the grave too and joined him by the headstone.

There was a sticker on the top corner: a barcode. Did the cemetery barcode their graves here to track its. . . occupants?

"Nice," Penny said. "Freaking vandals. Who thought a grave was a good place to market their crappy product?"

Max grabbed his phone—a new one that his dad had given him as an early Christmas present along with his replacement laptop, Winston.

"I wouldn't," Penny said.

Max opened the barcode reader app and lined up the square reticule of the camera with the block of code. A red line blinked in the center and a web address flashed briefly before loading the page. It looked like an IP address, not a domain name, like a server on the Deep Web.

A password field appeared. Max sighed and showed it to Penny.

She raised her eyebrows.

"Evan," Max said.

"But how? I mean. . . ." She gestured at the mound of dirt at their feet, decorated with a fresh bouquet of roses. Max hadn't thought to bring anything.

Max was pretty sure Evan had something to do with this, because no one trying to advertise a product or service would require a passcode to access the website—and it wouldn't be on the underground internet used for acquiring all sorts of illegal goods that was the Deep Web.

He quickly tried all the passwords Evan had used to-date, but none of them worked. In a fit of pique, he typed in max.

A black video window popped up with a swirling circle in the middle as it buffered.

"Come on, Evan. Three letters? That's not very secure," Max said.

Penny crowded close, her face inches from Max's. They waited for the video to load, looking at their own faces reflected in the glossy black screen.

When red had inched about halfway across the progress bar, Evan's face appeared in a burst of pixels.

Max clutched the phone tighter, thinking he was going to

have to watch Evan's suicide again. But even though this video was lit exactly the same, and Evan was wearing the same outfit from the night he'd died—hardly conclusive, because he always dressed that way—Max knew this was something different when he heard his friend say, *"Hey, Max."*

Max paused the video.

"I need to sit down," he said.

Penny sprawled with him on the grass beside Evan's grave. She put an arm around him. He pressed Play.

"Long time no see, huh? I know you're watching this after I'm. . . ." Evan swallowed. *"After I'm gone. I'm sorry for what I'm about to do—what I've already done to you and my folks and my online friends. I'm sorry for* everything.*"*

Evan's voice broke. He pushed up his glasses and rubbed his fingers against his eyes. *"No, don't do this,"* he muttered. Then he looked up again, and his eyes had lost some focus. He was looking past the camera.

"It has to be done, and if you don't understand it yet, you will one day. God, that's such a cliché, isn't it? But you will." Evan shook his head. *"This sucks. I had big plans for us. We could have done so much together."* He gave a weak smile that seemed somehow painful. *"We did do a lot, didn't we?"*

Evan let out a long, shuddering breath. *"So, a contact of mine was instructed to place this link where you'd find it, after the presidential election. I know whatever happened, you did your best. You always do. So. . . Thank you. Not just for this, but for being my best friend."*

"Shut up," Max said, barely able to get the words out past the ball of emotion lodged in his throat.

"You're one of the only people I feel like I could trust with my—" He laughed. *"My life. And now with this, what's left of it."* Evan spread his hands. They started shaking and Evan stared at them until they calmed down. He squeezed them into fists.

"Don't worry about showing this to my parents. Oh, um, would you check on them once in a while? Mom. . . ." Evan looked away. The picture jumped and Evan was now more composed, but his eyes were red and puffy.

"Your mom's okay, Evan," Max said. "She misses you, but she's going to be okay." He'd been to visit the Baxters a few days ago. They were still a wreck, but knowing that their son had died trying to make a difference was helping them to pick up the pieces. They were talking about taking a long vacation, to get away from Granville and the media circus, and the memories.

"As soon as you accessed this video, a link was automatically sent to Mom and Dad and a few other people, with a different video and some other things they'll need."

On cue, Penny's phone beeped in her purse.

"Max, don't feel bad. We drifted apart a bit, but it's okay. Really. I'm glad you have your own thing, that you weren't dragged into this sooner and ended up hurt because of me. I hope you're happy. Good luck. You're going to need it without me there keeping you out of trouble."

Max let out a strangled laugh, half a sob.

"Take care of P-squared."

Max glanced at Penny. She blushed.

"I know you have a freakishly good memory, but I'm leaving you with something else to remember me by. I saved some things on the cloud for you." Evan's face was wet with fresh tears, but he didn't seem to notice.

"Link?" Max asked.

"And I have one last favor to ask. This one's easy: Hold on to some stuff for me for a while. You don't have to look for it. You probably won't find it even if you do. But it'll be with you, and you'll have it if you need it. But I hope you won't need it."

"God damn it, Evan," Max said. "What is it now?"

"Maxwell Stein, good-bye. It has been an honor and a privilege." Evan gave Max a goofy salute he'd copied from an old British science fiction show.

The video faded to black.

"Wait. What?" Max said. He tapped at the screen. "That can't be all."

Max's phone beeped and a message popped up: "This application is attempting to upload data to your phone. Accept?"

Max's finger wavered over the Yes button. He didn't know what Evan's program was sending, but there was a chance that the next time he visited this site, the data would be gone. It was now or never.

"Come on," Penny said. "Is there any question?"

He tapped Yes and file names flickered over his screen, too quickly to read.

"What the hell, Evan?" Maybe Evan wanted him to have his comprehensive digital porn collection.

After five minutes, the progress bar reached 100 percent. Then another box popped up: "Warning. Disk almost out of space. 35MB free."

Evan's data dump had taken up nearly 10GB on his phone's SD card. Which meant Max's phone was way over his monthly data allowance. *Great.*

He checked the website again, and it returned "HTTP Error 503 Service Unavailable." He'd made a good call grabbing the files while he could. All trace of them, and the video, was gone.

"What is it?" Penny asked.

Max thumbed through the files.

Folders full of images, and a few files that looked like junk, with no file extensions. He'd found that garbage data on Evan's four dead drops too, along with the code for SH1FT, but hadn't been able to figure them out yet. That was a problem for another day; he was tired of puzzles and riddles.

Max opened a photo named besties001.jpg. It was the same photo of him and Evan that Evan had modified to include his torrent file of data against Panjea and Tooms.

Max tapped the screen and the next image appeared, another picture of them from the same day.

He expanded the view and checked the previews of all the images. "They're all pictures of me."

Many of them had Evan in them, some of them were so recent that they even included Courtney, and there were even pictures of the soccer team. Evan had pictures of games Max didn't know he'd been to, and there were also scans of newspaper clippings about the team—all the ones that mentioned Max, even briefly.

As Max clicked through every photo in the folder, all 217 of them, he realized he was crying. Tears splashed against the screen. He swiped at it with his sleeve.

Evan had always acted like he didn't care about Max playing soccer. He'd been downright unsupportive, even jealous of all the time it took away from their friendship. But he'd collected all of these over the last few months and had been following his games.

There were other folders too—filled with things that had meant something to Evan. Things he loved. Mix CDs of his most-listened-to music. Video files: pirated movies, favorite episodes of TV shows, YouTube clips. E-books and scans of comics.

Penny was looking at her phone. "Is it okay if I play this later? I kind of want to watch it alone. Not. . . here."

"Of course. You want to go back to the car?"

"I want to save it," she said. "I mean, yes, for later. But also literally. I'm going to make sure I record a copy of it while it streams."

"I wish I could have done that."

"You have a photographic memory."

Max smiled. "Yeah, I do." And this video was going to replace the last image he'd seen of Evan, which had launched him on this whole adventure.

Max got up and brushed off his pants. He helped Penny up. Then he tore the sticker off Evan's headstone, crumpled it up, and stuffed it into his pocket.

"I thought I was getting over it, but. . . are you all right?" she asked.

Max swung his backpack onto his left shoulder. "I think I will be," he said.

As they walked back to the car, Penny slipped her hand into his. He smiled. His new life was different, and very strange, but it had potential.

ACKNOWLEDGEMENTS

"WHAT IS *THE SILENCE OF SIX*?"

This book resulted from the collective talents and support of a multitude of people who contributed in many ways, large and small. Even I don't know all their names, but I owe a debt of gratitude to each and every one of them.

Writing a book is like assembling a jigsaw puzzle that has lots of pieces, and some of them are missing, and a few pieces from other puzzles have gotten mixed in, and you might even be looking at the picture on the box upside down. But you start at the edges, you work your way to the center, and you rely on others to help spot holes and figure out where everything belongs.

Biggest thanks to Marshall Lewy, for always keeping the big picture in mind and for excellent guidance and extraordinary patience in getting us there over many drafts. My editor, Kristy King, was brilliant and insightful, helping to fit all the pieces together and making the book greater than the sum of its parts. My amazing copy editor, Liz Tingue, went to heroic lengths to make sure that some embarrassing mistakes were never leaked to the public. I appreciate everyone at Adaptive Books for their creativity, enthusiasm, and tireless collaboration in shaping this story; I've learned so much from them along the way, while also having tremendous fun.

As always, I'm extremely grateful to my author friends, accomplished storytellers who encouraged and advised me throughout this project, especially Tiffany Schmidt, Elisa Ludwig, Paul Berger, Tom Crosshill, Kris Dikeman, Devin Poore, Lilah Wild, and Fran Wilde.

Cheers to Eddie Schneider, the growing forces at JABberwocky Literary Agency, and Tigger too.

Last but not least, thank you to my family for understanding why I was often writing in coffee shops instead of interacting in the real world—and for not holding it against me. . .much. All my love to Mom, Cora, Taylor, John, Kate, Mark, Liz, and Caroline.

ADAPTIVE WOULD LIKE TO THANK STEPHEN HAUSER, whose provocative question *What is the Silence of Six?* planted the seed for this story.

www.fawkesrising.com
www.fullcortpress.tumblr.com
@yourewelcomeSOS

Also Available from ADAPTIVE BOOKS

PRAISE FOR COIN HEIST:

"A group of teens hatch a plan to save their financially distressed school by robbing the Philadelphia Mint in this fast-paced adventure. . . Ludwig's exciting storytelling and some romantic subplots maintain intrigue throughout."
—*Publishers Weekly*

"Jackpot! Smartly plotted, morally fascinating, and featuring the most engaging crew of prep school outlaws, Elisa Ludwig's *Coin Heist* is a heist story with heart."
—DIANA RENN, author of *Tokyo Heist* and *Latitude Zero*

"The voices of the characters are distinctive. . . diverse representing a realistic group of teens. *Coin Heist* plays with some recognizable conventions of heist novels but adds in a few twists of its own. A fast paced, fun summer read not to be missed." —*Hypable*

Learn more at www.adaptivestudios.com/books